Victorian Venus

edited by Travis Perry
with Adam David Collings,
Kat Heckenbach,
Cindy Koepp,
L. Jagi Lamplighter,
and Kristen Stieffel

Table of Contents

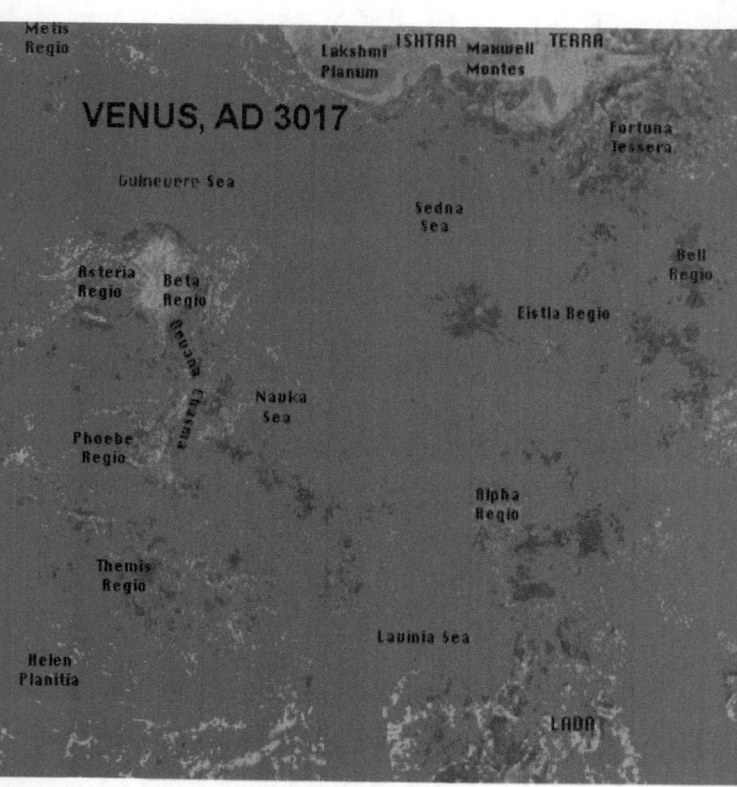

VENUS, AD 3017

Melis Regio

Lakshmi Planum

ISHTAR Maxwell Montes TERRA

Fortuna Tessera

Guinevere Sea

Sedna Sea

Asteria Regio

Beta Regio

Bell Regio

Eistla Regio

Devana Chasma

Navka Sea

Phoebe Regio

Alpha Regio

Themis Regio

Lavinia Sea

Helen Planitia

LADA

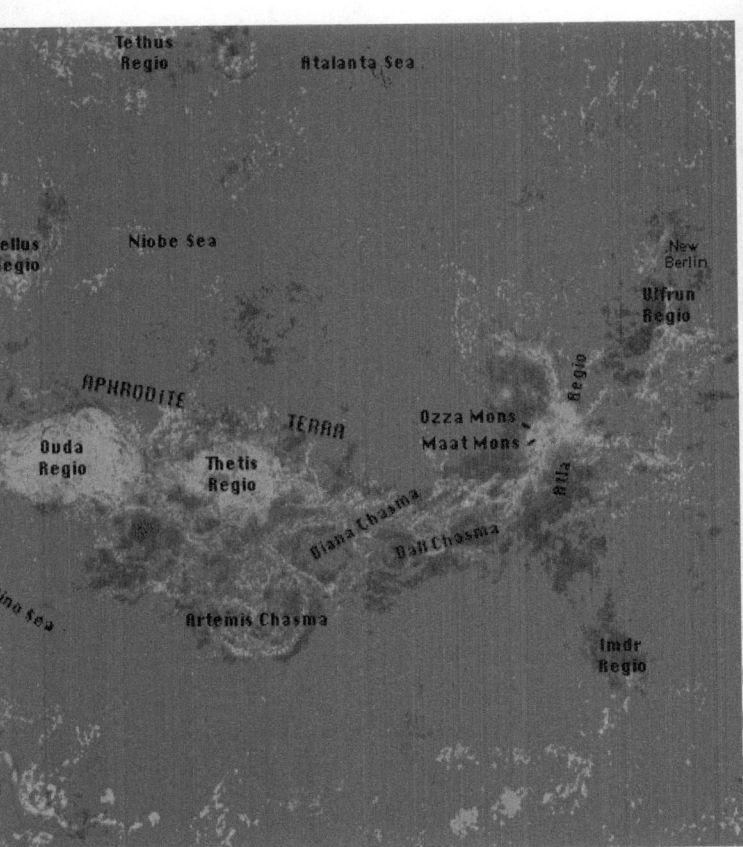

A Mighty Airship
by Travis Perry

"A mighty fortress is our God," reverberated through the steel framework of the Airship *Indomitable*. For men who had every reason to believe each breath could be their last, they sang with astonishing harmony. As if they were the New Berliner Cathedral Choir. Ironically.

The airship shuddered as it passed over the heat of a flaming sector of burning New Berlin. Burning because airships like the Indomitable had dropped incendiary bombs on it.

Black bursts of flak filled the view from the cockpit where Captain Adam Goodwin steered the craft. Four gray streaks cut across the sky behind the flak, evidence of the New Berliner Jet Fighter Squadron.

The control wheel shaking in his hands, Goodwin, pilot and commander of the craft, did not join the echoing voices. "The Lord is my Shepherd, I shall not want..." he breathed. A fiber-optic-view window showed the right rear octant of the vessel erupt in the pale flame of exploding hydrogen gas.

The vessel shook and shifted right, nose up. Goodwin twisted hard to the left and pushed the wheel in, forcing the surfaces to fight for level flight. A pair of jets from the Berliner squadron flashed into his field of view, having flown underneath his craft from rear to front, already firing as they went. Singing crewmen in lower decks below fired water-cooled machine guns back at them, tracers helplessly seeking targets that had gone past them before human hands could react.

⁂

Fourteen months earlier, the plans for the *Indomitable* were rolled out in front of Goodwin for the first time on an ornate redwood table in the plans room of the Tethus Junior Staff College, where he served as a professor of airship tactics.

At first glance he whistled low, "That is not a New Berliner design."

"No," replied Heinrich Mansfeld.

Goodwin glanced at each of the three men across the table from him: Mansfeld, who shaved his chin but otherwise sported lamb chops and a bushy black mustache, in civilian suit and tie; to his right General Jobs, tall and stiff in his crisp blue uniform, his white mustache neatly trimmed; to his left a man in colonel rank he'd never met before, with a full, red beard, all three of them in contrast to his own clean-shaven face.

"This is rebellion," he said to them. "Isn't it?"

Silence stretched out long, the dampened clatter of booted feet on granite floors sounding from the other side of closed double doors behind Goodwin's back. Mansfeld's eyes met Jones' and the general eventually stretched out an open palm towards the engineer. As if to say, "You take this."

Mansfeld turned back towards Goodwin, "Of course this is rebellion. The days of New Berliner domination over us are over." The engineer's thick New Berliner accent provided a high level of unintended irony.

VV

The shaking airship over New Berlin inspired Goodwin's thought: *that's one cell gone, seven left.* Carbon fiber cloth separated the hydrogen zeppelin into distinct regions, so if one blew, the explosion would be contained in that one area, instead of the entire airship going up in flames.

The vessel shook again and the lower right front cell blew from a flak burst, the expanding gas making the metal framework shriek. Which actually stopped the singing of the men. But only for a moment.

Now the craft listed even more to the right. Goodwin strained upward against the belt that kept him in the command chair, seeking leverage to twist the vehicle to left. A second pair of jets streaked his way, these coming in from eleven o'clock high. "Oh dear Lord!" exclaimed the navigator from the seat behind his   chair.

The upper gun turrets were already wrecked by New Berliner sniper-grenadiers, who had fired shoulder-mounted rockets no one in Tethus even knew they had from the top of the cathedral itself. Men in the remaining lower airship turrets fired at the jets, even though their angle was bad, flashes of tracer bullets leaping up into the sky.

The jets streaked in, like a lightning strike that had grown white vapor trails. The one on the left suddenly transformed into an expanding ball of orange and red, with tints of jet-fuel blue. "They got him!" shouted navigator Harvest pointlessly.

"The body they may kill," thundered the manly chorus from the deck below. Tracer rounds erupted from the jet on the right, which streaked by Goodwin's front windows before he realized the lower front left section of the airship had caught fire from the enemy bullets. It exploded, shaking the craft.

VV

Three months before that day, Goodwin stared out the window of the officer's car of the troop train he rode on the northeast line towards Lake Earhart, which had become the site of a secret airship facility. Duke Schmidt, the New Berlin-appointed governor, like Mansfeld the engineer, was fully engaged in the rebellion. He'd been the one to order the construction.

As Goodwin stared out the train window, the locomotive engine not three cars in front of him belching black charcoal smoke while blowing its steam whistle, he pondered, *I wonder what it is about Tethus that inspires such loyalty from New Berliners? American-style coffee?* He chuckled to himself at that. The coffee was the one thing every outlander always complained about.

"May I join you?" a voice from behind him asked with an English accent different from that of Tethus.

He turned and noted the brown wool uniform coat and gold buttons and shoulder braids of a Tellus major. The officer car was only three-quarters filled with seats—there were plenty of other places to for this major to sit. Plenty of other men in powder blue uniform with silver buttons for him to sit beside, some closer to the entrance.

"Of course," said Goodwin. He offered his hand, "Adam Goodwin, formerly of the Tethus Junior Staff College."

The major muttered, "A moment," then the car's porter loaded his large boxy personal luggage in the bin over Goodwin's head. The major then sat down and took the hand Goodwin had held out the entire time. The major with slicked back hair appeared to be smiling broadly, but it was hard to be sure because of the massive walrus mustache he sported that covered his mouth. "A pleasure, Captain. I've read your book on airship tactics."

"Oh. I'm a bit surprised. I didn't realize I had any readership at all. Outside my own students and fellow instructors, of course."

"You sell yourself short, my dear chap! Your insights on lift and survivability were absolutely brilliant."

"Ah. I thought what I was saying was merely logical. Obvious really."

The major leaned towards him. "You won't think me guilty of flattery if I observe the very greatest minds *always* think their work is 'merely logical?' By the way, I'm Henry Stone." And having said that, he finally released Goodwin's hand. But he leaned in even closer and whispered, "Say, you wouldn't know much about the rumor we are to fly around the entire *world* to catch the New Berliners by surprise, would you?"

"Um...that's classified."

Stone backed away and then slapped Goodwin on the shoulder, "Of course it is! Sorry. I'm sure my superiors know all about it—they would have to for our air fleet to meet yours—a lowly liaison officer like me doesn't hear about such things. But, having read your book, I simply wondered if a tactical wizard like yourself had been in on the planning."

"Um...that's classified."

"I'm sorry," said the face with grinning eyes and the general outline of a mouth hidden by whiskers. "Let us change topics of conversation. Do you fancy the majestic contest of skills that is cricket?"

Something about the entire conversation bothered Goodwin...he paused and drew in a deep breath, as if carefully considering the merits of the game commonly played in Tellus but not Tethus. Something didn't seem quite right about this major. But he didn't know what to do about it other than engage him and see if he could learn something specific.

"I'm sure it's no surprise for me to say that I've always favored baseball."

The major grinned at him in the exactly same way as he had before. Exactly the same. As if practiced.

VV

After the explosion, the airship's nose pitched down and the entire vessel began to lose altitude, fast. *Well, at least it isn't rolling as bad anymore,* thought Goodwin as he pulled back on the wheel and shouted down the gray tube to his right that carried sound to the senior engineer, the best one in the fleet. "Can we get more out of the engines, Chief?"

"For only a minute or two, sir, then they'll blow. We're already in the red on our RPMs."

Goodwin paused, "Give me everything—a minute or two is probably all we've got."

"Yes, sir!" replied the chief.

After a few seconds, the airship surged forward, pressing Goodwin back into his seat. *What did he do? Spray ether in the fuel line?*

They'd already dropped their bomb load over the city center and now Captain Goodwin, anxiously straining to see through the smoke and flak ahead of him, perceived the western outskirts of New Berlin, nearly directly underneath. The city below seemed to be rising up to meet them. Fast.

A pair of jets streaked off to the far left, while a solitary fighter appeared in the upper rear right fiber-optic-viewer, high above them, a spot at this distance with a white tail behind it. Diving down, straight at them.

"Navigator! Where's the New Berlin River?"

"Uh, north, sir. To the right. You should be able to see it!"

Goodwin deliberately increased his rate of descent by lowering the horizontal surfaces, gaining speed from falling, while cranking hard to the right. The *Indomitable* complied with a groan. The jet above stayed on their tail, diving. Its bullets poured into the upper rear right octant before it streaked off, still going down as it moved past them in a blur.

A sudden ball of flame and smoke arose from the edge of the suburbs of the city below them. Their altitude had been too low for the jet pilot to succeed in pulling back up after his attack on them. Astoundingly, the upper rear right octant of the *Indomitable* that he'd fired into didn't blow—but it *was* leaking.

Their airship had crossed out of the flak zone, out of the city proper. Goodwin caught a glimpse of the green of the New Berlin River, just as he knew the other pair of jets he'd already seen were circling for another attack run from behind. He pushed the pilot's wheel forward, throwing away even more altitude for a bit more speed.

The left engine ceased to turn just as the airship nicked the top of a tall pine tree on the river bank, right before passing directly over the

15

stream. "Brace for impact!" shouted Goodwin an instant before the *Indomitable* crashed hard into deep green water.

At the same moment the zeppelin plummeted downward, the low fuel warning light of Baron Von Artemache's jet flashed on, the needle in fuel gage on the dashboard nearly *LEER*. Empty. Which left about five minutes flying time left.

"Let's turn around," he broadcast to his wingman in a Paleo-German that Martin Luther would have understood. Or Adolf Hitler.

"Ee," came the reply in Modern. Modern language was against protocol. Artemache ignored the breach as he pulled the joystick around.

As the pair of jets streaked back over the city, the baron noted the anti-aircraft guns had stopped firing. All twenty-two airships from the Tellus-Tethus alliance had either passed all the way across the city or had been destroyed. The raid that intelligence had warned of had come and gone. Some seven or so airships that first hit the city succeeded in crossing, before the jets scrambled into the air.

Von Artemache's sister squadron of jets was hunting them down at that moment.

Intelligence had warned of the enemy's approach from the east, but not that they would be virtually immune to ground-based anti-aircraft fire.

The seven of them made it (for now) plus the last, which had just plunged into the New Berlin River, which flowed westward into the Vinmara Sea. Technically it had made it as well.

New Berlin itself, mightiest city-state in Aphrodite Terra, built on the central slopes of the Ulfrun Penninsula, had long been prepared for an attack coming from the west, the direction of both Tellus and Tethus. But three days ago they'd received intelligence that the alliance had flown their airships all the way around Venus to attack from the east...giving not much time to reposition their air defense artillery.

Flames leapt upward and smoke rose from the center of New Berlin as Baron Von Artemache flew overhead. He knew well that for fire crews on the ground, the battle was far from finished. Bombs of the type some of the airships had succeeded in dropping made flames that would burn long.

17

But for him it was over. After just short of four minutes past the low fuel light engaging, his craft was in line with a military runway at the south of the city. He flipped the switch to lower his landing gear. His Earth-designed ME 262 touched down with a squeal of tires and rolled towards the hangar.

He dismounted the aircraft and left it to the ground crew. Normally he would wait for his wingman, but not today. His long, powerful strides took him in the direction of the "Forschungsflugzeughangar"—the aircraft research hangar. It was massively tall, in the brick dyed red to match Earth designs, made huge for the accommodation of zeppelins. Five minutes passed as Von Artemache marched there, it progressively growing taller and taller.

The hangar doors, more than ten stories tall, were closed. A door nearly in the front right corner of the building was open. Artemache strode through it, barely noting the sign above the door: DIE VERGANGENHEIT IST DER SCHLÜSSEL FÜR DIE ZUKUNFT. "The past is the key to the future."

Several strides past the door, he saw Dr. Kopfstein. He had blueprints for the ME 280 rolled out on a wooden table, several technicians gathered round as the portly man in thick eyeglasses, with a clean-shaven face and long white hair combed backwards, himself a stereotype of what a German scientist should look like, pointing out a design feature of some kind at the underbelly of the aircraft.

"Herr Doctor, may have a word?"

Without looking up, Kopfstein rasped, "Whatever it is that's got you upset, whatever it is you have to say to me, Erich, you can say right here and now. My assistants know all about your peculiarities by now."

"Very well," he unconsciously slapped the aviator gloves he held in his right hand into his left palm. "The Alliance have modified the zeppelin plans, Herr Doctor. Sleek design, suitable for an atmosphere denser than the one they were originally planned for. Fast for airships, probably a different engine design. No gondola. Carbon-fiber in the outer fabrics.

Separate cells of gas, preventing a single good hit from taking out the entire craft."

"And yet early reports are the Messerschmitts were very successful against them."

"Yes. We were successful. But we had losses. And bombs were dropped on our capital, in spite of our efforts, because it took us time to scramble into the air. The jets are better than the airships, but they could be better still. More sweep to the wings, stronger materials—especially in the engines. Better weaponry. Missiles. These are all things that we could easily do. But we haven't!"

The doctor looked up at the baron for the first time. "I've told you before. We are developing things according to schedule. Not too fast, unless we make the mistakes our ancestors made."

Artemache drew in a deep breath to calm himself. "Herr Doctor, we are using designs first made over one thousand years ago. We are wearing clothing—speaking language—that is over one thousand years old. The designs you are peering over were only a few years from breaking the sound barrier. When looking a thousand years into the past, what difference does a few years make? The defense of New Berlin demands better aircraft!"

The doctor stared at him icily for several seconds. "I will pass on your observations, Captain Von Artemache. Was there anything else?"

Artemache's fist tightened over his gloves. "That is *Baron* Von Artemache. Perhaps I ought to speak to my cousin the Kaiser about this."

"Second cousin," replied Kopfstein, looking back down at the blueprints.

Artemache's jaw worked in frustration. "Isn't respect for the landed aristocracy supposed to be a big part of this historical sham we are all engaged in?"

"Of course, Baron." Dr. Kopfstein stood straight, clicked his heals together, and snapped his arm upward at a 45 degree angle in a crisp military salute. "May I return to my work of building better military aircraft for the defense of our nation, Herr Baron Captain?"

"Ee," replied Artemache, not returning the salute before pivoting on his heel and storming out of the hangar.

VV

The green waters of the New Berlin River contained God knows how many industrial toxins. Good thing they weren't getting wet in the pilot's cabin, though the men from lower decks had to evacuate upward as waters poured into the airship before they could seal their firing positions.

Goodwin feared for a little while that once the damaged calls filled up with water, the airship would sink. But even though water rushed in, they still had three cells completely undamaged and another still holding at least some hydrogen, even though it continued to leak. That which may fail to be lighter than air was still much lighter than water.

The airship rolled back and forth clumsily on the river. Drifting downstream, with any luck it would eventually reach the sea and freedom. Though it would be rather unbelievable if the New Berliners made no effort to sink them or pick them up in a patrol ship. Or cruiser. Or would send them to the bottom of the river with one of their "new" diesel-electric submarines.

"Get me the chief engineer!" he ordered the navigator, Flight Lieutenant George Harvest.

"Yes, sir," came the answer. The lieutenant glanced down at his maps and compass, now rendered largely useless as they drifted inevitably westward, and exited their shared cabin. Goodwin could have at least attempted to shout down to the chief himself. But he needed to find something for Harvest to do—all hands needed to contribute in a situation like this.

Several minutes passed before the soaking wet Chief arrived. "Captain Goodwin, sir," he said.

23

"Chief, I keep waiting here by the radio in case we get a signal. In case you were wondering what I'm still doing in here."

"Sir...you do as you see fit. I follow orders."

Goodwin nodded. "We need some kind of engine to steer us. More than one if you can figure out how. I can't believe we haven't been set on by a New Berliner patrol ship already. I mean, at least *some* part of their fleet must be able to go upriver, right?"

The chief let out a heavy breath as his head lowered. "Sir, um...that will be difficult. Both outboards are in the water. Their blocks were hot, too, then suddenly in cold water. I wouldn't be surprised that they're cracked. And the left side had already stopped turning."

"I understand it's a long shot. But finding some way of driving ourselves forward might make the difference between life and death. I've got a hunch you can come up with something, since you are probably the most resourceful man I've ever met. Just make sure that the machine guns still above the water line have crews. If there's any way to move ones below the water line up, we need to do that. Other than covering that, take the rest of the men as you see fit to recover the engine. We need to make this airship into a motorboat. Understood?"

"Yes, sir," the chief saluted but didn't wait for the gesture to be returned before stepping out of the cabin and shouting. "Smith, Edwards, Hardy, Tombs! I've got a special mission for you from the Captain!"

VV

Von Artemache did not report to the head of the squadron, like a fighter pilot was supposed to do. He strode to Kaffee Road (what had once been "Coffee Road"), at the northern edge of the flight zone. More than one soldier in spiked helmet cast astonished looks at his flight uniform. Pilots, as officers, would normally change to a dress uniform before leaving the field. Plus, it was odd to be out walking around so soon after the "All Clear" siren had sounded.

On the street he caught a horse-drawn cab, the driver just emerging from a bunker by the airfield. He fished a copper ten pfennig piece from an upper flight uniform pocket for payment. Most cabs in New Berlin were horse-drawn. Efforts to use steam-powered cars as cabs had mostly failed for economic reasons. But some steam cars did ply the streets on a normal day—though none were in view at the moment. A pair of steam-powered fire engines in red huffed by, off in a rush to fight city fires, but that was all.

In spite of New Berlin's decision to advance to diesel engines and even jets for military use, most of the city was still steam-powered. Though unlike the Germany of over a millennium ago, not a single one of the steam engines anywhere were powered by burning coal. Ethyl alcohol was the most common fuel used to supply external combustion for most purposes, though burning wood or making it into charcoal was also used. The planet Venus didn't have a single natural seam of coal.

At his order, the cab driver took him to the nearest city rail, the gray horse pulling the black cab trotting down the basalt cobblestones of the street. At the station, he paid a one-mark paper note to mount a charcoal-burning train. The man behind the window assured him the rail was operational as far as he was going and rail service was about to re-commence. The train belched black smoke as it pulled out from the platform.

Dismounting the train at National Avenue, Von Artemache from there walked the three blocks towards the domes of the Kaiser-Palast, none of which had been struck during the air raid, though the gardens on the other side of palace burned with an orange visible all the way from the opposite side of the palace. Clearly at least one of the zeppelins had tried to hit the Kaiser's home, but missed.

As he approached the stone fence surrounding the Kaiser residence with its wrought iron gates, the main entranceway,

27

where a squad of guards in long gray overcoats and spiked helmets snapped to attention after staring at his uniform for a moment in puzzlement—before they recognized the two pips on his shoulder marking him as a captain. He sought out the coat braid marking the senior non-commissioned officer present.

"I need to see the officer in charge of the guard, please."

The sergeant, his brows knit in apprehension, saluted. "Sir, I am not certain he is immediately available. There is some concern of further air raids and the safety of the palace."

"I flew one of the jets overhead that defended this palace and this city. I am reasonably certain the raid is over. Plus, the "All Clear" has sounded, as you must have heard. Get me the Officer of the Guard."

"Yes, sir!" the sergeant saluted sharply and Von Artemache casually returned it. The sergeant pivoted on his heel and marched off. Several minutes passed before he returned. Minutes in which the enlisted soldiers remained standing at attention—which Von Artemache allowed them to do without comment.

When the sergeant of the guard returned, his officer was walking in front of him, a captain.

The pilot reached out to shake the hand of the man who was technically the same rank as himself and told him, "I am Baron Von Artemache, here to see my cousin the Kaiser."

VV

The nose of the airship bobbed up and down regularly, both above and below the waterline. Goodwin was especially aware of this because his control cabin peeked out from the very nose of the craft. His lower windows were permanently below the dark green waters, while the upper ones splashed under and out of waves repeatedly. Fortunately, a design intended to resist rainstorms made all the window seals good and tight. Only a tiny trace of beaded water had entered the cabin thus far.

Goodwin had issued his orders and knew there was nothing to be directly gained by leaving the flight cabin and watching. The chief was an extremely competent man.

Still, he might have to relocate. *If* the crew succeeded in getting a working engine running on what remained of the airship, it seemed unlikely he'd have effective control from this cabin. Though that in and of itself was a question worth discussing. What would be effective controls of such a means of propulsion? The air surfaces of the zeppelin would be mostly useless, though they could turn water to a degree. The motor itself would probably have to be pivoted. Probably this would be something the chief would already be thinking about—he needed to know for sure what the chief had in mind.

He walked out of a cabin framed with thin steel beams coated with carbon fiber. The airship sloshed, jolting him sideways at the edge of the doorway. Of course, the same thing could have happened in the air with an unexpected change of wind. Still, the New

Berlin River flowed faster and with more turbulence than he would have expected. That had to be good, right? The faster the river, the quicker their voyage to the sea would be...

After about twenty feet the passageway split into a Y. He took the right, since the tilt of the craft put that section of the airship higher. Two of the engineers in coveralls carrying toolboxes were walking his direction. The twist of the craft and the mild jostling in the water made the short walk an exercise in balance. Goodwin breathed a sigh of relief that he managed to stay on his feet. It wouldn't do to fall down in front of the men.

He passed by with only an "Excuse me, Captain" on the part of one of them. A bit further ahead, daylight illuminated a steel ladder angled upward to an open hatch. He climbed it, noting the rungs were wet and slippery. He took his time on the way up. Again, it would set a poor example for the men to break his back while falling down a ladder.

The top rung was followed by the outer skin of the aircraft. Its carbon-fiber technology hadn't been shared by New Berlin when they'd rebuilt the industries of Tethus and Tellus and so many other Venusian city-states in accordance with to their own distinct concept of what was historically "good." But New Berlin wasn't the only city to have records remaining from the technological past...

Captain Goodwin pulled himself onto the aircraft surface on his belly, careful because of the downward slope of the artificial terrain on his left, the movement of the airship, and the wetness around the hatch. He raised his head after coming to his knees. About one hundred yards distant from the airship, on the steep and grassy green bank of the river, a flock of sheep grazed. And a shepherd boy stared at him in astonishment. Goodwin offered him a friendly wave. The boy waved back feebly, his mouth still open.

He strode carefully across the surface of the craft, noting three ropes anchored to outer metal rings he knew existed but which were barely visible. Three men were cranking on come-alongs not far in front of him, while the chief's focus was in the water.

Goodwin walked up to the chief. Lieutenant Harvest was standing beside him, staring into the water, his shoulders slumped.

"Lieutenant, I'd like you to take charge of the efforts to reposition our machine guns. We probably need some mounted on top of the craft. Speak to..." He turned to the chief, who finished his thought:

"Harrison."

"Yes, Harrison. Ask me if you have any questions. But first, talk to Harrison and get his thoughts."

"Yes, sir!"

The navigator set off towards the hatch Goodwin had just come up. The chief gave an understanding nod to the captain. "Always good to keep a man busy, but we might have to inspect the Lieutenant's handiwork, sir. He's not an expert in fields of fire that I know of."

"We'll be able to. The ships I'm worried about would be pretty much immune to machine gun fire anyway."

The engineer nodded again, his eyes turning back to the waters. One man came up for air in the river, spewing green water. Through the murky river a dark squarish shape was visible in front of him, not more than a few feet down. The engine.

"You've got it that far along already, Chief? I'm impressed."

33

"We got some good swimmers on this crew, Captain. That was the hard part—deep underwater unbolting the motor from the side strut and getting all the lines attached. We're also trying to recover the other, but I think that one may be a lost cause."

Goodwin continued to observe the crew ratchet up the engine out of the water, onto the skin of the craft. As they did so, the propeller, which had been horizontal under the water, rotated to stand straight upward. It was hand-crafted from wood, and much taller than the engine itself.

The weight of the ten foot long motor (still encased in its housing) dented the aircraft's skin. It was one of the first internal combustion engines built in Tethus in fact (prior engines had been steam-driven external combustion designs whose ancient blueprints had been shared by New Berlin engineers), heavier than it really should be, since it was based on ancient designs of something much lighter called the "Liberty Engine." Based on it, but more than double in total size, since the original had used 12 cylinders and this had 24.

Goodwin looked up from the engine and considered their situation. Sundark would be coming soon, which would make river navigation more difficult. The *Indomitable* could run aground in the river if it got any shallower. Or catch on the side of the river bank if it got any narrower. They were rather closer to the north bank now than they should be...

His thoughts were interrupted by a repetitive squeaking sound to the north, accompanied by the *whoosh-whoosh* of a large steam engine under load. Then he saw a smokestack moving downriver on the north side, poking up above the river bank. It was nearly parallel with their position along the river, belching white smoke, still a bit upstream from them.

The vehicle mounted the top of the bank, huffing steam, blowing smoke, it's front tires of synthetic rubber and its rear the treads marking it as something Goodwin had seen on paper but never in person—a New Berlin steam-powered half-track. Its smokestack rose from in between the open-roof driver's cabin and the open bed rear of the vehicle, which contained around a dozen New Berlin soldiers in their spiked helmets and gray coats. At the rear of the vehicle on a tall tripod was a mounted machine gun of the rotary barrel type—a *Gatling* of some kind.

As the steam half-track, chewing up the ground of the river bank, pulled up alongside them as close as it could get, the soldier manning the machine gun pivoted it on the tripod in their direction. And began rotate the gun's handle, spraying bullets in their direction.

♥♥

Baron Von Artemache twisted in the plush green velvet bench as if arguing with himself in his mind as he waited for the Kaiser. He couldn't believe the ridiculous rules he operated under. Modifications of original designs had happened with ground craft, with ships, too, on occasion. Why should aircraft be strictly exempted?

And now, part of the city burned. Who knew how many New Berliners had been killed? It could have been prevented.

"Ludicrous!" he exclaimed out loud in Modern, inspiring a passing elderly manservant carrying a silver platter with gleaming coffee service to stare at him, the man's eyes open wide in astonishment.

"This place was originally named for New Berlin, Wisconsin! Not Berlin, *Berlin!*" he added to no one in particular, his head turned to his left, where sunlight poured in from a glass window with multiple small panes. This time it was a young Army lieutenant in crisp dress uniform on his right that stared at him while walking over the intricately designed and sparkling clean tile, down a hall lined with mostly very accurate reproductions of paintings from over a millennium ago.

In his flight uniform, he was a completely incongruous element in this place. And would have been even if he hadn't been talking to himself out loud, peppering his outbursts with prayers to God for help.

He didn't care in the slightest. Like in the philosophy even more ancient than the painting reproductions—Plato—it was the substance of things that mattered, their immaterial truth. As was also true in the spiritual realm of the Christian Faith as far as he was concerned—service belonged to God and not to men. The substance mattered, not the outward or exterior form. He strove to live his life so he would never care for appearances or what people thought of him. He always did his best to say what he believed and act as he believed he should, no matter what. People often thought him strange, even insane. But he was a superb fighter pilot.

37

"Come now, cousin. I have a good reason to be waiting for you," he muttered in crisp German, calming himself. He remained in his seat, unmoving, for long hours, long after the sky turned black with the commencement of a night cycle.

VV

Bullets sprayed in the water behind the engine, sweeping up towards it and the men hauling it up. Goodwin anticipated it raking through them all and rather helplessly flung himself to the top surface of the airship. Then he realized he saw the man behind the gun on the halftrack fall backward. There had been a single *crack* from behind him in the midst of the enemy fire.

He rolled to his side to look behind him and saw one of his junior mechanics kneeling down with a bolt action rifle in his hands—a rifle he'd barely noticed earlier. In the same second he looked back, the corporal finished closing the bolt and squeezed the trigger again.

He flipped over the other way and saw men with spiked helmets pouring out of the back of the half-track with rifles of their own.

"Harvest!" he bellowed, the Lieutenant and his machine gun placements nowhere in sight.

OV

Artemache had nodded off, his head hanging down between his knees, his legs splayed wide, when a voice called to him. "Cousin?"

He looked up and saw the Kaiser in the light provided by overhead lamps (as latter sundark had come), his fresh young face peering at him in obvious concern. Standing next to him was the portly and gray-haired Duke Wasserstrand—in German *"Harzog"* Wasserstrand, just as in the same German his title was *"Freiherr."* Wasserstrand pulled out a pocket watch from his upper military uniform pocket and peered down at it through the monacle clenched by his right eye, his face impatient, his entire presence apparently unaware of his multiple outrageous anachronisms.

Artemache held himself back from replying in Modern: *"Ja, mein Kaiser, ich bin hier um dich zu sehen."*—I am here to see you, my Kaiser. While using the informal pronoun of close friends. Or cousins.

39

"*Und was kann ich für Sie tun, mein Cousin?*"—what can I do for you, my cousin, replied the Kaiser—taking the opposite approach, using a formal pronoun but a familiar title. Both distancing and belittling.

Artemache drew in a deep breath. This wasn't going to be easy.

VV

Goodwin remembered he had a sidearm at his belt and pulled it. His Single Action Army, a.k.a. "Colt Peacemaker" was copied from a design even older than the airship plans New Berlin had delivered to Tethus. He didn't have much chance to hit anything with a revolver at the range of over 50 yards. But he could draw fire away from the one corporal on his side who was effectively engaging the enemy.

He stood and dashed five paces away from the corporal, firing one time as he moved. He stood and held the revolver in front of him with both hands and tried to aim. He pulled back the hammer with his left thumb and squeezed the trigger with his right index finger. The .45 caliber weapon kicked back hard as he sent lead towards the New Berliners, the black powder smoke from the fired cartridge rising over him, clearly marking his position.

"Harvest!" he bellowed and fired twice more.

Behind him (he didn't dare glance back to see from where) a voice shouted out, "Here, sir!"

In front of him the chief barked, "Back over the ridge of the ship, boys! Outta the line of fire!"

Goodwin was vaguely aware of movement and his own ragged breathing. He was good at keeping a cool head, but the adrenaline of the moment made his peripheral vision disappear. Staring down a tunnel of red, New Berliner soldiers dropped down to the ground and lined up rifles to fire at him and his men; he had 3 rounds left. He breathed deep to calm himself, and did his best to actually *aim* the last shots he might ever fire.

One round and the gun kicked back. Dark smoke erupted from weapons of soldiers returning fire. Probably Model 1871 Mausers. Single shot weapons. Not hitting him yet. Thank God.

His second round fired and the soldier he'd aimed at in gray coat and spiked helmet hit the dirt. He didn't know if he'd hit the soldier, or only gotten close enough to inspire him to jump to the ground in a heap. Black smoke erupted from soldiers firing his way and it felt like something pulled at his flight jacket.

Last shot and he remembered the enemy Gatling. He swung his weapon towards it, shifting his tunneled vision. A New Berlin soldier had moved into the firing position behind it. Before he could squeeze the trigger, the soldier fell. It would seem his corporal with the rifle got him. But he hadn't heard the shot.

Another New Berliner, the last one still in the back of the half-track, lunged towards the machine gun. He shifted his aim and pulled the trigger with a simultaneous and contradictory sense of inner peace coinciding with adrenaline tremors running up and down his legs. The spiked helmet smacked the gun as the man fell, throwing up a splash of blood. But Goodwin could not say if he'd hit the soldier or his corporal had done so again.

From behind him, Harvest bellowed, "Get down, sir!" He realized he might as well; out of rounds to fire; he hit the deck.

From behind him a machine gun began to roar. One of the modified Maxim guns, hurling .303 British rounds of ancient design. Goodwin was afraid to roll back to look, because the rounds were going right over his head at the enemy and rolled on his side he be closer to them. Facing the New Berliners on his belly, he saw dirt on the shore torn up by the gun behind him, in the area where the spike-helmeted soldiers taken firing positions. Several rifles fired back once more not obviously hitting anything. But they fired only once.

When the weapon behind him stopped hurling rounds in a roar, he dared to roll over to look. Flight navigator Harvest and three crewmen were at a gun mounted on a tripod. Harvest was *not* the one pulling the trigger. The trained gunman, Harrison, who'd come from one of the lower deck placements, he was in that position. A cloud of black smoke trailed away from the gun placement, rising and pushed upriver by the prevailing breeze.

"Well, hello, Lieutenant."

"Hello, Captain. My apologies at the delay in getting the gun up here. I heard you shouting."

"Um...yeah. Thank God you're here now." He breathed deeply to alleviate his body shaking. But his mind was altogether calm. "Continue setting emplacements. We want fields of fire all around the ship, even though sundark is about to come and our chances of an

43

enemy attack will go down. Do you understand how to overlap fields of fire, Lieutenant?"

Harvest bit his lower lip, "I'm not sure I do, sir."

The Corporal behind the Maxim gun, Harrison, spoke up, addressing Navigator Harvest. "I know how, sir. I can help ya."

"Excellent," said Goodwin. "Move sharply, men. More of them could be coming along at any moment."

VV

"So you are telling me that Tellus and Tethus have come up with airship designs *we* didn't give them," the Kaiser said.

Artemache drew in a deep breath. He'd only stated this twice before. *But I must remain calm. There is a time for everything under the sun, as the Scriptures say. Now is the time for calm patience*: "Yes, my Kaiser. Carbon fiber fabrics. Individual cells within each airship, preventing the explosion of one part from destroying the whole. Sleeker design. Faster engines—not steam-powered. No gondolas."

"How could they conceive of such things?" whispered the Kaiser, clearly to himself.

"I do not know, my Kaiser. But perhaps records of the past from some city-states other than New Berlin were also preserved, even if incomplete."

The young Kaiser drew in a short breath. "Then why would they be living in barbarism before we came to enrich their lives, as we did for the entire planet?"

Artemache hesitated. He knew the true answer to this question but did not want to insult his cousin. Still, the virtue of honesty *demanded* he say something. He managed to frame it as a question, "Could it be, my Kaiser, that the other city-states of Venus love their homes as much as we do?"

Wasserstrand snorted, "Miserable savages! They don't know what's good for them. New Berlin is acting in *their* best interests. Someone needs to take leadership of this planet and ensure its proper development! Are any of *them* going to do that?"

With several things he could say, all true, Artemache steered straight for getting what he wanted, "Whatever their reasons, they pose a threat to us. Given their unexpected advances, we need to respond with advances of our own."

The Kaiser looked upward towards the ceiling, his face illuminated by lamps mounted on the walls burning hydrogen gas. His eyes were sunken in, his face very pale. Tired. The burden of near-total rule weighed heavily on him. "I suppose we should look into it. I could form an advisory panel. Herr Doktor Kopfstein could head it up..." His voice trailed off.

"My Kaiser, please not Kopfstein. I've already discussed this with him and he was skeptical."

Wasserstrand snorted again. "Rightly so. I think we need to see evidence, first, that such 'advanced' designs actually exist—and are not mere the delusions of a single fighter pilot."

"I'm not the only one that saw them," replied Artemache sharply. "Thousands of people must have."

"Proof," growled Wasserstrand, "Where is your proof?"

"I imagine a great deal of it rained down on the city as debris, since we shot down fourteen of them here!"

"Ha! How can you be so sure of the number?"

"I counted some myself—but I am mostly repeating what the Imperial Intelligence Services gave for numbers—"

"Yet that same service reported not a single word on your so-called 'advanced designs'—why would they miss such basic facts?"

Artemache paused. He had no idea why—in fact, it was rather astonishing they hadn't reported them. Then he came to himself. "Duke Wasserstrand, it isn't at all *important* that intelligence failed. Not at this moment anyway. That is an investigation for someone else. I am here to request authorization to accelerate our pace of aircraft development."

"That is a risky thing you propose, *Frieherr!* All these matters have been carefully weighed out by experts," replied the duke, his face flushing red. "We need solid evidence before we can even discuss acting."

An inspiration flashed through Artemache's mind. "Proof? Would an intact enemy airship qualify? I think I know where to find one of those...in the New Berlin River!"

◊◊

The *Indomitable* had made it to the New Berlin River estuary, mere miles from the sea, when the crew finished bolting down the single fully-functional recovered engine as an

47

outboard motor. Repairmen, gunners, and bombardiers had worked together as a seamless whole to make it happen, even after sundark. In addition to being brilliant with equipment, the chief was a master of motivating and efficiently employing men.

But while watching them work, it suddenly struck Goodwin there were too many men onboard. Twenty-eight were too many (by some miracle, all of them were still alive). With automation, the number could be reduced to two or three. That would greatly reduce the weight of the craft—crew not only weigh a good deal, they need quarters and food. And then...the airship should be filled with helium rather than hydrogen...well, it still wouldn't be a good match for a jet, but it would fly much, much better. And be more resistant to enemy fire. With more gun placements, it might work...

Concerning machine gun placements, those Harvest had set up had been in position for several hours. After that, Goodwin had directed the navigator to use his binoculars to scan for enemy vessels and ground forces in all directions. Looking out towards the sea at that moment, he announced, "Sir, I see the silhouettes of ships on the horizon. Moving our way."

Goodwin looked out west towards the ocean. It had been sundark during most of their trip downriver but was sunlight again. He saw tendrils of black smoke rising in the distance—at least some of the ships Harvest saw must be steam-powered to belch such smoke. Finding ships at the mouth of a river leading to an upland city-state was hardly unusual. In fact, it was unusual that they had seen *no* ships before now, not going upriver, not going down.

"Warships?" he asked, though he thought he already knew.

"Yes, sir. I see deck guns on most of them. Big ones."

"How many ships do you see, Lieutenant?"

"Seven...at least seven. Maybe more."

VV

When Baron Von Artemache entered the zeppelin hangar, still in his jet pilot flight suit, Kopfstein met him near the doorway. The baron blinked in surprise, "Yes, Herr Doctor, what is it?"

His eyes went past the doctor to the zeppelin his cousin had given him control of for this mission, the *Kaiserin* herself. The hangar was lit up with electric lights, as it was latter sundark. The zeppelin had already lifted off the hangar floor as its crew pumped it full of *Wasserstoff* in preparation for his flight.

"It seems I underestimated you," stated the master controller of New Berlin's technological plan.

Artemache's eyes met the doctor's for a second and then looked back at the airship inside the massive hangar. He was trying to compute in his head wind speed plus the *Kaiserin*'s top speed divided by the distance down the river the enemy airship must have gone based on average hourly river flow. "What?" he asked distractedly.

"I underestimated you. I never believed the Kaiser would listen to you. And now he's recalled a naval squadron and given you control of our finest airship. As part of putting you in charge of recovering the enemy airship."

"Well, my goal is not all the way met. First recover the airship, then we can talk about design improvements. But yes, it is an encouraging start. Thank God." Artemache stated all of this with his eyes still fixed on the zeppelin that would be his command center for the recovery operation.

"I will never underestimate you again," stated the professor icily.

Artemache met Kopfstein's gaze. "This was never about *you*, Herr Doctor. I only care about the defense of our city-state. And for doing what I believe is right. You don't matter to me in the slightest. I mean that with all of my heart."

"Pray that you recover the airship, Baron. If you do not, you will belong to me."

The baron didn't take the time to ponder what in heaven that could mean. He walked right past the corpulent scientist, political insider, and planner. He saw a captain walking across the floor towards him in a zeppelin commander's uniform. An old classmate.

"Manny, how good to see you! Now I know what the Air Force does with pilots who aren't good enough to fly jets!" He grinned broadly as he said it.

ᘯᐺ

The outboard motor roared and the *Indomitable* surged forward...but not very quickly. Goodwin bit his tongue to stop himself from

51

cursing. Perhaps it was a matter of building momentum.

Two minutes later, no significant change in speed accomplished, plugging his ears with his fingers to drown out the engine's cacophony, he strode towards the chief across the rocking top surface of the airship. "Whadya say? Ten knots faster?"

"At best, sir," shouted the chief to be heard over the engine roar.

Goodwin had seized on a plan to turn a sharp right after leaving the estuary, to hug the coastline in order to escape the New Berlin naval squadron. But to make that work, the *Indomitable* would have to move faster than the naval ships.

"What do you expect the naval vessels can do, Chief? Twenty knots?"

"I'd say at least twenty-five, sir."

This time a word slipped out. "Damn!"

The chief nodded in understanding, even though Captain Goodwin had ever heard him curse, not even in the smallest way. "What are your orders, sir?"

"Give me a minute, Chief," he shouted back.

VV

Kapitän zur See Schmidt studied the estuary with binoculars from the bridge of the heavy cruiser that served as command post of his squadron, the *Vizeadmiral Scheer*. His entire naval squadron had been ordered to evacuate the region in anticipation of enemy bombing.

Terraformed Venus was an ocean world, a world in which naval vessels mattered. They plied between isolated city-states on what had once been high peaks and plateaus on the planet. Most naval vessels, even those of New Berlin, had wooden hulls. Though many of the wooden ships also had steam engines and paddlewheels to drive them.

Schmidt commanded one of two "all iron" squadrons that had been recently built by the naval shipyards at New Hamburg. These were considered vital for national defense in case the scattered city-states of Venus had mounted a naval attack on New Berlin—hence their evacuation at the time of anticipated bombing. Just in case.

Schmidt had not enjoyed being evacuated. His ships were made of steel for a purpose, to be resistant to enemy attack. They were armed with deck guns; they should have had the chance to participate in the fight. Still, it was not his job as a New Berlin naval officer to question his orders. But rather to obey them.

So when the wireless radio on his bridge had tapped out in the rhythm of ancient International Morse Code orders to return to the estuary and capture—not destroy, but capture—an enemy airship floating downstream, he did not protest the plan openly, even though it contained the objectionable element of his squadron being placed under the command of a lowly Air Force Captain (an Air Force rank equivalent to his own would be a Colonel). Whether the man was a Baron or not.

He simply ordered his wireless telegraph crewman to acknowledge the orders. And then turned back home, full steam.

"Do you see what I see, *Fregattenkapitän?*" This was to the commander of the Scheer itself, standing next to him on the bridge, also studying the mouth of the estuary with binoculars.

"*Jawohl mein Kapitän.* They have mounted an engine as an outboard motor. And it looks as if they are driving their half-sunken airship straight towards us!"

"*Ja,* I see the same things. This will be an easy day."

The *Kaiserin* had taken off in the sundark hours before Schmidt arrived at the estuary of the New Berlin River. Baron Von Artemache sat in the assistant navigator's chair in the forward gondola.

The slow pace of the zeppelin—and its silence—gave it an otherworldly majestic quality. At least from his point of view as a pilot in the developing jet fighter program. The reproduction ME 262 he flew howled into the air, yet had a fragile engine that had to be handled gingerly. Like flying in a bullet made of glass.

By contrast, the *Kaiserin* seemed like an invulnerable mountain that drifted in the sky. Or a cloud.

But it, like the original zeppelins, lifted in the air by hydrogen gas displacing the oxygen, nitrogen, and carbon dioxide that made up the atmosphere of Venus. An atmosphere that had once been 92 times denser than Earth's. The terraformers spent a lot of effort degassing the planet, sending a portion of its carbon dioxide all the way to Mars, in a process no longer understood. Still, the atmosphere of Venus remained over three times as dense as that of Planet Earth, increasing the lift properties of displaced air. And of air flowing over a wing, for that matter.

These should be filled with helium, history be damned, thought Artemache. It was rather astonishing the Tethus and Tellus airships hadn't already done so, since they'd done so many other re-designs. Though it could be because making hydrogen only requires processing abundant water via electrolysis, while gathering atmospheric helium takes fractional distillation, something they may not have been prepared to perform.

"Your first time in a zeppelin?" asked its captain, Manfred von Holstein, interrupting Artemache's thoughts.

"Um, rode a blimp when I was fourteen. So not quite the same. But like this time, I couldn't hear the engines. It's a strange experience for me."

"It must be quite different than flying a jet."

"Or a flying boat. That's what I requested for this mission, by the way. Denied. But I'm grateful to get anything at all."

"A flying boat? Pfft! Such a thing does not move with the majesty of this craft."

"No, but I don't see 'majesty' as of particular military value," replied Artemache dryly.

"Pfft!" answered the captain.

The hydrogen gas street lights of New Berlin were still off post-air raid, but orange light nonetheless illuminated the underside of the zeppelin. From fires still burning in the city. The Kaiser had declared war on the Tethus-Tellus alliance, of course. Running the declaration through the *Reichstag* in the morning was a mere formality. But specific plans for an armed response had yet to be devised.

Artemache's thoughts for some reason he could not identify drifted to more than twenty thousand kilometers overhead, to an orbiting panel of thin, sun-blocking material responsible for sundark during this daylight half of the month. The ancient terraformers had sped up the rotation of Venus, but only to 28 Earth days, making eight of these "months" per year ("months" are what the ancients called them, even though they really should have been called "sols" in the terminology of the time). Each month with fourteen days of light and fourteen of darkness. Winds blowing through the still thick atmosphere and the worldwide ocean did much to even temperatures between the fortnight of daylight and the fortnight of darkness. Still, the orbiting panels blocked four hours of sunlight out of every twelve in latitude-specific bands on the daylight side, while radiating infrared beams back on the night side of the planet. Once the night panels had also rained down light, according to history. But that system no longer functioned.

After the United Nations Wars destroyed space transportation and left most people on Venus in a low-tech state, most of them content to fish alongside the planet's many beaches, the failure of the overhead lighting system signaled the elders of the city of New Berlin that it was not possible to remain free of the technology everyone blamed for the excesses of the past. Not forever. Someday the heating system would fail as well.

The key was to return to the past, but not all the way. To rebuild technology in a society that made technology work—but without going too far, culturally. Because at some point, advancing technology had seemed to make everyone go insane. New Berlin had good records and a devoted citizenry. They worked hard to imitate the past of over one thousand years ago—and saw to it that other city-states of Venus did the same thing.

Artemache liked to read. He knew that those who lived at the time of the United Nations Wars would have seen the culture New Berlin imitated, that of nineteenth century Earth, as inherently destructive, as "evil"—even though they bizarrely avoided using that term. Of course they were wrong, everyone accepted that. Nothing in the nineteenth century could compare to the rank brutality of the twenty-fourth. Not even slavery and racism. Which of course, New Berlin rejected.

Still, hasn't evil always been a part of the entire human race? Didn't the era of early technology have its own forms of wickedness and excess? Couldn't New Berlin achieve its goals, or at least attempt to, without slavishly worshiping the past?

These questions not even Baron Von Artemache pondered too deeply. In the end, he was an officer in the New Berlin Air Force. He understood what his duty to his city-state was—in this case, to capture an enemy zeppelin. Nothing would dissuade him from the pursuit of that goal.

Kapitän Schmidt peered through his binoculars from the bridge of the *Vizeadmiral Scheer*. He pulled his eyes away from the lenses, rubbed them, and looked through them out the window again.

Eyes still fixed to the binoculars, he spoke with the sharp tone of command even when asking a question: *"Fregattenkapitän* Arbeiter, do you see what I see?"

"Mein Kapitän," the more junior naval commander answered with a voice tremor, "I do not know. What is it you see?"

Schmidt lowered the binoculars and glared at Arbeiter. But the ship captain did not notice, still peering through his own binoculars. "What *I* see, sir, is that it seems as if the enemy airship is sinking. While it is still coming towards us."

VV

The wireless telegraph tapped out its staccato message on the console to Artemache's right, on the bridge of the *Kaiserin*. The operator read the paper ribbon coming off the device. "Sir! *Kapitän* Schmidt reports the enemy airship is sinking as it approaches their squadron. He requests instructions."

Von Artemache turned to his left to address the airship captain, "Manny, how far away is the shore?"

"We'll arrive in about fifteen minutes."

"Fourteen thirty-two...thirty-one...thirty...twenty-nine—" replied the navigator.

"No need to keep a running count," said Artemache mildly. He scratched the side of his head. *Sinking as it approaches?*

"Wireless operator, please request Schmidt to explain how the airship can be *both* sinking in the ocean *and* approaching them?"

Long moments passed as the operator tapped out the message and then received the reply. "The message says they have mounted a single motor. Which remains above water, pushing the craft as it sinks. It is approaching them. Schmidt again requests instructions."

Artemache felt his face flushing red, "Tell him he needs to capture them!"

VV

Beads of cold sweat ran down Adam Goodwin's face in sympathetic harmony to beads of water running down from the ceiling and across the glass of the *Indomitable's* cockpit.

The craft creaked and leaked. Salt water lapped up to Goodwin's ankles.

Dear God, dear God, I pray that I have not killed my men. No matter what happens to me, may they survive.

The airship's steel frame groaned in reply. Somehow the outboard was still moving the craft forward. It was impossible for him to estimate speed very well—they of course had no periscope. But it couldn't be much more than 5 knots. About all he could do is try to manipulate the aircraft's turning surfaces to provide some form of steering. His main task was to keep heading out into deeper water, to prevent the ship from a turn that would lead it back to shallow water. The window allowed him to see enough to attempt that, though the compass helped, too.

It was a crazy idea, almost certainly doomed to fail. A crazy idea, one that had caused the chief to raise his eyebrows at him. But then he shouted the men into executing the plan.

The *Indomitable's* windows and doors sealed tight to increase its aerodynamic traits and to shut out the worst that rainstorms could throw at them. Still, nobody had designed their airship to be a submarine, with only the section with the outboard motor high enough that the motor itself was out of the water. Submerged, the airship was bound to take on more water, to sink *more*. To wind up at the bottom of the ocean.

Thank God, the sea was calm, with low waves. Or it would have been impossible to even try this. The motor could keep running while exposed to some water, as in a thunderstorm. But immersion in salt water would probably be too much for it.

So—with no way to keep leaking water out and it being vitally important they not sink more—all they had to work with to maintain their balance in the water was the carefully-designed motor intended to push hydrogen from one cell to another. The chief had taken direct control of the mix, and judged by *vibration of the frame and motor* their relative depth, while his crews executed his other plans.

A crazy idea—which for now was working. Captain Goodwin sweated and prayed under his breath, as he guessed and steered his way in the direction of deeper water.

VV

The *Kaiserin* made good time on the prevailing high winds blowing from East to West, over 150 kph. Soon, the New Berlin River estuary was visible. The New Berlin Navy docks were on the left of the river and the fishing town of New Muskego lay on the right, northward. Neither of these did much to disrupt the natural flow of the river, perhaps rather surprisingly, considering how industrial New Berlin had become upriver (to the point of coloring the river green with algae blooming from consumption of whatever-it-was in the water).

The sun had been rising in the sky for three of the twenty-four hour days the inhabitants of Venus had taken with them from their former home on Earth. At seven days the sun would be at its zenith, at "noon," so it was not halfway there yet. It had risen high enough to be out of Von Artemache's eyes when flying west, which was good. But still, they were in the cooler, early part of the month.

The airship steered out over the river, its commander slowing the engines, which were far enough back to nearly be inaudible, even though they carried the noisy, internal combustion type. The airship seemed to drift forward on its own.

64

"Any word on the airship location?"

The wireless telegraph operator replied, "They say it is still heading straight for their squadron, only the outboard motor above water."

Artemache scanned from the direction of the river outward in a nearly straight line towards eight steel-sided ships, which had pulled in parallel to the shore in a double line of four ships each. The motion of the engine and the spray of water it left made it easily visible, in spite of it being relatively small from their height. Its motion forward was quite slow in spite of the fury of the engine's spin.

"Operator, do our ships have any nets? They could simply fish the enemy aircraft out of the water."

The *tip-tip-teep, tip-tip-teep* of the machine signaled its message being sent. Artemache frowned. Really, the rest of the military should be allowed voice radio, like his jet had.

At the relative crawl in communication speed, the answer came back, one letter at a time. Eventually the operator answered. "Sir, they say they do not."

"How about grappling hooks? Cables? Anchor chain? Surely they've got some way to fish this vessel out of the water. Tell them to figure that out and pull alongside the enemy vessel. Then pull it up."

He turned to his left. "Manny, can you bring us a whole lot closer to the action? Would it be safe to make our height one hundred meters, just over the outboard motor?"

"*Jawohl,* Karlo," his friend answered. "We'll be in place a in a few minutes." The navigator opened his mouth as if about to give the exact count, but a stern look from the airship captain warned him not to.

As he watched through the binoculars, the motor slowly approached the side of one of the warships, as if about to crash directly into its side.

VV

Kapitän Schmidt no longer looked through his binoculars. The above-water outboard motor was easily visible, churning up a vast amount of spray as it slowly pulled forward. It would soon impact the side of the Scheer.

Rhythmic clattering from the communication station was given a sudden interpretation by the wireless telegraph operator. "Sir, the airship requests us to use grappling hooks to pull up the craft."

Schmidt looked up towards the airship flying in from the east. *The Air Force. They know nothing.*

"*Fregattenkapitän* Arbeiter, would you use grappling hooks at this time, if the choice were yours?"

A look of consternation passed over the face of the more junior officer, as if this were a test he would be wise to fear failing. Which, of course, it was. "*Nein, mein Kapitän.* The, uh, spinning outboard motor could catch the lines. It's a hazard to the men."

"Quite right," Schmidt nodded in approval. "What happens if the motor hits the side of our vessel?"

"Their forward progress ends. They, uh, either sink or, um, come up if they can."

"At which point *they* will turn off the motor."

"Uh, yes sir—that would seem entirely natural."

"That is when we will deploy the hooks."

"*Jawohl, mein Kapitän.*"

"Sir!" called out a deck officer. "The outboard is turning." And so it was, as if

67

someone below water could see the Scheer's shadow. The turn was a slow one, but just might manage to get the outboard in parallel with the ship instead of on a direct impact course.

Schmidt looked at Arbeiter expectantly, his right eyebrow raised.

Arbeiter spoke in reply to the look, "Helmsman, reverse starboard motor, half speed. Port engine forward, half speed." The Scheer would spin in place in the water, blocking any escape the pathetic outboard motor and the airship below it could attempt.

VV

Baron Von Artemache watched the slow turn of the outboard motor from the forward command gondola of the *Kaiserin*. He didn't bother to issue an order to the naval craft to block the movement, since he observed the Scheer begin to spin.

As the Scheer pivoted in place, blocking the movement, the outboard turned once more, in the opposite direction. But only for a short time before the motor cut off, the rotation of the propeller blade winding down to a halt.

68

Their airship now hovered in place over the site, spinning their motors so the *Kaiserin* was facing back the direction it had come from, so its engines could resist the prevailing wind. The airship captain and navigator did a superb job balancing the forces, so they hovered motionless over the site, only a bit more than one hundred meters in the air. They were far enough out into the ocean that the waves weren't particularly hard. The mostly submerged airship below remained in roughly the same position relative to his gondola. As if the outboard motor hovered below them.

Artemache walked over to the side window to peer down at the deck of the Scheer, rubbing his chin. "Where are the grappling hooks? Now would be the perfect time to throw them."

He scanned the deck of the Scheer for motion of sailors preparing to obey his command. He saw nothing significant.

"Telegraph operator, please signal the naval squadron and ask just when it is they intended to capture the enemy vessel."

The operator beat out the message. Silence from the machine was the only immediate reply.

"Operator, please request confirmation that the last message was received."

The message sent, a brief tapping came in reply. "Message acknowledged as received, sir. Not answered."

Artemache suppressed an urge to signal again. The commander of the naval squadron *did* outrank him and perhaps that was the issue here. He'd give them a bit of time before evoking the name of the Kaiser.

After several minutes of hovering, Artemache finally observed sailors moving on the deck of the Scheer in large numbers. They opened storeroom doors and began to lay out chains with hooks on their ends. Frustrated at their slowness, he nonetheless managed to refrain from comment. Slow compliance was better than no compliance.

But below them, just behind the motionless outboard motor still bobbing slowly above water, large bubbles of air broke the surface of the ocean, as if the waters had suddenly begun to boil. With astonishing speed, the outboard motor sank below the surface.

"They've scuttled their ship," breathed the captain of the *Kaiserin*.

"*Gott in Himmel!*" shouted Artemache, half a prayer, half a curse. "Operator, order the

Naval squadron—as directed by the Kaiser himself—to pull that vessel out of the water before all the men inside it are dead!"

The sailors complied with the order. Eventually. But were slow to start.

Though as much as they threw their hooks into the water, working with vigor once they actually began, they seemed to touch nothing other than the ocean bottom. They labored continuously until the next sundark, after which a late-to-arrive U-boat took over the search of the ocean floor. But still found nothing.

After just over an hour into the attempt to recover the *Indomitable*, Artemache took a rope ladder down to the deck of the Scheer and exchanged sharp words with *Kapitän* Schmidt, winning the naval commander's life-long enmity. Which would lead to no less than three formal complaints being lodged against him.

Without the proof of advanced enemy airship development that he'd been sent to recover, not even the Kaiser came to his assistance in full. Von Artemache wound up being demoted to Flight Lieutenant.

But he still continued to fly...

VV

Water poured into the *Indomitable* to a terrifying degree at first. Captain Goodwin had to abandon the cockpit and navigate based on the airship's specially-designed compass alone.

He would never have believed the chief and his men would be able to recover and adapt the remaining engine to propel them forward, combining it with a water pump designed to clear rain water so that it took in and squirted out water at a high rate. The motor had been recovered entirely underwater by the heroic action of the crew.

The chief also sealed the region of the ship that had been fired into and lost its hydrogen without exploding, the upper rear right octant. That area had naturally filled with ordinary air, which now provided air for the motor and which the chief planned to augment with a snorkel. The motor had been placed inside it, running on only eight good cylinders that worked the pump mechanism. However, as much water as the pump pushed, the airship's forward progress underwater couldn't be more than one or two knots per hour.

They'd released enough hydrogen to sink, but not all of it. Goodwin and his men clustered in the service access between the separate hydrogen bladders and breathed increasingly stale air. No one felt like singing, but the whispers of quiet prayers landed on Captain Goodwin's ears unceasingly—a different type of music, both more beautiful and more terrifying.

Standing on the part of the accessway behind the growling motor in the upper octant, Goodwin held the handle the chief had adapted to direct the flow of water, standing under the only functioning light bulb in the area, continually monitoring the compass direction. Westward, ever westward.

Moving through the crowd of men in the crowded access way, a dark shape that manifested itself as the chief came close to the captain.

"Sir, I've identified the excess weight we can cut from the ship."

"Do you have any idea if it will be enough to raise us to the surface?"

"Not sure, to be honest, sir. But have faith. If it works, we saved our ship. If not, we go on to a better eternity."

Goodwin smiled. "Uh, that's not the most comforting thing I've ever heard from you, Chief. I don't want to be responsible for the deaths of all these men."

The chief patted his shoulder. "Have faith, sir. Are you ready for me to start?"

Goodwin fished out a pocket watch from his flight uniform. "Yeah. It will be sundark by the time you finish. And then we will either rise above water or we won't. In either case, we should be beyond the horizon from where the New Berliners were. God only knows if they will figure out what happened to us."

"Yes, sir."

He almost added, *thank God for you, Chief.* But he kept it to himself.

It was a lucky thing—no, providential—that the frame of the Indomitable had been bolted together rather than riveted. Even though he'd complained about it at the time of manufacture, because rivets are stronger.

Within the hour, every last one of the crew of the Indomitable felt themselves moving upwards as the extra parts of the airship without lifting gas were dropped from the main frame of their craft. After a very long time that probably was only a minute or so, the craft shifted in direction to the right. It also seemed to be bobbing slightly. That probably indicated that they had broken surface.

There was one way to be sure. "Open the door," commanded Goodwin.

Saltwater poured in the sealed doorway, but immediately stopped. A fresh ocean breeze filled the craft.

One of the crewmen began to sing. Several others joined in, in astonishing harmony. "Praise God from whom all blessings flow, praise Him all creatures—"

"Quiet boys, quiet!" barked the chief. "We don't know where the New Berliners are."

Goodwin overrode him. "Let them sing, Chief. Just for a bit."

END

The Gaslight Jungle
By L. Jagi Lamplighter

"Are you certain the archbishop was not mistaken?" Charles Fairweather asked cheerfully, as he peered into his mirror and adjusted his clerical collar.

"Beg your pardon, Parson Charlie?" intoned Deacon Abimanyu, in his lyrical Vasilisan accent. A native of the tropical island, his skin was a deep tan.

Abdu, Charlie's dark-skinned manservant from the jungle isle of Umay-ene, stood behind him holding out his master's black frockcoat. The long cherry and magenta rays of late afternoon sunset lit the servant's white garments until they seemed to smolder.

Through the window, the light of the soon-to-be-setting sun reflected off the rain-washed gardens and jungles of the Island of Vasilisa, petals and broad leaves glittering as if set with fiery gems. Beyond, the waves of the Navka Sea leapt like rosy flames. Across the sea, however, bright daylight from the east still bathed the upper slopes and crater-peak of great Ushas Mons.

Of course, the sun would not actually set for a day or two yet.

Charlie spread his arms and backed into the waiting coat. "He didn't look, oh, I don't know, as if he had suddenly lost his marbles?"

"I saw no misplaced marbles," replied Abimanyu. His black frockcoat was a twin of the one Charles was now buttoning. "Did you mean the children's toy? Or the building material?"

"I meant his sanity, old friend." Charlie tapped his noggin with two fingers.

"Come now, Parson Charlie," The deacon scratched his nose so that his hand hides his smile. "You will do fine in this new life."

"You just say that because you want your dressing room back," Charlie gestures at the handsomely-appointed chamber, one of many in the mansion Abimanyu had inherited from his father, a rajah.

"Do not despair." Abimanyu spread his arms. "The archbishop is not a cruel man. He has given you three weeks to decide. If you truly feel that you are unfit for the task, he will release you from the obligation."

"Great. I can escape by admitting I'm a hapless lout," sighed Charlie.

No longer struggling to hide his smile, Abimanyu said kindly, "I will miss you, my friend. You have taught me so much. But when the archbishop says it is time to go, we must go."

"But..." Charlie paced back and forth across the dressing chamber. "Abi, I have done well as a missionary into the wilds. Everyone— my father, my grandparents, even my great uncle himself—said I would fail, but I did not. I have even helped a few."

"A few? You have achieved wonders, Parson Charlie! Did you not lead me to salvation? All the good I do is thus attributed to you as well."

"You must take credit for your own good, Abi," laughed Charlie. More seriously, he added, "I feel at home in the jungles and the barren places. I could understand if he wished me to take on some new horizon: to set up a church in Cape Juno or to blaze a trail into inmost Phoebe. But why take me away from where I have been doing good and send me back to civilization?"

"I think you may find, Parson Charlie, that wherever there are men, there is jungle. Some jungles are a tangle of trees, but the jungles that grow in men's hearts can be just as

78

treacherous."

"Perhaps," replied Charlie, glumly.

"Remember the three rules of Taming the Jungle, friend Charles, and all will be well." Abimanyu counted on his fingers. "Rule One: *Never show fear,* as the Lord commanded Joshua. Rule Two: *Give all to God,* as did Daniel and all the holy prophets. Rule Three: *Never appeal to authority if you can appeal to the spirit God put in man.*" He waggled a finger at Charlie. "The conviction of one's own conscience lasts far longer than a conviction from a magistrate."

Abdu handed his master a silver cross hanging from a chain. Thanking him, Charlie slipped it around his neck and arranged it upon his breast.

"You will do well, my friend. Mayhaps you will meet a good Christian woman or," a wistful note of hope came into Abimanyu's sing-song voice, "a fallen woman to redeem. Maybe a beautiful temptress, such as that Audacia Dangereyes—you know, that woman from Tethus you always warn your flock against who preaches free love? She is a firebrand! A man could do worse than the likes of that for a wife! Train her up! Rid her of her wicked ways! Every day a great adventure!"

"Maybe for you, Old Boy," laughed

Charlie. "Not my cup of tea."

Abimanyu shrugged pleasantly.

"Nothing to be done, then." Giving the mirror one last cursory glance, Charlie straightened his frockcoat and sighed. "Hasting Abbey, it is."

VV

Dusk was falling on the town of Hastings Abbey as Charlie stepped from the crowded train, his travel bag and dragon-headed cane in hand. The sun had fallen beyond the horizon, but the remaining twilight allowed him to make out most objects. Gazing at the dim, maroon-gray sky, he guessed that at least eight hours of twilight remained before the fall of the dark fortnight.

The crowd pouring from the rail cars was twenty times the size he had expected. Yet, when he looked at the village, he saw few new structures. He glanced around at the surrounding countryside. To the north rose the hill upon which sat the old abbey—now Hastings Manor. To the south, the vast, mountainous bulk of an ancient, crashed, atmospheric mining ship—now just a rusted bulk—was silhouetted against the twilit sky.

80

Where did this crowd of humanity live?

It was nearly dinner time. Charlie expected to see his fellow travelers shuffle off to their homes, wherever they might be. Instead, they made a bee line for the long queue coming out of O'Leary's Tavern and Travelers Inn. They were almost all men, clad in worn work clothing. He could think of no nearby industry that might offer employment for so many men. Apparently, a great deal had changed since he had last been in this part of the world.

Making his way around the workmen, he headed down an alley that, if his memory served, led to the country lane he sought. His dragon-headed cane made a pleasant *konk* as it struck the cobblestones. He walked quickly, eager to reach his destination. Already, the chill of the coming dark fortnight was descending, and his black frockcoat was made for warmer climes. Just a mile away, the rectory awaited and, as soon as he could stoke the fires, a hot bath.

"Ow, Gov'nor," came a sultry feminine voice. "Lookin' for a good time?"

A provocatively-dressed young woman sauntered forward, giving him an unconscienceably bold eye. Her bright garments

81

displayed entirely too much of her ample charms. Charlie froze, taken aback to see such a sight in this once-decent town. Encouraged, she strutted forward, swishing her hips.

Suddenly, she stopped.

"Churchman," she pouted, her eye resting on his white collar and the silver cross upon his chest. A painted eyebrow rose hopefully. "Unless…"

Charlie's voice was pleasant yet firm. "Put such thoughts from your mind."

"Just my luck." The young woman stuck out her hip and rested her fist upon it. She blew a stream of air that sent a lock of her auburn hair flying.

Charles continued forward, his cane clicking rapidly against the cobblestones. Abimanyu was right. The jungle was here, too. Only Charlie found he preferred the open danger real savages to rubbing shoulders with the dregs of humanity.

Thinking of Abi, however, brought a smile to his lips. His friend would never have allowed an opportunity to reform a lady of ill repute slip through his fingers. The Vasilisan deacon had a warm spot for them in his heart. Abimanyu's own mother had been less than reputable before she had come to the notice of his father, rising to become the rajah's head concubine. Abi actually believed such women could be redeemed.

Charlie's footsteps slowed. In honor of his friend, he should at least speak civilly to the misguided young thing. Maybe, she could answer some of his questions.

"Er…Miss?" He turned back, putting down his bag and pointed his cane back towards the inn. "Can you tell me what those men are doing? The ones lined up outside the tavern. Is the food at O'Leary's as good as all that?"

She giggled. "Auch, no! It's payday."

"Payday?" Charlie repeated. "They are paid at the tavern?"

Her auburn head bobbed up and down. "He's a wily one, O'Leary. Handing out pay to hungry men, after a long day's work, right next to a keg on tap. 'Tisn't much left afterwards for those lads to bring home to their wives."

"You mean, they drink a goodly portion of their paycheck before they leave the Tavern?"

The young woman made a sour face, "Clever as a snake, is our O'Leary."

"Clever…" discerned Charlie, "but you don't like him?."

83

Alarm flared in her eyes. "Not one word against 'im will ye 'ear from my lips! 'E was good enough for 'is lordship. Guess 'e's good enough for the rest of us."

"His lordship?" Charlie gestured his cane at the abbey, where it presided on the hill, visible above the village. "You speak of Lord Hastings?"

She nodded again. "Only the old lord's done and croaked."

"My condolences. Who's in control at the moment?"

She shrugged. "'Is lordship 'ad a son once, but 'e died, in the wars. They say there's a great nephew, but who knows if 'e'll ever come. 'E's in service to the queen or something."

"In service to the queen, you say?" Charlie borrowed Abimanyu's habit of scratching his nose to hide his expression. "And no one left in charge in the interim?"

"O'Leary, maybe."

Charlie sighed. "What is your name, Miss?"

The girl struck a saucy pose. "Lola."

"Lola." He repeated the stage name sardonically. "If you say so."

"New here, are ye?" Lola looked him up and down. "Come to fill our empty pulpit?"

"Not exactly," Charlie answered both questions simultaneously. "I visited a few times as a boy." He gave the young woman's attire a dubious frown. "Things have changed mightily in the last decade. When last I visited, your profession was not practiced in Hastings Abbey."

"Profession?" She tucked her flyaway lock of hair behind her ear, struggling to appear offended. "The 'uman body is a Temple of God. Shouldn't we give it the worship it deserves?"

"Good Lord!" A muscle twitched in Charlie's jaw. Things were worse than he had expected. "Audacia Dangereyes's vulgar notions have made it to Hasting Abbey!"

"I don't know who this Dacia person is, but Madam 'Olland says it's a woman's right to find her pleasure where she may. It's good for the propagation of the 'uman race."

"Did she indeed?" Charlie replied dryly, leaning both hands upon his cane.

"Yes, she did," Lola cried excitedly. "She's amazing. She predicted that Lord 'Astings would be able to restart the mine, and it came true!"

"What's this now?" Charlie asked, his interest suddenly piqued. "The silicon mine Mt.

Tam? Is it running again, after all this time?"

She nodded cheerfully.

"So that's where all these men are coming from!" he exclaimed. He swung his cane back the way the train had come, as if indicating the vast, white expanse they both knew lay in the miles beyond. "I thought that mine was spent!"

"They's workin' it again now. All thanks to Madam 'Olland and her spirits!"

Charlie froze. "Spirits, you say?"

"You don't believe in spirits?"

"On the contrary," he said forcefully, "I have lived in the wild places, below the equator. I have seen things that would make a strong man's blood turn to ice. I have lived in Dione and Umay-ene and Vasilisa. In Umay-ene, they believe in sprits, and they do strange tricks with snakes and nails. But in Dione, they worship them. A dangerous land for missionaries. I have seen a stone idol turn its head, and a good man carried, screaming, into the sky."

"Oh," murmured Lola, subdued.

"If this Madam Holland trucks with spirits, she is not someone to be admired."

"Well, 'is lordship would say otherwise." The young woman said tartly. "'E thought the world of 'er."

86

"Did he?" Charlie replied dryly.

"'E did. 'Is lordship didn't take his tea without first consulting Madam 'Olland! And another thing." Lola wagged her finger at him. "A churchman like you should know better than to chastise a Temple of God, like me. After all, did not our Lord himself tell men not to throw rocks at a woman whose only crime was sharing that which the Lord had given her?"

Charlie's eyes rolled heavenward. *"Father,"* he prayed, *"this brings abuse of Your Word to a new high. Or should I say low. Protect your faithful from such folly."*

He had been right to have reservations about the archbishop's request. Civilization was a cesspit, and that Dangereyes woman's ideas— represented here by some old hag of a medium—were among the worst it had to offer. Give him an honest savage any day!

It was time for him to be on his way. As he bent to retrieve his bag, however, he noticed something that stopped him in his tracks. Charlie sighed. He had been so looking forward to getting out of the chilled air and into that hot bath, but it looked as if Abimanyu would win this round. This might not be the jungle, yet the time had come to apply Rule Three.

Straightening, he rested his hands on the dragon-shaped grip of his cane. "Did this Madam Holland tell you what Our Savior said next?"

The young woman shook her head.

Charlie gazed steadily into her eyes. "He said, *Go and sin no more.*"

The young woman took a step back, as if struck.

"Lola." Charlie gestured at the alley. "Is this any life for one in your delicate condition?"

The young woman hand flew to her slightly-rounded stomach. "This? Oh, this ain't nothin'. Madam 'Olland, she knows how to remove any unwanted obstructions."

"Remove the obstruction?" Charles struggled not to raise his voice. "And did Madam Holland tell you what Our Lord said about children?"

New life was precious on the savanna. Once, Charles had seen a young Umay-enes mother throw herself in front of a great, clawed tiger to save her child. The tiger had mauled her, permanently damaging one eye. Yet, that mother, Mirembe was her name, had worn that injury as a badge of courage. She was accorded a heroine among her people.

That was how mothers were supposed

to act. They were not supposed to throw the child to the monster with their own hands.

Lola tossed her head and quoted primly. "'E said, '*suffer the little children to come unto me.*' That means 'E wants them to go to 'eaven. To be with 'im." Her voice wobbled. "Right?"

"That is not what He meant, and you know it." Charlie's voice cracked like a whip.

"Wh-what did 'E mean, then?"

The pastor drew himself up, until he seemed to tower above the young woman. "Do you know what else Our Lord said? He said, *'It were better for him that a millstone were hanged about his neck, and he cast into the sea, than that he should offend one of these little ones.'*"

The young woman began to cry. She pressed a hand against her abdomen. "But…what else can I do? I ain't got the money to go 'ome again! 'Sides, there's notin' there for me. I used the last of what my dada left me to come 'ere, because I 'eard there was work. 'Onest work. Only, when I get 'ere, they weren't 'iring women."

"Do you have any relations?" asked Charles. "Someone who would accept you in your…um…" He gestured at her again, "current condition?"

"I got an aunt. Lives in the Anake

89

Island. I could tell her my man died. But I ain't got the fare for the train, much less the ferry." The young woman wept openly.

Charlie handed her his handkerchief. "What's your real name, Miss?"

The girl too it and blew her nose. "Lily Ainsley."

His bath would have to wait. "Come to the station with me, Lily Ainsley. I shall buy you a ticket all the way to the Anake Archipelago. Your child deserves a better life than this."

VV

The third time Charlie bought a ticket for a young woman of ill repute, O'Leary came looking for him.

It had been five days since he had arrive in Hastings Abbey, and the dark fortnight had fallen. During the four hours when the orbital panels reflected heat from above, the streets were bearable. The long hours in between, however, grew so cold that Charlie's breath formed puffs of mist. After the warmth of Vasilisa, so close to the equator, this place seemed bone-chilling.

The town still ran on a twenty-four hour day. During the "daylight hours", the ubiquitous gas lamps that lined all the village streets were at their brightest, giving the village square a festive and prosperous feel. During the "night hours", however, only one in four streetlights was lit, and many smaller alleys and country ways kept no lamps burning at all. It was one of these dark places that O'Leary picked for his confrontation.

The innkeeper did not come alone. In the light of O'Leary's lantern, Charlie could see that the short, wiry man was flanked by two huge bruisers, both carrying thick clubs.

"Top of the long night to ye, parson." O'Leary spoke with a Bellian accent. "I must ask ye to stop mettlin' with me girls. Your do-gooding is cutting into me profits."

"I beg your pardon, Innkeeper," Charles replied mildly. "But they are not 'your' girls. We are each made in the image of Our Father in Heaven. No man owns another."

"Own them? Not at all. They are all their own little ladies, just as Madam Holland has instructed them," O'Leary chuckled. "Such a useful bint, that one. Fillin' the girls heads with such nonsense as makes them cooperative to me purposes."

"Madam Holland is a wicked woman," Charlie gritted his teeth. "I intend to see her influence undone. But first, I must ask you to curtail your less scrupulous practices, Innkeeper."

"Perhaps ye have been misinformed," the little man said, his friendly tone was belied by the malicious gleam in his eye. "I am not merely the innkeeper. That is but a small part of the O'Leary concern. I am the overseer for the Hastings Silicon Works. His lordship himself, may the old gent rest in peace, appointed me."

"Oh? And Lord Hastings said, 'Take young women who come seeking work and put them to a disreputable use?'"

"Not in so many words, no. But he didn't tell me otherwise, neither."

The little man smirked and crossed his arms. He made a gesture with his head. The walking walls of muscle took a step forward and smacked their truncheons against their hands.

Never show fear.

Charlie had spent over a decade in the most remote parts of their lovely planet. He had faced a village of fume-maddened savages in the wilds of Manatum, a twelve-foot tiger in Umay-ene, and monstrous beasts that were the results of early biological experiments gone wrong upon the slopes of Ushas Mons. Two overgrown country louts failed to intimidate

92

him.

"Oh, you will need to do better than that," chuckled Charlie.

O'Leary's victorious grin twisted into an ugly scowl. "Get 'im, boys."

The two louts lumbered forward. Charlie put one hand on the top of his cane, right below the dragon's head. With a twist, he loosened the outer casing and drew the blade hidden within. Taking a fencer's stance, he pointed the blade directly at O'Leary's nose.

"Still time to walk away, O'Leary," he said lightly. "I would hate to damage your, er," he looked the men up and down. "footmen."

One of the large louts scowled angrily, taking the term as an insult. The other chuckled.

"No fear, boss," said the second one. "'E a churchman, not a gentleman. 'E won't know what to do with that pig-sticker."

The first man lunged forward, swinging his club. Charlie had reach on him by at least two feet. With a precise, rapid motion, he stabbed the man's hand. The bruiser shouted in surprise, his club falling as blood gushed from his injury.

The second man lumbered forward with more care. He swung his truncheon to and fro, hoping to block the sword. Charlie danced back

93

to maintain his distance, waiting for an opening. Sure enough, the thug swung his weapon in a wide sweep, leaving his body unprotected. Charlie stabbed him in the thigh, twice.

He did not make the cuts deep. He still held out hope that O'Leary would realize that he was outmatched and call off his dogs, and Charlie would not be required to kill either of them. To emphasize this point, Charlie lunged forward and gave both thugs a cut across one cheek, leaving behind a slanted bloody line.

The second man screamed now, as well, grabbing his bleeding cheek and his leg.

"Boss, he's too quick for us!" cried the first one, cradling his wounded hand, blood running down his cheek. His truncheon had rolled away into the darkness.

Charlie stayed alert and kept his distance, until he saw the opening for which he had been waiting. In a flash, his sword was at O'Leary's own throat. The overseer squawked. A tiny trickle of red appeared upon the pale skin of the overseer's neck, before his lantern dropped, and the light went out.

Venus had no moon. Nights were always dark. But in the pale starlight, Charlie allowed himself a slight smile.

"Unfortunately for you and your men, I

was a gentleman before I was a churchman."

"Eh! Whot's all this now?" a new voice sounded in the darkness.

Lamplight spilled over the combatants from a lantern in the outstretched hand of a portly man with a mustache. His coat bore a crest over his breast. Charlie recognized the wyvern upon the crest as the coat of arms of the House of Hastings.

"The sheriff, are you?" he asked cheerfully, backing up and wiping off his blade with his handkerchief.

"That I am. That I am! Sheriff Oaks. And who might you be?"

"Some new parson," spat O'Leary.

"Not exactly. You see I'm here to decide—" began Charlie.

The sheriff interrupted him. "Mr. O'Leary, I didn't see you there! I am sorry, sir!"

Oh, oh. That was not good.

"Sheriff, aren't you going to arrest this man?" asked Charlie. "He set his thugs upon me."

"Now, Oaks!" O'Leary spread his hands. "Ye know how things are. Besides, look what he did to me men!"

The sheriff hrumfed and hawed. He looked from one bleeding bruiser to another.

95

"Well, now. Well, now. Violence in the streets. In Hastings Abbey. Can't have that. Can't have that."

Charlie bit back an oath. He did not know which was more despicable, the petty greed of the overseer or the obsequious corruption of the sheriff.

"See here, now..." Charlie began.

Then he paused.

Abimanyu's voice echoed in his mind, repeating the words of the Third Rule. Slowly, Charlie lowered his hand and regarded the sheriff thoughtfully.

"Sheriff, I believe you know who is telling the truth here," Charlie said calmly.

The portly man licked his lips and looked nervously back and for between Charlie and O'Leary. "His lordship left Mr. O'Leary in charge."

Charlie took a deep breath. When he spoke, his voice was very calm and very firm. "Were I you, Sheriff Oaks, I would give more thought to our Living Lord than to a dead one."

"Has the heir come?" The sheriff looked around, as if expecting to see another man.

Charlie pointed up. "I meant Our Lord above."

96

"Oh, that's precious. He's talkin' about yer soul, Oaks," guffawed O'Leary. "Thinks yer going to put yer soul before yer hide."

"He will if he's wise," said Charlie. "Better a poke now than a flogging that never ends."

"W-what if the new lord agrees with the old one?" asked Oaks, his voice unsteady.

"There are four possibilities," said Charlie. "You please Our Lord above, and the new earthly lord is pleased, too. You please Our Lord, but the new earthly lord is not pleased—either way, Heaven smiles upon you. You betray Our Lord above, but the new lord below approves, gaining you a few soft days on earth and a bed of nails hereafter. Or, finally, you betray Our Lord, and the new lord agrees with Him, gaining you a bed of nails here and hereafter. And you're sacked. Do you have other work lined up? The mines perhaps? I hear they take able-bodied men."

The sheriff loosened his collar and swallowed.

"Do your duty," Charlie instructed. "Take Mr. O'Leary and his...staff and lock them up."

Oaks was sweating now, a fat bead of perspiration running down his brow. "Look, here, parson. I've known Mr. O'Leary a long time now—"

"Then you know exactly what kind of man he is."

"I don't want any trouble."

"Then why did you become sheriff?" Charlie gazed keenly at the man, even though he could hardly see him, as the lantern was shining in Charlie's face. "Did you set out to be a weak man, who did the will of a wicked one? Or did you, once upon a time, believe in something higher, finer? Justice, even?"

The sheriff blinked at him, as if from far away. "I…"

"Come on, Oaks. Ye know me. Ye're not going to let any stranger come between us, are ye?" coaxed O'Leary. "Lock him up for disturbing the peace, and let's get back to business as usual. It's not as if ye'll be breaking a commandment."

Charlie's voice carried through the dark night. *"Thou shalt not bear false witness."*

O'Leary laughed, "As if that's going to motivate the old dimwit!"

"Dimwit?" the sheriff drew himself up. He sounded calmer, like a man of authority. "The parson is right. I did take this job because I wished to see justice done. I wanted to do daring deeds as in the tales of old. You may be short for an ogre, O'Leary, but you're just as wicked."

"What? Ye would not dare!" cried O'Leary, pulling himself up as high as his short stature allowed. "Ye'll be sorry ye laid hands on me when Madam Holland gets wind of this! Don't tell me ye've forgotten what happen to Parson Marsden, when he went up against her!"

Fear crossed the sheriff's face, but the confidence in Charlie's eye stiffened his resolve.

"Tut. Tut. Off to jail with you." The sheriff gestured the overseer along. "Your associates as well. Parson, if you and your blade would care to help me see them safely there?"

OV

The next morning—or what passed for morning, as the sky was still black as graphene paint—Charlie paid a much-overdo visit to the old parson. Leaving the rectory, he followed the gaslight, winding country lane that led through the town and then up the hill. The oldest houses, from the first landing days, were closest to the center of the village. Squat and hexagonal, they were made from the same kind of concrete as the long-lasting Roman coliseum:

limestone mixed with volcanic ash. Only there were no sea creatures on Venus whose crushed shells could form limestone, so the early colonists had used a native stone much like dolomite.

These first houses were uniformly matte black, the color of the impenetrable graphene-dichalcogenides layered paint with which the colonists had coated everything. This wonder substance, so plentiful in the early days due to the ease of making graphene from the excess carbon dioxide, had, at one time, both protected the structures from the sulfuric acid winds present in those days and produced electricity from the sunlight. Weather and time had long since ended the lifecycle of the energy-producing function, but the tradition of not putting anything between the black surface and the sun remained.

Farther from the center of town were winter gardens from the Period of Occupation. Sheets of transparent graphene had been set into a latticework, forming greenhouses—some rectangular, some geodesic. Within, bright illuminated both gardens and living quarters. Some of the winter gardens had been very large, containing the first forests. Had it not been dark, Charlie knew he could have seen the

100

struts of old, broken domes jutting up above the trees.

The country lane wound its way up the hill, passing large estates lit with brilliant gaslight. Like many of the finest houses from the Age of Expansion, they were built entirely of wood and painted with brilliant colors, red, green, or blue, to contrast the matte black of the colonial buildings. Wood had been so rare in the early period of colonization, before they had developed varieties of trees capable of adjusting to the 28-day light-dark cycle, that building a wooden mansion had been a display of ostentatious wealth. Nowadays, when lumber was less dear, the well-to-do still built houses in a fashion—tall turrets, dormer windows, bright trim of a contrasting color—to imitate that first period of wealth and leisure. Charlie, himself, had grown up, some eighty miles from Hastings Abbey, in such a mansion.

The old parson lived in a gatehouse on one of these estates. Upon knocking, Charlie was ushered inside by a woman who might have been a servant or a daughter. She led him to an old withered man, unable to rise from his bed. With her help, Parson Marsden sat up and greeted Charlie amicably.

Charlie had put off this visit because he

feared that Marsden might remember him from his occasional childhood visits to the village. Particularly, from the time that he and two friends had fallen into the river that ran behind the rectory. Marsden had rescued them. Charlie did not wish to be recognized until he made his decision about staying, but he need not have feared. The old man's kindly smile showed no sign of recognition.

Parson Marsden could trace his family lineage all the way back to the very first colonists, back when they lived in balloon-like cities in the upper atmosphere, even before the great mining factories went into production or the orbiting panels were in place to help cool the planet. Back then, the lower atmosphere was so thick that it would have crushed a steel vehicle. The upper atmosphere, however, was similar in pressure to that of the old home world, so there was no fear of extreme pressure or explosive decompression. All a man needed, in order to leave the safety of the balloon-city, was a covering to protect himself from the corrosive sulfuric acid. Few living today could trace their ancestry back so far.

"Charles Fairweather, at your service." Charlie bowed.

"Fairweather?" the old parson's brow

102

raised. "Any relation?"

"To whom?" Charles asked pleasantly.

"No matter." Marsden struggled to sit up farther. The woman put another pillow behind him. "Beth tells me you're staying in the rectory."

"For the time being. The archbishop sent me." Charlie said. "He told me Hastings Abbey was severely in need of leadership and moral direction," Charles gave the old man an apologetic smile. "I thought he was exaggerating until I arrived."

"He is not," Marsden said sadly. A coughing fit interrupted him. "How can I aid you?"

"Tell me," asked Charlie, "all these newcomers are working here at the factory, and yet there are precious few new houses. Where do they live?"

The old parson sighed. "Ten men to a house, sometimes more."

"You mean, they are all pressed together?" Charlie asked, aghast. "Why did Lord Hastings not invest in more accommodations?"

Marsden shook his head sadly. "His lordship was not himself in his last year or so. Between O'Leary and that Holland woman, I fear they bewitched him. It may be that he even gave the orders for the needed work to be done, but the money made its way into his overseer's pocket and conveniently failed to come out again."

"Despicable," Charlie shook his head in disgust.

"It is more than just housing," Marsden continued. "There are not enough shops in town to provide even basic needs like food. O'Leary runs a company store. Half the village owes him their next several paychecks."

"O'Leary will trouble you no more," Charlie said firmly.

"If the new heir does not arrive in time to appoint a better man to the bench," said the old parson, "O'Leary will be released. The current magistrate is O'Leary's creature."

"Ah." Charlie shifted uncomfortably.

"But O'Leary is the less dangerous of the pair," continued Marsden. "It is Holland who you must watch out for."

"This Madam Holland is a fan of Audacia Dangereyes, I gather?"

"Dangereyes?" Marsden asked. "That woman who ran for president of Tethus?"

Charlie nodded, "Only politics is merely the tip of the iceberg that is Mrs. Dangereyes. It

104

was she who brought false adultery charges against the world-renowned preacher, Reverend Walston Crocker Brown. And she singlehandedly destroyed the Tethus stockmarket back in '07."

"That was her!" Marsden cried. "The medium who told Cornelius Bildervan that spirits had given her some marvelous business tip, when, really, she had it from the doxy of one of Bildervan's rivals?"

Charlie nodded.

"How does a free love advocate come to accuse somebody of adultery?" asked Marsden.

"Word is that she hoped that if one of the foremost moral authorities of our day was discovered to be practicing free love, it would help her cause. He was found innocent."

"Abominable," muttered Marsden. "I had no notion all this was accomplished by one woman. Are you certain that stories about several women have not been conflated by rumor?"

Charlie shook his head. "I've been following her exploits for years. I saw her once, when I was a boy, on a stage in New Francisco. She was an actress then. Quite a good one, mind you. I saw her in *New Newyork by Gaslight*.

105

She stole the show, which is why I remembered her."

"As to our Madam Holland," Marsden said slowly, "I suppose you may be correct that she fancies herself to be Hastings Abbey's answer to Audacia Dangereyes."

"You say Holland is more dangerous than O'Leary?"

"O'Leary's allies are merely flesh and bone. They obey him out of fear and greed. That woman has allies that are of air and darkness."

"I was afraid of that." Charlie nodded.

"She took a disliking to me." Marsden paused, coughing. "When she first came three years ago. She did not like that I preached against her wicked ways. First, I suffered an unexpected, accident. My pulpit collapsed while I was preaching against her, throwing me to the ground. Then when I would not relent, I suddenly developed with a mysterious wasting disease no doctor can put a name to."

"She hexed you."

The old man narrowed his eyes. "You believe me?"

"I have seen many unusual things in the long jungle nights, where there are no gaslights to pierce the darkness."

IV

The time had come to bell the hag.

Charlie strode down the country lane, swinging his cane in a circle every third step. In his other hand, he held a lantern. There would be at least eight more days of darkness before the sun shown again, and the street lamps were spotty on this side of the village. When he came to the lane leading to Madam Holland's cottage, he slowed and approached more cautiously.

There was nothing that angered him more than those who preyed upon innocents, and the tangled web of corruption in Hastings Abbey led here, to the house of the medium. He would put an end to this, catch her at her crime. Then he could report to the archbishop with a clean conscience that there was no more here for him to do.

He knocked upon the door. A dour servant led him to a drawing room. Charlie walked around the chamber, examining the furniture and the tea service on the mantelpiece. A mural covered one wall, showing a village reminiscent of Hastings Abbey but twice as large and more prosperous. The furnishings of the room were all tasteful but worn. Two hearths burned brightly, one at either side of the chamber, but that was the only sign he could find of ostentatious wealth.

Charlie sat down upon the green velvet divan, puzzled. Where was the queen spider hiding all the riches she had stolen from the people of Hastings Abbey? He had half an hour to find something—he had asked Sheriff Oaks to meet him here—or he would end up looking the veriest fool.

Footsteps sounded, and Madam Holland appeared, a vision in scarlet. She was garbed in a silk turban, a quilted dressing gown, and fringed shawl of the most vivid red. At first, Charlie thought that she was rather portly, but it was merely that she wore three layers of robes. That and the two burning hearths suggested that perhaps she, too, was troubled by the cold.

Gliding across the floor, she struck a dramatic pose, popular with actresses of Charles's mother's generation. To his surprise, he saw that she was not an old hag. In fact, she was a handsome woman—with a face Charlie had seen in daguerreotypes and on handbills, and, once, long ago, with his own eyes.

"You are Audacia Dangereyes!" He cried, jumping up. "You are she herself!"

"I beg your pardon," she intoned, glaring down at him like a *grand dame*. "You have mistaken me for someone else."

"I have seen you before. I saw you when but a boy in *New Newyork by Gaslight*"

"Ah." She struck a new but equally-dramatic pose. "Was I magnificent?"

"As a matter of fact, you were. But that is neither here nor there. I have come to put a stop to your abuse of the people of Hastings Abbey."

"I know who you are!" she thundered suddenly. "You're that meddling parson!"

"That would be me," Charlie acknowledged.

"Why are you here?"

"To speak with you. I had heard so many things about you."

"Ah, of course. Are you ready to leave your repressive ways and open up to the world of free love?"

"No," replied Charlie, pleasantly. Looking back at the wall, he realized suddenly that the painting did portray Hastings Abbey. He recognized the church spire and the town hall, but what were all those other buildings?

"Interesting landscape here on your wall." He nodded in its direction. "Looks a bit like the village…only larger."

Mrs. Dangereyes made a sweeping gesture toward the mural. "This was our dream. Our vision of the Hastings Abbey that could be. With the proceeds from the new factory, we hoped to expand the town, making it both prosperous and beautiful. The plans were drawn up. We had even hired an architect. Just as the work was scheduled to begin, Nigel fell ill." She bowed her head dramatically, but Charlie thought, for just an instant, that he saw real grief amidst the show.

"By Nigel, you mean Lord Hastings?"

"Nigel Fairweather, the eighth Earl of Hastings, my friend, my lover, my soulmate."

"Ah. I see."

Charlie glanced around the room again, perplexed. He was still casting about for some evidence of her wrongdoing. He knew she was up to nefarious deeds—O'Leary and Parson Marsden had both implied as much—but how to prove it. Perhaps, if he tried bluffing and pretended that he already knew, she would let something slip.

"Sheriff Oaks is on his way," he said truthfully. "Your reign of wickedness shall end."

"I? I have done no wrong!"

"We shall see when he arrives, shall we not?"

Audacia Dangereyes seemed nervous, then her eyes fell upon her coffee table. Suddenly, she seemed to swell, to grow taller. It might have been Charlie's imagination, but the shadows in the chamber seemed darker. "Parson, you have interfered quite enough! You will drop your charges against Mickey O'Leary!"

"I shall do no such thing," replied Charlie.

"Oh, I believe you shall!" thundered the turbaned medium. "Be gone, meddler, or die!"

The room suddenly became stifling. The shadows, now as dark as pitch, moved toward him of their own accord. Charlie choked, no air reaching his lungs. His vision started to fade.

Running. Away. That was all that mattered. Away. Away from this witch. Away from this town. Away from…

Charlie tripped and rolled across the hard dirt of the lane. He lay on his back in the dark, panting and staring of at the stars. His shoulder and his hand ached from the fall. *What was he doing here?* Why had he…?

Oh. Charlie climbed slowly to his feet, rubbed his shoulder, and—after a search in the dark— replaced his hat. Then, straightening his

111

clerical collar, he turned and marched back toward the cottage.

As he drew closer, a cold sweat broke out upon his brow, and his hands began to tremble. Charlie stuck them in his pockets. He recognized this dread. He had encountered it before. But shaman and witchdoctors were a part of the jungle. How had such a power spirit made its way into the heart of civilization, and would this dark power yield to Charlie's authority as a churchman?

Another step closer, and his legs trembled as well. Another man might have panicked and run again. This time, however, he knew what to do. He threw his whole soul behind the Second Rule: *Give all to God.*

Dropping to one knee, he held up his silver cross he wore around his neck and bowed his head. He began to pray aloud. *"Yea, though I walk through the valley of the shadow of death, I will fear no evil: for thou art with me; thy rod and thy staff they comfort me."*

The ominous shadows around the cottage remained, but the sense of dread paralyzing Charlie's own limbs gave way. Standing and brushing off his knees, he strode purposefully toward the cottage.

Audacia Dangereyes seemed mildly

surprised to see him when she opened the door; however, this only threw her for a moment. Drawing herself up, she began chanting, dark shadow leaping around behind her in a manner that could not be accounted for by the two hearth fires. Again, dread assailed Charlie, but this time, he just shook it off.

"Please!" He gave a snort of distain.

Audacia seemed to grow taller. The shadows raged and roared. The cottage shook. But Charles was not swayed. As the howling and shaking reached a fevered pitch, he brandished his silver cross and commanded in a loud voice:

"Get thee behind me, Satan! Be gone in the Name of Jesus Christ!"

There was an ear-splitting roar. The floor beneath him trembled. Then, all was still. The room was bright again, the two hearths crackling cheerily.

Audacia Dangereyes staggered backwards, dazed. "They're…gone."

"And good riddance." Charlie stood and brushed off his knees.

The ex-medium blinked. "Truly, I don't know whether to curse you or weep with joy."

"Wh—I beg your pardon?"

"They were cruel task masters.," She

113

dropped down to the divan, looking much reduced and not at all dramatic. "I...shall not miss them."

"Then you are well rid of them," said Charlie, adding cheerfully, "I shall not drop my charges against O'Leary in any case."

"O'Leary can rot in Hell!" Audacia Dangereyes spat.

"But..." Charlie gazed at the despondent woman, who now sat staring blankly at her hands. "You were about to call down the wrath of the inferno upon me to aid him."

"Only because he is blackmailing me!" She gestured at a letter on the low coffee table. Charlie picked it up. It read:

> *Madam Holland,*
> *I know the location of the document for which you have been searching.*
> *If you arrange my release, I will lead you to it.*
>
> *Your ob'd,*
> *Mickey*

Charlie folded the letter and lay it down

again. "Of what document does he speak?"

"Nigel promised to leave me a tidy sum. I had planned to use it to travel a warmer land, nearer to the equator. When his will was read, I was not mentioned."

"Ah. So, O'Leary pocketed it?"

"That was what my spirits told me," intoned the woman.

Charlie gazed at her speculatively. "Your spirits… And they predicted that the old mining ship could be restarted?"

Audacia laughed bitterly. "No. I claimed that because no one wants to hear a woman's ideas, but spirits fascinate all. Cornelius Bildervan found a new technique for getting more out of old mines. I passed what he told me onto Nigel."

"You have done this town good, then. Perhaps that will weigh in your favor upon Judgment Day. Of course, you could still increase your chances by repenting and taking up a good Christian life."

"Shall I?" Her head snapped up. "And support myself how? A woman possessed of spirits is allowed to speak in public. It is thought to be the spirits speaking. But a woman alone? What hope has she of supporting a family? Why do you think so many sell their bodies?"

"That is an interesting point but it will be no concern of yours," he assured her with a pleasant smile, "You will not need to take care of yourself any longer…for you will be in jail."

"Jail!" her face grew pale. "No! I cannot go! Who will…" She bit her painted lip and then rose with a sigh. "Come. You might as well know all…"

Audacia Dangereyes led him to another room. It was simply appointed, with toys and books such as one might find in a nursery. Two people resided within. The first was a pale young woman in a simple black gown. The second was a toothless man with only scraps of hair, who babbled like a child. Charlie took him for aged at first, but looking more closely, he realized that it was a young man but a simpleton.

"Meet my children, Zola and Byron." All the fire had gone out of Mrs. Dangereyes. "My parents were snake oil salesmen who drifted from town to town. My father was generally good-natured, but occasionally he would beat one of us to a bloody pulp, while my mother stood by and laugh. As a child, I so wished to escape this life. And so, when a doctor who had treated me for an illness proposed marriage, I was ecstatic. I thought marriage would be the answer to all my hopes and dreams."

"But, it wasn't?"

"Three days, we were married. Three days, before he returned to his mistresses and his drink. He was twenty-eight. I was fifteen."

"Fifteen?" breathed Charlie, shocked.

"Zola, such a good girl, cares for her brother, while I strive to provide for us. Byron… Well, you can see how it is with him." She turned away, pained. "Had I had a better husband, one who was not such a sot, I might have had a son who was healthy. You wonder why I preach free love? Why should a girl, unwittingly married to a blackguard, be constrained to serve him and bear his weak offspring for the rest of her life?"

Zola picked up a red rubber ball and threw it to her brother. Byron caught it awkwardly, an expression of child-like joy coming over his features. He began to clap and laugh, rocking back and forth and giggling like an infant.

Charlie looked at the pathetic creature and shuddered in distaste. In the wilds, such a waste of flesh would have been… He froze. Did he really feel nothing but disgust for this

117

poor imbecile? What had become of his Christian charity? Did not this young man deserve pity? He had noted, with pride, that human life was precious on the savanna, but, truth be told, food was scarce there. None would be spared for a child who could not contribute to the tribe. If a child like Byron had been born in the wild, he would be dead by now.

Could he, himself, have spent too much time in the jungle?

Turning to his hostess, he gaped, awed. The most beautiful woman he had ever seen stood before him. Her expression was gentle and filled with the most feminine of graces. It took him a second to realize that this was the same jaded harpy whom he had so long despised. She was looking at her son. Her gaze held no pity, only motherly love. It was the sort of expression an artist might crave, were he seeking a model for a portrait of the Madonna.

Charles had seen such this expression once before, upon the face of Mirembe. He had rushed to the young mother's side as she crawled, bloody and mauled, away from the corpse of the tiger that now served as a pincushion for the spears of her tribesmen. Despite her injuries, she had gazed down at her

118

little son with just such love.

Many a mother might have abandoned a son such as Byron. Audacia must have had many opportunities to do so. But she had not.

Suddenly, Charlie saw everything in a new light.

Instead of a hag who contaminated all she touched with long-reaching tendrils of seduction and corruption, he now envisioned Audacia as a young mother, courageously guarding her young against a ravaging beast. Mirembe had faced a physical danger, and her tribe had been there to save her. The monster young Audacia had faced had been entirely spiritual. No tribe had risen to protect her from the blows fate had dealt her. She had had to fight for her family's survival as best she could. The wounds she took had damaged her spiritually, blinding the eye that should have helped her stick to the narrow way.

Abimanyu had been right. Wherever there were men, there was a jungle. In Umayene, Vasilisa, and Dione, the dangers were violence, wild beasts, and the elements. Here, in the civilized world, the dangers were moral, but just as much courage was needed to face them.

Gazing at the helpless young man, clapping with joy over his red rubber ball,

Charles Fairweather made his decision. He loved the church, but the task the archbishop had requested of him was the more important. He would stay.

But what of this woman and her children? He turned back to where Audacia, no longer a vision of mother-love, stood in her scarlet turban. The hatred he had felt toward her—that had led him to preach against her in his sermons for so many years—was gone. But that did not excuse her many crimes, the lives she had ruined, such as Parson Marsden's. She still must be punished for her crimes. She could not be allowed to merely set up shop elsewhere and begin again. Too many girls like Lily Ainsley had been ruined by her preaching. The time had come for it to stop.

And yet, he gazed at the sad, toothless young man happily clutching his ball.

"Perhaps, it need not be prison." He frowned thoughtfully. "Perhaps, you could be transported instead, with your family."

"To the penal colony at Lada?" Audacia's face became ashen. "Lada is so cold! Byron would never survive."

Charlie paced back and forth, pondering, while Audacia and Zola watched him anxiously. What to do? True, she was the

120

victim of her circumstances, true. The moral
wounds she had received made her unfit for
decent society. On the other hand, she was a
handsome woman with a mother's heart and a
heart-wrenchingly sad past. What a shame that
her spiritual wounds could not be healed. If
only she could be redeemed, brought back into
the bosom of the church.

Suddenly, he laughed out loud. "I
cannot allow you to remain where you will do
harm. However, I will allow you to keep your
freedom, so long as you promise never to step
back upon civilized soil. You are hereby
banished from the civilized lands. If I hear even
a whisper of your activities again, I shall carry
through with my charges. And I am sure, by
then, I shall have gathered much more evidence
of your wrongdoings."

"B-but…where shall we go? How shall
we pay for our travel?"

"I shall buy tickets for all three of you.
You will travel in comfort."

"Tickets to where? Could our
destination be near the equator? With flowers
and tea and exotic spices." Audacia gave a sad,
wistful sigh. "And sunlight. Warm, warm
sunlight."

"How would Vasilisa do?"

Her face lit up. "Yes! Oh, yes."

Charlie took a piece of stationary from a small desk, dipped the nearest quill into the inkwell, and wrote. Straightening, he blotted the page and handed it to his hostess.

"Once you reach Vasilisa, go to this address and ask for Abimanyu," his eyes danced. "He will take care of everything."

The door of the cottage burst open. Audacia and Charlie rushed into the drawing room to find Sheriff Oaks panting on the front stoop. A handful of stalwart lads followed behind him. The light from the lantern in his left hand glinted off the metallic threads in the wyvern crest emblazoned upon his right breast.

"Everything all right?" The sheriff called. "We heard a disturbance."

"All is well, Sheriff Oaks," Charlie replied cheerfully. "Alas, Madam Holland shall be leaving us. She is planning a long journey. For what it's worth, however, I shall be staying."

"You'll be moving permanently into the rectory, then, will you?"

"I fear the rectory must remain empty a while longer. You see—" Charlie played with the dragon grip of his cane, though, truth be told, it looked more like a wyvern. "I am Lord

Hastings' heir, his long-lost great nephew. I am the new Lord Hastings."

END

The Great Game
by Kristen Stieffel

The marketplace biddies were atwitter over a new ship come in—not a cargo ship, but a navy schooner from Parga. Kimberly O'Hara left the marketplace and sprinted down the brick-paved street toward the docks. The colonel would be pleased if she could bring him news. Drunken sailors had a tendency to share news they shouldn't, and that always carried a good price.

Summer had come at last, giving Kim eight weeks of freedom from the dour Roman-church boarding school Colonel Crayton had sentenced her to. She had left behind the ridiculous uniform—the oversized white blouse and constricting twill jumper in an awful shade of brown—and had donned instead her trusty dungarees and a blue collared shirt.

She slipped into an alley that afforded a clear view of the ship. It flew the blue-and-white Pargan flag, all right, and a dozen sailors in crisp white uniforms walked toward town, laughing amongst themselves.

Kim followed them up the street into the *taberna*. While they took over all the tables at the front, she sped along the bar, pretending to ignore them, and took a seat at the end, where she could watch and listen.

"Ah, Kim, you need to run along." The barmaid swiped the clean bar top with a towel. "With new sailors in town I can't have you taking up a seat."

Kim reached into her pocket and drew out a 20-Pfennig coin. "Can't you bring me a cup of *cafe con leche*?"

"Pfft." The barmaid pocketed the coin. "*Nur, wenn du es Kaffee mit Milch nennst,* as our dear leaders would have it."

"*Ja, Danke.*" Kim grinned. The barmaid shared Kim's disdain for the New Berliners and their imposition of their language and culture all across the planet. Kim's island home, Asteria, had been a lovely spot before those *chicos* showed up.

The Pargan sailors said little of value until they had gone through several pitchers of beer.

Then one of them, in words fouler than even Kim was accustomed to, described what he thought ought to be done to the Zirkans and their allies from Tethys. "They think they can protect their ships by flying zeppelins above the shipping lanes?" He made a sloppy, spit-spraying farting noise. "We'll annihilate them."

One of his shipmates shoved him almost out of his chair and told him, using some earthy epithets, to shut up.

By the time their drunken carousing had them mauling waitresses and seeking prostitutes, Kim had heard enough. She left an extra 10-Pfennig coin for the barmaid. Rather than run the gantlet of groping sailors to go out the front, she ducked through the door to the kitchen. There, the smells of burnt bread and seared chicken enveloped her, along with the humidity and heat common here late in the fortnight of daylight.

An old woman idly flipped pieces of chicken on the grill. She glanced Kim's way and startled. "*¡Mira! ¿Qué haces aquí, vagabunda pequeña? ¡Sal!*" She jabbed a fat finger toward the door.

Kim waved at the cook, never slowing her brisk pace. "*No me importa, abuela. Simplemente de paso.*"

"*Sal de mi cocina. ¡Ahora!*"

The cook was still yelling when she sped out the back.

VV

Kim jogged through alleyways up the

hill to the Montecito neighborhood of Nuevo Barcelona where the *burguesía* had their homes. None of the cold, gothic stonework of the New Berliners up there. It was filled with white stucco and red tile roofs, as an Asterian neighborhood should be. The arched portico at the front of the colonel's house was not for her. She ducked around the back. The wooden gate was locked. She leaped, caught her hands on the top edge, and climbed over, dropping into the shadow on the other side.

She waited. Not a sound arose, either from the guardsmen or the kitchen staff. The colonel really ought to do something about his security. Kim straightened and strolled through the kitchen garden as if she were at home.

Through the wide windows of the kitchen, she could see the staff inside working. Much as she'd like to stop and visit with them, going that way would just slow her down. She walked around the side of the house, to the colonel's study, where a pair of French doors opened onto a terra cotta patio. The doors stood wide open, as they often did, to catch the evening breeze that blew in from the Hecate Sea. Thin white curtains wafted in and out of the open doorway. Within was silent, which might mean the colonel was alone. But it was no guarantee. He was posing as an Asterian, but unlike the natives, who babbled constantly, he could hold his tongue as easily in company as he could in solitude.

Kim paced quietly up to the doorway and peeked in. Colonel Crayton hunched over his desk, reading something. She slipped through the door and into the armchair near the window. She sat back and waited.

She could be silent, too.

A full minute, maybe more, passed before he startled, squeaking the springs of his wooden swivel chair. "Gracious heavens, Kim! You'll give a bloke a heart attack sneaking up like that."

"Oh, come now, *patrón*. You've always been a great supporter of my sneaking."

"You'll be the death of me, you scamp." He pushed away the papers and turned to face her. "What sneaking have you been about today, eh?" The colonel was a pudgy fellow from Tellus with thinning brown hair and a bushy mustache. When he leaned back in his chair, the springs squealed again. Outside his compound, he spoke perfect Asterian and passable German. But within his home it was usually Modern, and occasionally English.

"A navy schooner from Parga docked

128

this afternoon."

His eyebrows shoved the skin of his forehead toward his hairline. "And?"

"The sailors say they're going after the airships from Tethys. The ones guarding the shipping lanes."

"Yes. After the bombing of New Berlin, retaliation was inevitable." The colonel sighed. "If they discover the Tethysans have an airship base on Zirka … things could get ugly."

"You didn't see the Masacre de Bolos. Things are already ugly." On the bocce lawn north of the city, four of her compatriots had been killed during a protest against the New Berliner occupation. In the years since, she'd dedicated herself to ridding the island of the invaders.

"Too right, young miss." He hefted himself out of the chair and tugged the bell pull beside the fireplace. "You'll stay to dinner, I suppose?"

She hadn't expected much. Still, dinner would be enough. "If you'd like me to, *patrón.*"

"Yes, Kimberly. We've much to discuss. You won't mind if Barbara gets you cleaned up and changed for dinner?"

"No, sir. Of course not." She'd far rather pass the evening with Barbara than the

129

colonel, but they generally came together. Not that they were a couple. As far as she knew. Their cover story had them as siblings, though they were actually from different city-states.

The idea of Barbara as the colonel's consort almost brought a laugh. They were allies, not friends.

The colonel wore a civilian suit of tan linen. She'd never seen him in uniform. According to Barbara, he was retired. But his retirement was not at all quiet. He returned to his seat and pulled the papers close again. "What news do you hear from the Statthalterhaus?"

"Very little. The staff there are not ones for spilling secrets. All I hear from them in the marketplace is idle chatter. Herr Statthalter must run a very strict organization. Or at least, his housekeeper does. They all fear her. Most of the staff is Asterian. Only the housekeeper and a couple of others came with him from New Berlin."

"Interesting. And do any of the staff know you?"

"Oh, no, sir. They're all respectable types."

"Heh. Indeed, you ragamuffin."

Just when she thought she was

becoming fluent in his language, he would throw out a word like that. It was as if he knew he had to keep her off balance.

A rap at the door.

"Come in," he called.

A footman in a dark gray suit opened the door. "You rang, Colonel?"

"Ask Pastor Fisher to join us, and inform the cook that we'll have a guest at dinner."

"Yes, sir." The footman departed.

Once his footsteps could no longer be heard in the corridor, the colonel leaned forward. "I am pleased to hear that you are unacquainted with the Statthalter's staff. That's ideal, actually."

"Why?"

"Because one of my informants at the Post Office intercepted a letter from the Statthalter's housekeeper." The colonel picked up a paper from his desk and brought it to her. "What do you make of that?"

"Ugh." Kim took the paper and studied it a moment. Like everything from the New Berliners, it was in German. She struggled a minute to make it out. The handwriting was schoolbook precise, but for Kim words on paper were always harder to comprehend than spoken ones. Pastor Barbara said that was because she didn't learn to read at all until she was nine. "I have a hard enough time reading Modern. Can't you just tell me what it says?"

"You'll need to improve on your German, young lady. It says a girl of fine deportment is needed to serve in the Statthalterhaus, and so on."

Kim dropped the paper to her lap. "What does that have to do with me?"

"What does it indeed." The colonel tweaked her nose, a gesture she hated. "You little minx. Can't pass for a boy anymore."

She was painfully aware of that. "Doesn't make me any less able to run your 'errands.'"

"Never said it did, my girl." He grinned. "Might make you even better able. You're a daring soul. Never yet shied away from an assignment." He sat in the big armchair near hers. "And this will be a very daring assignment indeed."

"I'll do whatever you like, *patrón*." She folded her arms. "Within reason."

He chuckled warmly. "I daresay none of it will be reasonable. Quite unreasonable, in fact. Nevertheless, I shan't do your dignity any more harm than you have already done yourself."

She unfurled her arms, gripping the arms of the chair. "What about my dignity?"

"By Jove, child, you can't expect to have any left after a life of scampering about these streets as a tatterdemalion."

She didn't know that word, either, but Pastor Barbara would. Kim would ask her later. "What's the assignment?"

"You're going to become a maid and infiltrate the Statthalterhaus."

Just as the door opened, Kim laughed. "I know I can't pass for a boy, but I don't think I can pass for a 'girl of fine deportment,' either. You have the wrong *chica, jefe*."

"Nonsense. Barbara can teach you what you need to know." The colonel looked toward the open door, where Pastor Barbara Fisher stood. "Isn't that so, Pastor?"

"That has always been my goal." Pastor Barbara closed the door behind her and stepped into the center of the intricately patterned rug that covered the floor in front of the open patio doors. She extended her arms.

Kim ran to hug her. "I have missed you, Pastor Barbara." They hadn't seen each other in months. Pastor Barbara had gone up to Mount Rhea for some purpose Kim was not allowed to know.

"I've missed you, Kimberly." Pastor Barbara was from Tethys. Not quite as old as the colonel, she was still old enough to have a sprinkling of gray hairs on an otherwise brunette head. A tall, thin woman, she wore a plain dark-blue dress that lacked the bustle most fashionable *burguesías* wore. "You've grown."

"Yes, ma'am." Kim now stood almost as tall as the pastor. She glanced at her bust, which strained at the buttons of a shirt made for a boy. "In more ways than one."

"That was inevitable." Pastor Barbara smoothed some of Kim's wild auburn locks behind one of her ears. "Has the colonel told you his plan?"

"Only a little." Kim gestured Pastor Barbara into the side chair, and drew up a footstool to sit on. "I don't see how I can get this job. Won't there be more skilled maids applying for it?"

"I think not," the colonel said, "Since we intercepted the letter, and you have one advantage."

"What?"

"You're a polyglot, you little minx." He poked at the letter again. "*Fließend Deutsch erforderlich.* Which means …?"

134

Kim screwed up her face. "Something about German being required."

"Yes, *fluent* German. Have we not been training you to this for years?"

They had, ever since the colonel had discovered her in the marketplace, running errands of all kinds—some not entirely legal— for all sorts of people. Including one of his informants at the port authority. Kim prided herself on being friendly to everyone. Or at least, pretending to be. And that meant learning their languages.

Even German.

◯◯

Pastor Barbara took Kim to the bathing room. Kim cleaned up and let Barbara wash her hair with a soap that smelled of lavender. Then she rinsed it with rosemary tea and sat Kim on a stool while she combed her hair out.

"Honestly, Kimberly." Barbara worked at a thorny tangle at the back of Kim's neck. "How do you let it get this way? You've only been out of school a few weeks."

"My hair goes its own way. I can scarcely stop it. If the schoolmistress would let me cut it off, it wouldn't be so bad."

"You cannot go about with short hair anymore, Kimberly. It's not ladylike."

She huffed. "I don't want to be ladylike, and I hate the boarding school, *Pastora*. I just want to study with you."

"Silly girl. Who says you can't do both?"

Being cooped up in that giant stone building wearing the awful, stiff uniform was like being in prison. "How can I, if I'm working at the *Statthalterhaus*?"

"You won't be stuck in the governor's mansion forever. Once the assignment is complete, you'll be free to roam once more."

"Only until school starts again."

"Yes. That was our agreement." Barbara tugged on her hair again, ripping at Kim's scalp.

"*Pastora*, about the school … Isn't it awfully expensive? The other girls … they're all from the *alta burguesía*. Why would the colonel pay for it?"

"He doesn't."

"What?"

"The colonel did arrange with the Mother Superior to get you in. But your scholarship comes from my congregation."

Pastor Barbara's church was one of the stranger ones, and Kim had visited plenty. But the Congregationalists had been more welcoming to Kim than anyone else. And Pastor Barbara most of all. But this ... this was unexpected.

"Your people would do that for me?"

"I told them you were worthy of it, Kimberly." Barbara ducked down to look her in the face. "Don't you prove me wrong."

Kim straightened her shoulders. "I won't, *Pastora*. Thank you."

"You're very welcome, dear." Barbara twisted Kim's hair into a bun like her own and pinned it in place. "Meanwhile, we have to get you through this business at the governor's mansion." Barbara tsked. "You'll stay here a few days while we work on your deportment and teach you how to serve as a maid. Then, I'm afraid, we'll send you into the lion's den."

Kim actually preferred that to the boarding school.

◌◌◌

The guest room mattress was like sleeping on a marshmallow, and at first Kim didn't want to get up. But then the scents of one of the colonel's massive English breakfasts reached her. She tossed the quilted blanket aside. Her clothes no longer sat on the chair where she'd left them. If Barbara had taken away Kim's trousers and shirt, she would have left something in their place.

Kim pulled open the wardrobe doors. Inside were two crisp cotton dresses, one dark blue and the other forest green. She put on the green one. At the bottom of the wardrobe sat a pair of black boots—not buttoned ones like Barbara wore. These had laces. She put them on and laced them up and then jogged down the stairs.

Barbara met her in the foyer. "The first piece of deportment you must learn, Kimberly, is to not run everywhere. You must use a measured pace, especially in the governor's house."

"Yes, ma'am."

Barbara started down the hall. "We've been over your table manners before. Let's see how much you've improved since being in school."

With Barbara's back to her, Kim risked an eye roll. The things she put up with, just to aid the fight against the New Berliners.

In the dining room, the colonel sat at the head of the table with his newspaper. "Well, my little rapscallion, you've scooped the reporters, at least."

"Have I?" Kim waited by her usual seat on the colonel's left while Barbara walked around to his right side.

He folded the paper and set it aside. "*Der Staat* has no news of the Pargan naval activity."

Barbara drew back her chair and sat. "Of course not. Why would a state-controlled newspaper report that?"

"Just so." The colonel spread his napkin in his lap.

Kim sat and did likewise. "What will we do?"

"We have done what we can," the colonel said. "I have reported the information to my superiors. Now we await instructions." He picked up a little silver bell on the table and chimed it. "You look very respectable today, Kimberly."

"Thank you, sir."

He turned to his right. "Well done, Barbara."

"My pleasure, Colonel."

The cook brought the breakfast in, placing giant platters on the table. A maid poured coffee into each of their cups. While the servers were present, the colonel and Barbara spoke of trifles—the weather and such.

139

The maids left and closed the door.

The colonel took the serving tongs and helped himself to a generous portion of sausage. "Now, do you see what you are up against?"

"Sir?"

"If Barbara and I hold our tongues around the local help, when I trust they are very much on our side, how much more so will the Statthalter keep silent around the local help? You shall have to be very deft indeed to overhear anything."

Kim spooned some scrambled eggs onto her plate. "Haven't I always been deft, *patrón*?"

"Yes, indeed. That is what we are counting on." He took the eggs next. "But see here, Kimberly. You'll have to brush up on your German. You needn't speak it as fluently as you do Modern or Spanish or English. But you must have enough to understand what's said."

"*Ich habe ein wenig davon,*" she said.

"Of course you do, my little minx. By Jove. You'll be brilliant, as ever."

Kim grinned and looked to Barbara.

But the *pastora* looked sad. "Kimberly, please don't take this lightly. You treat it like

140

some great game, but if you're caught, it could be very dangerous."

"I think sometimes you forget my whole life has been dangerous." Kim heaped toast and sausage onto her plate.

Barbara sighed. "I don't forget. It troubles me. Often."

Kim dropped the tongs back onto the sausage platter. "Don't be troubled. I'm used to it."

"That's what's troubling, dear. But never mind. Just don't clatter the utensils."

"Yes, ma'am."

OV

For the next two days, Barbara and the colonel's housekeeper drilled Kim thoroughly on the protocol of serving. She learned how to carry a giant tray of food around the table without spilling, and how to clear the dishes without getting in anyone's way.

By the end, her head spun with all the tiny, eccentric rules. "How am I supposed to remember all these things?"

Barbara patted her back. "You've always been a fine actress, Kimberly. Just pretend you are me."

141

Kim laughed. That was the best instruction of the week.

Her final examination, as it were, was serving dinner to the colonel and some of his compatriots. She gathered none of them knew who she was. Barbara absented herself from this event. Kim would have preferred to have her there.

The cook, with a knowing smirk, handed her a silver tray that held a bulbous ceramic soup tureen. "There you are, dearie."

Tomato soup, no less.

Kim squared her shoulders. She could do this. She carried the tray into the dining room. There, the men—all men—sat around the table talking about nothing important. They looked like businessmen, or more likely, diplomats. They might have been discussing the need to protect Tellusan ships doing trade with Asteria. But now it was the weather, and things from the newspaper.

Kim reached the head of the table opposite the colonel.

The guest of honor wore a crisp white linen suit. He ladled out his portion of soup and she moved around the table, clockwise, serving from the left, as she'd been told, each man serving himself, as even the New Berliners did.

142

She reached the kitchen without having spilled a drop.

ᴏᴠ

The next day, Barbara instructed Kim to wear the dark blue dress and gave her a hat to match—a straw one with a narrow brim decorated with white cloth flowers.

In the foyer, Barbara tied the hat's ribbon into a bow under Kim's chin. "You'll leave your hat on from now until you return. Once you are living in the governor's mansion, it will be opposite. We leave our hats off at home, and wear them when we are out."

"*Si, pastora.*"

"And you should probably forgo Spanish from now on."

"*Jawohl.*"

The colonel plodded up the corridor. "All right then, there's your letter of recommendation." He handed Kim a stiff envelope of creamy paper. "Give that to Frau Wolkenhorst. My man at the postal service said she has written again about the matter."

They reviewed the story Kim was to tell, and then the colonel pulled a key from his pocket and put on his bowler. "Very well, then, let's go."

"You're coming with me?" Tailing her implied he didn't trust her.

"No, but if I drive you part of the way, you'll arrive fresh, and make a better impression."

"Oh." Kim turned to Barbara, puzzled.

Barbara hugged her. "God be with you, Kimberly. Take care."

"I will, Pastor. Thank you." Kim turned to the colonel, who opened the door and walked her out to his big black steam-driven horseless carriage. A cylindrical tank sat in front, and a black leather top covered the passenger compartment. She'd never ridden in such a vehicle before.

One of the footmen stood next to the chuffing vehicle. He leaned inside to look at something. "All warmed up, Colonel. Optimal operating temperature."

"Excellent, Rolando. Thank you." The colonel climbed into the driver's seat.

Rolando ran around the car and opened the other door for Kim. "There you are, *señorita. Buena suerte.*"

"*Gracias, amigo.*" She stepped up into the car and sat next to the colonel.

He glowered at her over the gold rims

of his spectacles. "By which you mean to say…"

"*Danke, Freund.*"

"*Sehr gut.*" The colonel pushed a lever, and the car rolled away, through the open gate into the streets of Nuevo Barcelona. Ten minutes later, the colonel stopped in a side street not far from the marketplace. He pulled the lever, and the car stopped with a hiss of steam. "You know how to reach the *Statthalterhaus* from here?"

"*Jawohl. Es ist gleich um die Ecke und—*"

"All right then, clever girl. Get on with it, then."

Laughing, Kim jumped from the car.

"More ladylike, please!" The colonel called.

She waved, and then struck off across the street to the market. Behind her, the steam engine rumbled as the car pulled away. Kim squared her shoulders, straightened her spine, and settled into her best Barbara imitation.

She breezed past the fruit and vegetable stalls, ignoring the hawking merchants.

"Your papers," a New Berliner shouted.

A few stalls ahead, where vegetables gave way to spices and dried peppers, a soldier grabbed a stocky young man by the arm.

The man yanked his arm away. "*No comprende, jefe.*" He sneered.

The soldier threw a right cross. The Asterian man staggered.

Kim ducked between two stalls, but kept an eye on the fight.

The Asterian drew a dagger from his boot and turned on the New Berliner soldier.

In an instant, the soldier pulled his pistol and squeezed off a shot. The bang reverberated through the aisles.

Shoppers screamed and ran. Merchants ducked behind their booths. Kim tucked into a crouch, her long skirt rumpling around her legs.

The Asterian lunged at the soldier, slashing at the soldier's arm. But the soldier kept hold of his weapon, pressing it into the Asterian's midsection. Another bang, more muffled, filled the marketplace.

The soldier stepped back.

The Asterian fell face-down onto the brick plaza. The fingers of his free hand clutched at the ground. Twitched a few times. Then stilled.

An uncharacteristic hush fell over the marketplace. The New Berliner, sneering, surveyed the scene.

Neither Kim nor anyone else dared to

move.

The soldier fired a final shot into the Asterian's head. Then he holstered his sidearm and walked away.

Kim held her place until he had gone. Then she ducked back out between a stall full of tomatoes and peppers and another selling various types of corn. Her stiff new shoes beat the brick pavers as she speed-walked to the nearest street.

Her limbs trembled. She breathed deeply to calm them, shoving the gory vision down into her memory with others like it. Such things could not be dwelt on if she wanted to keep her cool. Which was essential to prevent her from winding up like her compatriot.

She turned onto the road that used to be Via San Pedro but was now renamed Pederplatz. The governor's mansion was one of the gothic monstrosities the New Berliners had erected. Four stories of cold gray stone and mullioned windows. She couldn't go in the front way, so before reaching it she turned left and walked along its length and the surrounding wrought-iron fence with its spear-like bars. The next right brought her to the rear entrance. Her nerves settled, her cool Barbara-like persona in place.

147

A tall, broad-shouldered man stepped out of the guard shack as she approached. "What's your business, miss?"

"I was sent by Herr Van Oirschot to see Frau Wolkenhorst about a position."

"I need to see your papers."

Kim handed over the identification papers, which were just as forged as the letter from Herr Van Oirschot.

He looked them over and then opened the gate for her. "Through that door." He pointed across the courtyard to a stairwell that led down to a narrow black door, the top third of which was paned with four pieces of bulls-eye glass.

"Thank you, sir." Kim made a tiny curtsey.

He laughed and closed the gate. "No need to sir me. Good luck with the *übermammutfrau*."

Kim gave a little giggle and went on her way. She eased open the black door, revealing a large mudroom. A bench on one side had baskets underneath and shelves overhead. A long row of coat hooks lined the opposite wall. She shut the door and continued into a narrow hallway.

A short, round woman in a gray dress

and apron carried a wicker basket full of white linens. "*¡Mira!* Who are you?"

"I'm here to see Frau Wolkenhorst about a position."

"*Ah, bueno.*" The woman pointed with her chin. "Down this hall, third door on the left."

"Thank you."

"*De nada.*"

From the kitchen another woman yelled "*Kein Spanisch!*" in an Asterian accent.

The woman with the basket rolled her eyes. "*Spanisch ist hier verboten.*"

Kim shrugged. "*Natürlich.*"

"Oh, she'll like you all right. You do that *ü* thing properly." Basket woman winked and crossed the hallway to a narrow staircase and headed upward.

Kim walked down the hall to the indicated office, and kept to German. "Frau Wolkenhorst? Herr Van Oirschot sent me."

"*Ach!* Finally! Come sit." Frau Wolkenhorst was a tall, hefty woman with steely gray hair cut very short. She wore a brown tweed dress, and the collar of her plain white shirt looked painfully starched.

149

Kim sat in the wooden chair in front of Frau Wolkenhorst's desk, and handed over the envelope.

Frau Wolkenhorst read it and tossed it aside in disgust. "So you are the only one suitable, he says. What makes you more suitable than others?"

"My fluency in German, ma'am."

"You look awfully young. How old are you?"

"Nearly sixteen, ma'am."

"Pfft. A child. Why do you wish to work for His Excellency the Statthalter?"

"Because Herr Van Oirschot said I should, and I do as he says, ma'am."

"Do you? And how long have you been in service?"

"Two years, ma'am."

"Where was your last position?"

Kim spooled out the story they had prepared about her having worked for a now-deceased matron in the Montecito district. Should Wolkenhorst try to get a reference, Barbara would pose as the matron's now-unemployed housekeeper and provide a more glowing reference than already appeared in Kim's forged documents.

150

The interview went on for seemingly ages, though maybe it was only an hour. Finally Frau Wolkenhorst stood up. "Very well. You're the only one Van Oirschot has for me, and your German is good enough. You may have the job. Can you start tomorrow?"

Kim jumped from her chair the instant Wolkenhorst stood. "I can start today, if you like, ma'am."

Wolkenhorst's eyes narrowed. "Can you? That's unusual."

"I've been out of works for weeks, Frau. And Herr Van Oirschot said you needed someone right away. I'll have to run to my friend's house this evening to pack my bag, but I will be glad for the work, and she will be glad to have her spare room back."

"Ah. Very good. All right, then, let us put you to work."

Frau Wolkenhorst made her sign some papers first, but the colonel had prepared her for that, so Kim just did as she was told.

Wolkenhorst filed the papers in her desk. "Now let me show you where things are. Come with me." Frau Wolkenhorst walked out, and Kim trailed after her.

They passed through the kitchen and scullery, with Wolkenhorst pointing out workrooms and storage rooms. Then up the stairs where Kim had seen the woman with the laundry basket go.

"Ground floor is offices and rooms for entertaining. You will clean and serve here when ordered. Otherwise from these areas you will stay out."

"Yes, ma'am."

They passed a wide, elegant stairway carpeted in red. "You do not use these stairs. Ever. Except to clean them. You use the back stairs."

"Of course, ma'am."

The back stairs were hidden behind a white-painted door. Wolkenhorst took her up another flight. "The second floor contains offices for the governor's junior staff, and some meeting rooms. Also off limits unless you are ordered." Up another flight. "Third floor. Bedrooms for the governor and his staff, and also for dignitaries who are visiting. Off limits unless under orders." The final flight. "The top floor is bedrooms for the housekeeping staff. I shall put you in this room with Florina." Wolkenhorst pulled from her pocket a giant ring holding dozens of keys. She instantly found the one she needed and opened a plain wooden door. "Yours is the third room on the right

152

from the stairs. Remember that."

"Third on the right. Yes, ma'am."

Inside, a small iron bed stood against one wall. On the other, a pine wardrobe, and a little washstand in the corner.

"I'll introduce you to Florina shortly." Wolkenhorst strode into the room and pulled open the wardrobe. "Half of this—*Ach*." She shoved aside the dresses hanging in the middle of the cupboard to make room on the left half. "Will be yours."

"Very good, ma'am."

Wolkenhorst closed the wardrobe. "Any questions?"

"Will I have Sundays off, ma'am?"

"The afternoon—after church—yes."

"Excellent. And, begging your pardon, but how often am I to be paid?"

"You'll be paid twice a month."

"Thank you, ma'am. That'll be fine."

"Of course it will." Wolkenhorst left the bedroom and locked the door again. She escorted Kim back to the stairs. "The rest Florina can show you later."

"Thank you very much for showing me the room, Frau Wolkenhorst. It's very nice."

"Of course it is. It is in the governor's mansion."

They returned to the basement, to a workroom where the basket-toting woman and a maid were sorting laundry.

Wolkenhorst stopped in the doorway. "Florina Delgado? Come here."

The maid, a short, slight girl with pale blonde hair, looked up. "Yes, Frau?"

"Come. Here." Frau Wolkenhorst pointed at the floor in front of her.

The maid dropped the linens and rushed to the spot. She was just a couple of years older than Kim and wore a stiff black cotton dress with a gray apron. "Yes, ma'am."

"This is Kimberly O'Hara, our new maid. She will be lodging with you."

Florina smiled. "Oh, good. Pleased to meet you."

"And you," Kim said.

"Show her where to get a uniform, and where to hang her hat. Then take her with you on your afternoon chores and show her what needs doing."

Florina dropped a curtsey. "Yes, Frau."

Without another word, Wolkenhorst turned and walked away.

VV

Kim ate dinner with the rest of the staff. She held her tongue and listened, but learned little apart from the fact that Florina seemed enchanted by Diego, one of the footmen, who ignored her. The dinner was an awful mess of sausages and potatoes. Kim ate her fill anyway, as someone who for most of her childhood had never known when her next meal would come.

Afterward, while the others cleared the dishes, Frau Wolkenhorst approached. "Fräulein O'Hara, you may go now to get your bag. You must return by sundark. After that the guards will not open the gate for you."

"*Ja, gnädige Frau.*" Kim didn't bother to change out of the uniform. She went to the mudroom to get her hat, and hurried out to Montecito to report to the colonel.

She found him in the study, pacing. "Great heaven, girl! What kept you so long?"

Barbara jumped from her chair and hugged Kim.

"I told her I could start right away." She indicated the uniform—a stiff cotton dress and gray apron just like Florina's. "So she suited me up and put me to work. I only returned to pack a bag."

"Well done, Kim." Barbara stepped back. "Did she feed you?"

155

"Yes, but it was terrible. I've a mind to stop for *tapas* on my way back."

"When do you need to return?" The colonel glanced at the mantel clock.

"Before sundark."

"Then you'd best not waste time." He clapped her shoulders. "Good job, Kimberly."

"Just do be careful," Barbara said.

"I'm fine, *pastora*. So far it's all been very boring. Not even a sign of the Statthalter."

"Don't go out of your way looking for him." Barbara nudged her toward the door. "You'll only draw suspicion."

"I know, I know." Kim walked up to the guest room. "I need to pack my clothes, but what can I put them in?"

"I'll lend you my valise."

At the top of the stairs, they went opposite directions. Kim took out her dresses and folded them.

Barbara brought a brown case and helped her pack the things from the dresser. "I don't like this, Kimberly. It's too dangerous. But if intelligence from the governor's mansion can avert any more fighting—it will be worth it."

"Avert fighting?" Kim tucked some of her undergarments into the bag. "Won't the

156

colonel pass information to the military?"

Barbara sighed. "He probably will. It's all very…"

When she didn't finish, Kim offered, "Hopeless?"

"No. Never hopeless. But it is wearisome." She picked up the dresses and tucked them into the valise. "Sometimes it is hard to remain pacifistic when the opposition…isn't."

"Why should we be?" Kim related the shooting she'd seen in the marketplace. "That's the thing I can't understand about you." She took the comb and hairbrush Barbara had given her and put them in the bag. "Why you keep going on about pacifism when they've come into our land to kill us?" A vision rose in her mind of the man in the marketplace with his head blown in. She pushed it back.

"That's where you and the colonel agree." Barbara closed up the valise and stared blankly at its brass buckles.

"Why do you work with him if you don't agree?"

The pastor looked into Kim's eyes. "Pacifists don't fight with weapons, Kimberly. But we can fight. We fight for equality and for justice and for freedom."

157

"But how can you fight if you won't … fight?"

A hint of a smile played around Barbara's lips. "There are ways of fighting that don't require weapons." She picked up the valise and opened the door. "Your schoolmistress and the colonel have failed you, Kimberly." She walked out and down the stairs.

Remembering to moderate her pace, Kim followed. "How so?"

"They haven't had you read *The Art of War*."

That sounded like an interesting book. But the last person Kim would have expected such a recommendation from was Pastor Barbara.

VV

On Sundays the servants at the Statthalterhaus were expected to visit the Lutheran church with the rest of the Statthalter's staff. Kim sat through their dull worship service—why did they have to use the same pattern every time?—and then filed back to the mansion with the others. The Statthalter and his senior aides rode in gleaming black steam cars, but the lower-ranking servants had to walk, even Frau Walkenhorst.

After lunch was served and cleaned up, the maids lined up to see who would be assigned extra work and who would be released. Frau Walkenhorst read out the names of those who, for one infraction or another, were assigned some menial task.

"Florina!" the Haushälterin bellowed. "Twice this week your uniform was not pressed. You will shine the brass in the foyer."

"*Ja, gnädige Frau.*" Florina curtseyed.

Frau Walkenhorst corrected her pronunciation before moving on to her next victim. Once she had finished, she said to the rest, "You are at liberty until sundark. Do not be late, or you will be polishing brass a week from today."

Kim and the others answered in unison, "*Ja, gnädige Frau,*" and dashed to their rooms to fetch hats and handbags.

While the other girls babbled about shopping and other nonsense, Kim pulled her book satchel from beneath the iron bed she shared with Florina and headed for the door. Only when she saw the hatted girls in the corridor did she remember. She ducked back in and took her hat down from the top shelf of the wardrobe. For years, she hadn't worn more than an old black sailor's cap. Now she propped the little blue hat on her head as Barbara had showed her and tied the wide satin ribbon under her chin.

She walked out the gate with the others and continued alongside them to the marketplace. Their chatter was all about their shopping and never about anything they might have overheard while serving the Statthalter. Useless. Once in the familiar bustle of the market, Kim quickly lost them, and made for Montecito.

The colonel's office door was open as usual, though with no wind the curtains hung limply. He and Barbara sat on the patio, she fanning herself with a folding fan while he used one made of palm fronds.

"There's our girl," the colonel said. "How are things in your new situation?"

"*Aburrido.*" Kim walked inside, fetched a footstool, and carried it out to them, placing it between their two chairs. "Horribly dull, and I never get to serve the Statthalter." She sat on the stool. "And the ones who do never pay attention, so I don't learn anything from them." She slung the satchel off her shoulder and left it at her feet.

"Give it time, my girl," the colonel said.

160

"You've got to establish yourself with them, you know."

"I know. But Frau Walkenhorst watches us every minute. I can't even sneak around to overhear things."

"Let's be honest, Kimberly," Barbara said. "It's not 'overhearing.' It's eavesdropping."

The colonel harrumphed and straightened in his chair. "If we're to be honest, Barbara, it's spying."

Pastor Barbara looked sad. "That it is." She lowered her fan. "It's dangerous business, Kimberly. Do remember that."

"Always, *pastora*. I may be small, but I'm not stupid."

Barbara laughed. "Far from it."

"Too smart by far. Perhaps too smart for your own good." The colonel stood. "I suppose you ladies wish to get on with your lesson, eh? You may use the study as long as you like." He stood.

Kim shot to her feet also. "I'm sorry I didn't have anything useful this time, colonel."

"Can't be helped, Miss O'Hara. Can't be helped. Press on." He tipped an imaginary cap to her and walked through the study and the inner door, closing it behind him.

161

Kim sat back down and turned to Pastor Barbara. "What are we doing today, *pastora*?"

"I believe we left off at Romans 12, didn't we?"

"Yes, ma'am." Kim pulled out her Bible and notebook, and spent the rest of the evening walking through Paul's dense letter with her teacher. They reached the last chapter just as the orbiting panels that simulated night drew near the sun. Barbara glanced skyward. "You have to be back by sundark, don't you?"

"Yes, *pastora*, but we're almost done."

"We're nowhere near done. There's so much in Chapter 16, I can't even begin … Just do this. Tonight, read the chapter through and circle every name that belongs to a woman. We'll discuss it in depth next time. All right?"

"Yes, ma'am." Kim glanced over the page, picking out some of the names. "What if I can't tell whether they're female?"

"Make your best guess." Pastor Barbara stood. "I won't keep you any longer. Do you want me to walk back with you?"

"Not all the way, lest you be seen. But if you come with me as far as the *catedral*, that would be all right, I think."

"Very well." Barbara fetched her own

162

hat, and they walked up the Via Colina toward
the Catedral de Santa Inés. They talked about
the differences between the Lutherans and the
Romans and Barbara's Congregationalists.

Kim never much cared for any of the
churches. They'd run her out more often than
they'd welcomed her in. But Barbara's was
different. Different from the Roman *padres* with
their endless Latin recitations, and different
from the New Berliners' Lutheran formality. At
Barbara's little chapel, anyone who wished to
speak could, but no one had to. That seemed
the right way of doing things.

"I gather Colonel Crayton doesn't care
much for the Roman church." Kim said. "So
why does he attend it?"

"He doesn't, usually. Good Tellusian
that he is, he probably attended the Anglican
church at home. But here, we want to fit in with
the Asterians."

"He calls himself an Englishman,
sometimes."

"Yes, in his own way he's as fascinated
by his ancient heritage as the New Berliners are
of theirs."

"Is that why he's always calling me
Irish? What does that even mean?"

"With a name like O'Hara, you must be

descended from the people of Ireland. It may have been very long ago, longer even than colonization. I mean, my people were from America, but before that, they were English."

"But I'm an Asterian! That's all that matters. Isn't it?"

They reached the statue of Santa Inés in the cathedral courtyard. Barbara stopped and turned to face Kim. "Yes, that's what matters. That, and we are Venusians. When we can think that way, and not about nations or ancestry or sectarian differences, then we'll truly be a free people."

Kim slumped against Santa Inés's plinth. "Do you really think that will ever happen?"

"I do, Kimberly. I truly do. Maybe not in my lifetime or even yours, but I believe it will happen, even if it's not until the kingdom comes." She put her hands on Kim's shoulders. "No matter when, we just have to keep fighting for freedom and for God's kingdom as long as we are able. Yes?"

"Yes, ma'am." Kim hugged her. "Thank you for walking with me."

"My pleasure. You take care, now."

"I always take care."

"You do not. You get into more trouble

than a respectable girl should."

Kim laughed. "But it always turns out for the best, doesn't it?"

"It does indeed. Good night, Kim."

"Good night!" Kim turned and jogged half a block north, then ducked through a couple of alleys lest anyone should be following her. Not that she suspected anyone was, but it was more fun to return this way than to take a straight route. Though she wanted to take a long sprint and feel the wind in her hair, Kim restrained herself to a ladylike stroll up three more blocks to the Statthalterhaus. The sun still shone beside the panels, though the hills east of town were already cloaked in shadow.

At the back entrance guard shack, Kim showed her employee papers.

The guard glowered at the skypanels just as their shadow crept across the courtyard. "Cutting it close, Fräulein O'Hara." But he opened the gate for her.

She probably ought to spend more time getting to know him, and the other guards too, but that would have to wait. It was more important to get inside and be seen by Frau Walkenhorst. She paced across the rear courtyard as quickly as she respectably could, then slipped through the back door.

165

"Fräulein O'Hara!" Walkenhorst bellowed. "Where have you been?"

Kim froze in the mudroom. "I have been visiting my teacher, Frau Walkenhorst."

"You have no need of teachers now. I am your teacher, and the lesson you must learn is that respectable women do not remain out at all hours. You were expected back at sundark."

That she hadn't been shut out indicated that she had returned in time. But no one argued with the *übermammutfrau*. "Begging your pardon, *gnädige Frau*, I am a very foolish girl, and I suppose I need all the learning I could get."

Frau Walkenhorst slapped her. Kim stood her ground. She'd taken worse beatings than that.

"Have all the lessons you like on *your* time, but you be back to this house well before curfew, or you will be replaced. There are a hundred girls just like you who'd be grateful for the opportunity."

"*Ja, gnädige Frau.*" There wasn't even one other girl like herself in all of Asteria. Otherwise why had the colonel recruited her all those years ago?

"You've had one warning. There won't be another. Next infraction, you will find

166

yourself back on the street." The Haushälterin's voice turned to a sneer. "*¿Tú comprende?*" Her accent was terrible.

"*Ich verstehe, Frau.*"

"*Gut.* Now go."

Wolkenhorst blocked the way to the common room, where the rest of the staff usually socialized. So Kim climbed the stairs to her room.

Florina, already in her nightdress, was sitting cross-legged on the bed, reading one of her *novelas baratas*, with a lurid cover of a *salteador de caminos* riding through a dark wood. That she wasn't downstairs with the others hinted that Diego had rebuffed her or had in some other way embarrassed her again. "Did Frau Kommandant beat you too badly?"

"Hardly at all." Kim sat on the bed and took off her shoes.

"Lucky for you." Florina turned a page. "Where were you?"

"Visiting my teacher."

"Why?"

"I have a lot to learn, don't I?"

"I don't think so. You're smarter than anyone else I know." Florina turned a page.

Kim turned to the washbasin and cleaned her face and hands. The water was cold, but that was refreshing with temperatures rising. Soon the sunlight would cease, and a fortnight of dark would be upon them.

Florina lowered her book. "What sort of things do you study?"

That was a question not to be answered honestly. At least, not entirely. "The Bible, mainly."

"Sounds dull. Don't you get enough of that in church?"

Kim pulled her towel from the bar on the left side of the washstand. "Oh, no. My teacher is much more interesting than the pastors in the New Berliner churches."

Florina leaned forward, the book in her lap. Her voice dropped to a whisper. "So your teacher isn't Lutheran? Is she ... you know ... Roman?"

"*¡Caray, no!* She's Protestant." Kim wouldn't mention her Roman schooling or Barbara's congregation. The less said, the better. There couldn't be that many Congregationalists in all of Asteria, let alone in Nuevo Barcelona.

VV

On the third day of full dark, Kim returned from her furniture-dusting rounds without having seen a sign of the Statthalter. Frau Wolkenhorst seemed to deliberately schedule their work when the governor was out.

She put away the cleaning supplies, and turned to find Florina right behind her. Florina likewise stowed her things.

"Fräulein O'Hara. Fräulein Delgado." Frau Wolkenhorst stood in her office doorway with her clipboard. "If you have finished, you will now start on the fireplaces."

"But we cleaned those when the sun came up, and they haven't been used since," Florina said. "They can't be dirty."

What was she thinking?

Frau Wolkenhorst strode forward, and clunked her clipboard on the top of Florina's head. "They have collected two weeks' worth of dust, haven't they? Should I send your boy Diego to build a fire in Herr Statthalter's office and have the place smell of scorching dust?"

Florina blushed.

Frau Wolkenhorst drew back her shoulders. "Fräulein O'Hara, how many fireplaces have we?"

"Twenty, *gnädige Frau.*"

"And how many maids do I have here before me?"

"Two, *gnädige Frau.*"

Florina trembled, biting her lip.

"Ordinarily I would tell each of you to clean ten fireplaces, and then we would be done, no?" Wolkenhorst glowered at Florina. "You shall clean fifteen, Fräulein Delgado, and Fräulein O'Hara will clean the remaining five. And in the future, you will not question my orders. Is that clear, Fräulein Delgado?"

"Yes, *gnädige Frau.*" Florina dropped a curtsey.

"*Gut.* Get to work." Wolkenhorst walked out of the room and up the stairs.

"Why don't you work from the top of the house down," Kim said, "and I'll work on the ground floor."

"That means I'll be doing all the bedrooms, and you'll be stuck in the offices," Florina said.

"Yes." At this time of day, the bedrooms would be empty, which meant Florina was unlikely to be seen there. Kim knew that Florina lived in fear of running into the Statthalter or one of his aides. But Kim waited eagerly for such a meeting. "I don't mind."

Florina hugged her. "You're a good friend, Kimberly. Thank you."

"It's nothing." Kim crouched and picked up the bucket and a bag of cleaning

170

utensils. They walked upstairs.

At the ground floor landing, Florina said, "See you later," and continued upward.

"Right." Kim paced quickly down the hall to the front sitting room, which overlooked the Pederplatz. Her nerves jangled with anticipation, hoping for a glimpse of the governor. But no one was about.

She moved aside the fanlike copper screen that covered the fireplace. Kim whisked out the firebox with the broom and dustpan, reaching all the way back to gather up the balls of fuzz at the back. She emptied the dustpan into her pail, and then took out a rag and the polish and gave the fireplace screen a good cleaning.

Satisfied with her work, Kim replaced the screen and moved on to the library. And then the office. She took a deep breath and opened the door. She hadn't been in there yet. The outer room held filing cabinets on the left, the secretary's desk in the middle, and another door at the back.

The governor's skinny male secretary sat at the narrow writing desk with a cityscape of New Berlin hanging on the wall behind him. "Yes?"

"Frau Wolkenhorst sent me to clean the

171

fireplace, sir."

He opened a book, checked his watch, and nodded. "Very well." He drew a key from his waistcoat pocket and unlocked the inner door. "You have twenty minutes."

"Thank you, sir. It won't take that long." She walked in, casting an eye across the desk. It was utterly clear of any paperwork. She cleaned the fireplace as she had the others. Had she been left alone in the room, she might have risked searching the drawers. But the secretary stood in the doorway the entire time she worked, as if he knew she might do such a thing.

VV

Kim finished the fireplaces and returned her equipment to the basement.

Frau Wolkenhorst met her, clipboard in hand. "Since Florina is still working on fireplaces, you will sweep the carpet on the main staircase and scrub the foyer floor."

"*Ja, gnädige Frau.*" Kim collected the necessary tools and completed the tasks swiftly. They were similar to her chores at school, so she was well acquainted with the work.

When Kim returned to the basement,

172

Frau Wolkenhorst gave her a narrow-eyed sneer. "Finished already?"

"*Ja, gnädige Frau.*"

The *übermammutfrau* inspected the work as if she didn't believe it could be done in such a short time. "*Sehr gut.*" She showed no sign of emotion. "Since you have finished early, you may go to visit the seamstress to be fitted for your formal uniform. You remember the way?"

"*Ja, gnädige Frau.*" Early on, Kim had been sent to have measurements taken for a costume that she gathered was worn by those serving at formal dinners.

"Then go quickly, and return before dinnertime."

Kim was grateful for the chance to get out. She took the long way through the marketplace, though this yielded no gossip to speak of.

The seamstress shop sat on the Hauptstraße just north of the marketplace. The woman, a dour New Berliner with gray hair knotted in a tight bun, pulled out a black dress of fine cotton sateen with white lace collar and cuffs. Kim tried it on, and it fit perfectly. She saw little difference between it and the poplin uniform she wore every day, but the New Berliners rarely had rational reasons for their

173

demands.

Kim headed back toward the Statthalterhaus with the new uniform tied up in a parcel of brown paper and twine.

Screams echoed down the street.

She ran toward the sound.

People ran down the Hauptstraße, shouting.

"*Fuego!*"

"*Muerte a los invasores!*"

"*Fuego en el Staatspolizei-Station!*"

"*Viva Asteria!*"

Kim ran up the street in the direction of the police station. It was only a couple of blocks away from the Statthalterhaus. People ran past her on either side.

"*No, ve por el otro lado,*" someone shouted. "*Es un incendio.*"

She had no fear of fire, but as she reached the intersection of Pederplatz and the Hauptstraße, she staggered to a stop. Flames spouted from the station windows. In the street, an Asterian man held a rum bottle over his shoulder. A flaming rag hung out the top. He hurled the bottle through a window as a rattle of gunfire blasted from the building.

The man dropped, with several others around him.

174

Too late. There was nothing Kim could do here, no news to be gleaned that wouldn't be in the papers the next morning. Reaching the Statthalterhaus without crossing the path of the Staatspolizei-Station guns meant going around the block.

Kim turned and ran.

ОV

"Fräulein   O'Hara!"   Wolkenhorst barked.

Kim almost dropped the fork she was polishing. She jumped from her chair and stood at attention. "*Ja, gnädige Frau.*"

"Come here."

Kim left the worktable where she and the other maids were polishing every silver utensil in the house, and stood before the housekeeper.

Wolkenhorst looked her up and down. "Very good. Cook is preparing tea. You will serve the Statthalter and his guests in the front sitting room. You will be seen but not heard. Is that clear?"

"*Ja, gnädige Frau.*"

"Go." Wolkenhorst poked a sausage-like finger toward the kitchen.

Kim dropped a curtsey and went. In the kitchen, the cook and her assistant were loading up a trolley with the tea service and platters of cookies.

While she waited for them to finish, Kim cleaned her hands at the washstand by the door.

"There. It's ready," the cook said. "You may take it out now."

"Thank you, ma'am." Kim wheeled the trolley out of the kitchen and into the dumb waiter in the hall. She closed the door and ran up the back stairs to the ground floor. There she opened the dumb waiter, and hauled on the ropes. The compartment holding the trolley rattled and clattered as it rose. Once it was in place, she tied off the ropes and rolled the trolley out and down the hall to the sitting room.

Her nerves rattled like the tea cups on the tray. The one other time she had served the Statthalter, he had been alone in his office. But the sitting room meant he had company. Finally.

It had been two days since the attack on the Staatspolizei-Station, but no word of the event circulated in the halls of the Statthalterhaus. It hadn't been in the newspaper, either. As if the New Berliners thought that by ignoring it they could erase it from Asterian memories.

The sitting room doors stood open to the foyer, and voices murmured within. Kim slowed her pace, hoping to hear them before she was heard, but the incessant rattling of the cups made that impossible. The murmuring died before she entered the room.

Inside, Herr Statthalter sat in the big armchair near the fire. He was a tall, broad-shouldered man with close-cut blond hair and a clean-shaven face. Opposite him, in a similar but smaller chair, sat a man with olive skin, dark eyes, and darker hair that grew into huge mutton chops. His mustache was even bushier than the colonel's. A younger, clean-shaven fellow—the visitor's aide, maybe—sat on the couch with the Statthalter's secretary.

"Very good." Herr Statthalter barely looked her way. "Please serve our guest first."

Kim silently curtseyed by way of reply, and poured the tea. She passed cups first to Mutton Chop, then to Herr Statthalter, then to the guest's aide, and lastly to the secretary. Then she made her rounds with a tray of cookies.

"Leave the food on the coffee table, please." Herr Statthalter sipped his tea. "You may go."

Kim curtsied again, and moved the tea trolley off to one side of the room before walking out.

As she went, Herr Statthalter said, "Close the doors behind you."

She did so, silently.

It was as if Herr Statthalter knew there was a spy in his house.

VV

Kim returned to the silver polishing. Why every piece suddenly required attention had not been explained. They certainly didn't look dirty.

By dinnertime, they had finished. The kitchen maid put the polish away, and the scullery maid took the rags to the laundry for cleaning. Florina set aside the pieces that would be needed at the dinner table, while Kim returned the rest to their form-fitted trays. One velvet-lined slot for soup spoons, another for forks, and so on. Then she and Florina hefted the boxes and returned them to the storage room, which was across from the kitchen.

Cook's voice blared across the hall. "Is the gentleman from Parga staying to dinner?"

"Yes, he's staying the week," Frau Wolkenhorst answered.

Kim hesitated. She slowly slid the bin of silverware into its place in the storage room. That explained the silver polishing, and her need for a formal uniform.

Wolkenhorst continued. "And we have more visitors coming tomorrow from Chondi and Themis."

Florina stowed her box and left. Kim remained, pretending to inventory the room.

"We'll have six at breakfast," Wolkenhorst said, "eight at lunch, and twelve for dinner."

"And only a day's notice? You presume I have enough stores to feed so many!"

"I know what stores you have, since I ordered them." Kim could imagine Wolkenhorst ticking this item off on her clipboard. "You didn't accept a position in the Statthalterhaus so you could complain about having to serve dinner to diplomats."

"It's not the company that troubles me, Haushälterin. It's the short notice."

"It's notice enough. See to it." Wolkenhorst's heavy shoes pounded the pine floor of the kitchen.

Kim ducked aside, squeezing herself

179

into the corner next to the door. Wolkenhorst
would have to enter the storage room to see
her. She held her breath.

The footfalls clonked away down the
corridor toward the Haushälterin's office.

Kim let her breath out slowly and tried
to figure out how soon she could get out of the
house to see the colonel.

$\mathcal{VV}$

After dinner, the servants were almost
always at liberty, but with guests in the house,
there was no telling. The kitchen maids cleared
the table. Once Frau Wolkenhorst left the
room, the rest of the staff would claim the
servants' dining room for whatever
entertainments could be concocted. They would
play card games, or someone would read aloud,
or they would just share drinks and
conversation.

But Wolkenhorst remained in her seat
after the dishes had been cleared. Finally she
stood. "Fräulein Delgado."

Florina visibly flinched, then rose. "*Ja,
gnädige Frau?*"

"You will remain here in uniform and
prepared to serve if the Statthalter requires. Be

180

attentive to the bell."

"*Ja, gnädige Frau.*"

Wolkenhorst left the room, and Florina, trembling, fell back into her seat.

Kim patted her shoulder. "Don't worry, you'll be fine. He mostly ignores people anyway."

Florina pressed her hands to her cheeks and shook her head.

Diego sighed and stood up. "Someone needs a drink. You want *sidra* or *cerveza?*"

The cook slapped his shoulder with the back of her hand. "She can't drink, *imbécil*. If she gets called up and smells of beer, *die übermammutfrau* will never let her hear the end of it."

"Tea would be more calming," Kim said.

"Yes, we could all use some, I suppose, with a houseful of guests. I'll put the kettle on." The cook went out through the swinging door to the kitchen.

Edmundo, the most junior footman, sidled up to Kim. "Would you, ah, like a game of chess?"

"Oh. No, thank you. I have an errand to run."

His eyebrows shot up, crinkling his

forehead. "What kind of errand?"

Kim stiffened. "A personal one." With Wolkenhorst gone, the butler was the next most senior staff person. "Begging your pardon, Herr Jäger, but with it the dark fortnight now … when is our curfew?"

Jäger, a tall, heavyset man with gray hair and saggy jowls, pushed back from the table and unfolded a newspaper he'd stowed under his chair. "Eight o'clock."

"*Vielen Dank, mein Herr.*" Kim went to the mudroom for her hat.

Edmundo followed. "Sorry to intrude, Kimberly. I just … it's late to be shopping, isn't it? The marketplace will be closed."

"I didn't say shopping." She tied her hat in place.

"What, then?"

Kim's nerves jangled. Why did he care? Did he suspect her of spying? He couldn't. "How dare you pry into a girl's personal business!"

He flushed darkly and took a step back. "Very sorry, Kimberly. I just … how long will you be gone?"

"As long as necessary." She headed for the door.

"Ah. I see. Well …be careful out there.

182

It's dark."

It had been dark for days. "I may be a foolish girl, Edmundo, but I know the difference between day and night." She walked out without waiting for his answer.

Never had she so wanted to sprint. To run as fast as she could away from that place. Every one of Barbara's warnings chased her like dogs at her heels. Finally she reached the colonel's house. Scaling the fence was impermissible now, so she went to the front. The housekeeper showed her to the parlor, where the colonel sat with a fat book. "Ah, Kimberly. How nice to see you. Do have a seat." He turned to the housekeeper. "Ask Pastor Fisher if she'd care to join us."

"Yes, sir." The woman curtseyed and returned to the foyer.

When she'd gone, the colonel waved a finger at the doorway.

Kim jumped up, dashed over, and pulled out the twin pocket doors that closed the room off.

He abandoned the book on the side table and scooted forward. "What have you got, then?"

Kim explained about the visitors.

"Blimey. Doesn't leave us much time."

"It is important, though, isn't it?" Kim returned to her chair.

"Oh, yes, I daresay. Parga, Chondi, and Themis? If that's not the governor assembling a coalition to confront Tethys about overflying the shipping lanes, I don't know what is."

"So you think it's military activity?"

"My girl, with New Berlin, everything is military."

One door slid half-open, and Barbara stepped through. "Kimberly! What news?"

Kim filled her in.

"We can coordinate with Zirka, Phoebe, and Dione to counter this." The colonel slapped the arm of his chair. "They'll not cut off Asteria's trade with Tellus and Tethys, not on my watch."

"What will you do?" Kim asked.

"I shall do what I must. I will relay the information to my superiors, and then do as I'm ordered. As must you. Hurry back now, before you're missed."

"Almost all the servants saw me go. I said I was running an errand."

He frowned. "Oh, my. Bad form, that."

"It's impossible to sneak out unseen. The corridor to the exit runs right by the room where everyone socializes."

"No trouble." Barbara moved to the door. "Wait here." She slipped out again.

"Will you call up the airships from Tethys?" Kim whispered.

The colonel picked up his book. "As I said, I'll alert my superiors. They will decide whether to mobilize the military, and if so in what way."

Kim huffed. She provided the colonel with valuable information, but he rarely returned the favor.

Barbara returned in a few minutes with a brown paper parcel.

Kim turned it over. "What's this?"

"What do you think? It's a commentary on the Pauline epistles." Barbara winked. "But your co-workers don't need to know that."

VV

All the next day was a flurry of cleaning, serving, and cleaning again. The laundress—the basket-toting woman Kim had met the first day—complained that the representative from Themis used too many towels after his bath. "With no sunlight, how am I to dry them in time for anyone who wants a bath in the evening?"

Edmundo was sent to the marketplace to buy more.

Kim and Florina took turns ferrying the tea trolley back and forth from kitchen to meeting room.

As dinner neared, the clatter and chatter in the kitchen grew louder.

The kitchen maid pounded a giant pot of turnips with a masher. "Turnips. Hate turnips. Hate. Hate. Hate."

"You don't have to eat them, you only have to mash them," growled the cook. She opened the oven and ladled a sour-smelling marinade over the giant pork rib roast.

"The Statthalter asked for more tea." Kim emptied the dregs of the pot into the waste bin.

"*¡Caray!*" The cook slammed her ladle on the counter. "Does he not know dinner is coming?" She turned to the stove. "Put the kettle on yourself, Kimberly. I have to see to the *Spargel.*"

"Yes, ma'am." Kim filled the kettle and slipped it onto the back of the stove behind the large steamer set up to receive the white asparagus. Then she ducked out of the way and went to wash out the teapot while she waited.

Edmundo returned with his parcel of

towels. "Kimberly, there's someone at the gate for you."

"What?" Kim grabbed a hand towel and dried the teapot. "Who?"

"I don't know. She's arguing with the guard about needing to see you. A brown-haired woman."

"With bits of gray in her hair?"

"Yes, that's her."

"It's my teacher. She wouldn't come if it weren't important. Kim put the pot back on the trolley. "Thank you, Edmundo." She left the kitchen.

He followed her to the mudroom. "Listen, Kimberly, I know it's a busy day, but when it's all over, maybe you and I could … I don't know … go out for a walk or something. Get some fresh air and quiet."

"Yes, quiet. Quiet would be nice."

He grinned at her the same silly way Florina did to Diego.

Oh, no. She wasn't having a boy flirting with her.

"But I suspect we'll all be too tired for that." Kim opened the door, not even bothering to take down her hat. "I can't keep my teacher waiting." She opened the door and closed it behind her before he could speak.

187

Kim swept across the courtyard as fast as decency allowed, on the off chance that Wolkenhorst should look out a window.

Barbara paced outside the fence, wringing her hands. She turned back and met Kim's eye. She gripped the iron bars. "Kimberly! Come at once!"

Kim ran the rest of the way. "What's wrong?"

"I can't tell you here. You must come."

Something wrong with the colonel? She had never seen Barbara in such a state.

Kim ran to the guard, who opened the gate for her, one hand on his pistol, as if Barbara might try to assault him. "Should you be leaving, with the big doings going on?"

"I'll be right back." Kim had no idea whether that were true.

VV

Barbara put her arm around Kim's shoulders and walked her away from the Statthalterhaus. They turned a corner, passed a bank, and darted into an alley. When they emerged on the other side of the block, the colonel was waiting at the curb in his steam car.

Kim instinctively looked over her

shoulder to ensure they hadn't been followed.

The colonel sat in the back, Rolando in the front. As Kim and Barbara crossed the street, the colonel got out and opened the rear door. "Good evening, ladies." He tipped his hat as if nothing were wrong.

Barbara stepped up into the carriage, and pulled Kim in after her. The bench inside was padded and covered with black leather on the seat and back.

The colonel closed the door and got in front with Rolando. "The harbor. Fast as you can."

"Yes, sir." The engine sputtered and clanked.

"Where are we going?" Kim asked.

"A schooner is waiting to take us to Phoebe," the colonel said. "Until we get aboard, we'll say no more."

"But why are we leaving? I hardly know a thing."

"You told us the thing we most needed to know, my dear. An airship is on its way."

"What? Why?"

"To take care of the small matter of the Statthalter and his associates. No more." The colonel leaned out the window and looked to the sky. "As I said."

189

Kim leaned out and looked upward.

A gigantic balloon, thrice the size of a *goleta*, floated overhead. "*¡Dios mio!*"

"Let us not take the Lord's name in vain." Barbara didn't even look. "If you wish to invoke him, do so in prayer, for the cause has taken a dangerous turn."

"What do you mean?" Kim wailed. "What is it doing?" The airship flew in the opposite direction—toward the Statthalterhaus.

"My superiors determined that such an opportunity could not be passed up," the colonel said. "They ordered the airship to bring in … a deterrent to further oppression."

Kim turned and kneeled on the seat, looking out the narrow back window. They wouldn't. They wouldn't dare.

Barbara put her face in her hands.

As Kim watched, a large oval object dropped from the airship. A fat canister with pointed ends like a rugby ball, and stabilizing fins like those on the airship. It fell at a great speed, the wind whistling as it did. Another followed it. And another. A stream of them.

"Get down, Kim!" The colonel bellowed.

Barbara bent forward, head in her lap, hands wrapped on top.

Kim watched as the bombs dropped from sight. They disappeared behind the nearby buildings, into the block that held the Statthalterhaus.

A moment later, a series of roars echoed down the streets. Great balls of orange and red fire erupted from the spot, churning into a billowing gray cloud. The rear window glass cracked with the first blast and blew in with the second, shattering all over the seat and Barbara's back.

"NO!" Kim screamed. She turned around and grabbed the driver's shoulder. She scarcely noticed the cuts on her arm. "We have to turn back."

He kept his eyes on the road. "No, *señorita*. Sit down. Take care with that glass."

Barbara straightened and examined Kim's face. "Look at you. Lucky you didn't put an eye out." She pulled out a handkerchief and dabbed at Kim's cheeks.

Kim pushed her away. "Never mind that. I have friends back there. We have to go help them!"

"How could you be friends with people you knew barely a week?" The colonel pointed down a road that sloped toward the harbor.

"There."

The driver turned that way. The movement of the car sent glass shards off the seat and onto the floor.

"Some of them were good to me." Poor Florina. Would she be all right? With Kim absent, she might have been sent to wait on them. No, they would still be waiting for the tea. Maybe Florina and the others were safe in the basement. "It's not fair!" Hot tears streamed down her face, stinging. "They were just poor *trabajadores* like me. They don't deserve to die!"

The colonel turned in his seat. "Miss O'Hara! Enough of this outburst. The order came from far above me, and you will not question it."

"But …" Kim looked back again. The car descended the slope, and the landscape hid everything from her view except a pillar of billowing black smoke. "It's not fair," she whispered.

Barbara brushed away shards of glass with her handkerchief. Then she put her arms around Kim and held her. "War is never fair, Kimberly."

VV

Rolando let them off at the base of a gangway, unloaded the luggage from the trunk, then sped off again.

Kim watched the car pull away. "Isn't he coming with us?"

"He has other things to attend to." The colonel waved a sailor over. "Bring the baggage aboard." The colonel strode up the gangway.

Pastor Barbara's soft hand on her back propelled Kim up the ramp. Behind them, the sailor bellowed for help from his mates. Unlike the steel ships of New Berlin's navy, the Phoebean schooner was built of wood, painted blue near the water and white near the gunnels.

On the deck, an officer saluted the colonel, and with unflinching expression, looked Kim over. "This girl needs to visit sick bay."

"Yes, yes, show her down, would you?"

The officer extended a hand toward a door in the aft part of the ship, but Kim looked again over her shoulder. In the town, the wail of sirens overwhelmed distant shouts and screams and the roaring fire.

"Come along, Kimberly." Pastor Barbara wrapped an arm around her shoulder and pulled her toward the door.

193

They descended a steep staircase. Kim gripped the handrails, her knees wobbling. They'd bombed the Statthalterhaus because she'd told them when all the officials would be there.

It was all her fault. The fire, the screams, the dying.

All her fault.

Señor Jesús, perdóname.

VV

The ship's doctor was cold-handed with a disposition to match. He and his nurse—a sweet girl who reminded Kim too much of Florina—swabbed Kim's cuts with stinging solutions and covered her with bandages and plasters.

"Okay, you can go now." The doctor's accent was like Barbara's—Tethysan. "See the nurse tomorrow to have your bandages changed."

"Thank you." Kim slid down from the table and walked out of the little white room.

In the corridor, Pastor Barbara stood waiting. "How do you feel?"

"I don't know."

Barbara hugged her. "These are

194

unpleasant days." Her voice quavered. "But trust that Asteria can rebuild despite this violence."

"Rebuild?" Kim shoved her away. "With what? The New Berliners will just show up with more guns and bombs and those ... *volar cosas* ..."

"Airplanes. Come along." Barbara walked her down the corridor, down a ladder, and down another corridor to a little room. Two narrow bunks sat one above the other against one wall. "You and I will have to share the cabin."

"*Bueno, Pastora.*" Kim plucked at the skirt of her maid's uniform. "Do I have to wear this all the way to ... wherever we're going?"

"No, dear." Barbara took a key from her reticule and kneeled in front of a trunk opposite the beds. She unlocked it and pulled out clean clothes. "I brought some things for you. Hope you like them."

Kim shook out the skirt and blouse. They were all right. "Are there pants in there?"

Barbara sighed. "No more running about the streets pretending to be a boy. You'll dress as a lady."

Kim stifled the desire to roll her eyes. "Yes, ma'am."

"I'll wait in the corridor." Barbara grasped the door latch.

"You don't have to." Kim unbuttoned the top of her uniform. "At school we're six to a room. And I've been changing with Florina for days …" Kim dropped onto the bottom bunk. "What if she's dead? I wish you had warned me—"

"Kimberly, I didn't know myself until an hour ago. Please believe me. The colonel and I were powerless to stop it. We didn't have time to do more than fetch you. And frankly, we didn't have time for that."

"What?"

"Rescuing you was not in our orders. We were given an hour to board this ship. The colonel demanded more time. He said, 'I'm not leaving without my best operative, by Jove.'" Barbara's imitation of the colonel's accent was perfect. "And I said he was too right, so we came to get you. Waiting for us put the whole crew at risk."

"But Barbara, everyone in the house … Florina and the rest … they're probably dead, and it's all my fault!"

"No, Kim! No!" Barbara moved to sit next to her and hugged her. "Blame the general who ordered the bombing, or the Statthalter if you like, or the Kaiser himself. But do not blame yourself. You wanted what was best for your fellow Asterians—freedom. Right?"

Kim nodded against Barbara's shoulder.

"We must keep fighting for freedom. To give up now is to make everything that happened today pointless. You don't want that, do you?"

Kim soundlessly shook her head. Her throat constricted as if a boa had hold of it.

"You're a freedom fighter, Kimberly. Remember that."

"Yes, ma'am," she squeaked. She pulled off the uniform and dressed in the green gabardine skirt and white cotton shirtwaist Barbara had brought her. The buttons of the blouse didn't gape across her front as her old shirts did, and the narrow waist emphasized her bosom, which felt awkward.

The tiny mirror over the washbasin at the end of their cabin didn't afford much of a view. Still, Kim stared at herself for a moment. Freedom fighter. She'd borne a lot of epithets in her time, but that one … that one she could bear a long while.

END

Chasing the Sun
by Cindy Koepp

Uki packed the last of the carded fur in a basket destined for the dogsled. Spinning yarn from the soft undercoat of her dogs would continue as every night's project. The yarn made from malamute undercoat made beautifully warm clothing. Usually, the next step would be weaving, but that would no longer be a joy for her to look forward to. Her hundredth birthday was tomorrow, and the time had come for her to strike out on her own. Her people only survived by taking care of the children and the young. The scarce resources in the tundra wouldn't sustain the entire population if the elderly stayed on. Like everyone who reached their hundredth Venusian year, Uki would do her final great service to the community.

Her loom and spinning wheel were already marked for her granddaughter, a gifted weaver even at her young age. Uki stroked the smooth wood one last time. Real wood had to be brought in and purchased at too dear a price at the supply station for the tribe to replace it. Uki would miss weaving, but she could still spin using her caribou bone drop spindle. She'd leave the resulting yarn at the cave at Aqqut for her granddaughter, or any other weaver, to pick up and make into the useful things.

The cold wind whipped past her, reminding her that she needed to be going. She wanted to be well on the way when everyone awoke. No tearful goodbyes would haunt her memories that way. She'd miss her children and grandchildren, both adopted and biological, enough as it was.

Uki secured the last basket on her sled and checked the dogs, already hitched into their positions. Innuk, strong as any two men, led the way. Aga, too old for sled work, trotted alongside. It was her time to go, too, so they might as well go together.

Without even a single look back, she made a few soft kissing noises, and that was all Innuk needed to get the team going. She turned the sled northwest. The circumpolar route that way would be shorter, allowing her more time in a day to hunt, fish, and prepare food. The twilight of the coming dawn gave her plenty of light to see. The temperatures were warm enough if she dressed properly for it and cold enough for the snowy, icy ground to provide a good base for the sled. Staying in Venus' dawn twilight had kept her people alive for centuries now. They followed the sun around the world as it made its twenty-eight-day arc across the sky from west to east, running their sleds over the still frozen ground and staying ahead of the brutal cold that fell during the long night.

Checking her position against the dim stars of Qamautiik, The Sled, Uki continued onward. They were well in front of her, and she'd have quite a day's journey if she wanted to put them behind her again.

OV

Uki hooked up the last of her dogs to the sled and returned to Innuk in his lead dog position. He wagged his shaggy black tail and panted.

She knelt and her old bones creaked in protest. "Well, old boy, we'll reach Aqqut this year by my hundred fifth birthday, I think. Just a quick stop to shed some of this yarn we're carrying. Then onward, hmm?" *If I stay much longer than that, the tribe might catch up with us.*

Innuk barked once.

"I thought you'd agree." She ruffled the fur on his head and stood.

On her way to the back of the sled, she checked each dog's harness and neck lines then made sure everything on the sled was properly secured. Aga was curled up on the sled today. That made sense, she'd been limping pretty hard last night.

"Too much running on that bad leg yesterday, hmm? Well, you take your rest today. I think you've earned a day in the basket." Uki stepped up onto the runners and stretched the stiffness out of her own legs. Every year, the stiffness grew worse along with other joint aches and failing eyesight. She could use a day in the basket herself, but then who would guide the dogs? "Hike! Innuk, hike!"

He didn't need telling again. The lead dog started the team off at a good pace, fast enough to keep them in the twilight. There they still found enough snow for the sled, without the prevailing eastern winds that blew in warm air from the sun-lit lands melting it all. They stayed out of the full darkness where the deep cold would kill even the hardiest malamute.

As they went, Uki kept her eyes on the horizon to the south and west. Passing through Aqqut was inevitable, but treacherous. Any time her route crossed the path followed by the Inuit tribe, she risked encountering them. As much as she would have loved to see her family again, she couldn't bear the heartache. By now, they

201

would have assumed she had died in the elements, as so many her age did. There were undoubtedly children named for her, and the awkwardness of confronting them along with the grief of parting again outweighed the temporary joy of seeing them. Just like the last time around, she planned to reach Aqqut well ahead of her people, leave the malamute yarn she had spun in the cache, and continue on.

She approached Aqqut at the third hour of travel, when the stars of the Qamautiik constellation were directly overhead. Aqqut was a rocky outcropping, a sort of mini-mountain that created a bottleneck in the circumpolar routes. Anyone going around Venus' pole had to go through this natural gap, so it made a perfect place to store items a traveler would need.

"Whoa!" She stood on the brake.

As usual, she had to call a few times and toss the ice hook out before the dogs actually stopped, well past the cache entrance. Typical.

Uki shook her head and smiled. "Crazy dogs."

She carted the basket of finished yarn back to the cache, a natural cave in the rock outcropping, and dumped the contents into a larger basket. She took a quick look around at

202

the dried meat, finished cloth, garments, ropes, and other equipment. After a moment's hesitation, Uki darted back out to the sled and secured the now empty basket. Her goal was to add to the community stores from what excess should could generate, not take from them. Acquiring extra resources at Aqqut would defeat the whole purpose for heading out on her own.

Uki squinted into the east, but the tribe was not visible yet. Her plan would work if she got a move on, but first she inspected the dogs, their sled, and the rigging. She'd made her own *qamautiik* the old-fashioned way. Two long boards she'd gotten from the supply station made up the runners and the place where she'd stand during the trip. The bone cross pieces were roped together with woven grasses to form the base of the sled. She'd made it in the old-fashioned way years ago and kept up the maintenance so it'd last her several more years, if she managed to last that long herself.

"Well, time to get moving." She retrieved the hook and hopped onto the runners. "Hike! Innuk, Hike!"

No sooner said than on the way. Once through Aqqut and back in open terrain, Uki turned the team northward again, passing one of the only structures in the tundra. Aklaq had built an actual house up at this latitude to flaunt his rejection of his Inuit heritage. Now, whether taking the northern or southern circumpolar routes, no one could miss his sprawling home built of imported wood and stone. Gas-powered lights and imported charcoal heat protected him from the long nights.

Four years ago, Uki had bothered to stop and talk to her adopted grandson, a waste of time she vowed never to repeat. The dogs, given the command to pass on by the distraction, no longer showed any curiosity in the place.

When Qamautiik was behind her, Uki called the dogs to a stop, which took more than one try. After unhooking the dogs and checking each of them for injury, she unloaded the sled to get to the tent materials on the bottom. Setting up the tent wouldn't take long, but the dogs had stopped the sled a couple-minutes' walk from the rock formation that would give her some decent shelter from the winds. By the time she'd carted the caribou hides and sticks back to her campsite, she had little interest in hunting down a seal or trying to catch a fish, but it was either that or starve. The few bits of dried meat she had left wouldn't hardly feed her, let alone the dogs.

Uki headed back to the sled to collect her shotgun.

Somewhere nearby, the dogs barked in chorus. Her trained ear picked out five different voices. Una's deep-throated bark. Kanut's higher-pitched one. Naga, even his voice hinted at mischief. Aga, whose advanced age hadn't yet robbed her bark of ferocity, and Innuk, whose wimpy, almost whiny bark belied his great strength. Those weren't the happy barks of goofy dogs playing. There was threat and challenge in those voices, especially Una's and Aga's.

Moments later a sixth bark joined the chorus from the far side of the sled. Tamaiijja had once again found a place to hide nearby. She slipped out of the pile of baskets like a rust-colored shadow and came alongside Uki.

Uki grabbed her shotgun, a purchase she'd justified for hunting purposes before she'd left her people. "Come on, Tam. That sounds serious."

Tamaiijja took the lead, and Uki followed with the shotgun aimed away from them both. Her old knees protested the speed after a minute, but the pack counted on her for support no less than she counted on them. Tamaiijja led her off to the left and around a large boulder. The five dogs stood arrayed with Aga in the front and Innuk flanking her left shoulder. The other three formed a jagged line in both directions.

They faced two men, the taller one Inuit like her and the other pale-skinned and blue-eyed. Both dressed in the modern suits of outsiders. The men held pistols aimed at the dogs. These had to be Aklaq's men. Aklaq, the one child she had adopted that she took no pride in. No one else would threaten such fine dogs. As Tamaiijja darted forward to join her pack, Uki brought her shotgun up to her shoulder and took aim at the men. She walked through the line to stand even with Aga, and her stomach unsettled.

"Why are you here?" she demanded.

One pull of the trigger and someone would be dead or nearly so.

"Call off your dogs," the taller of the two demanded. He dressed like an outsider, but he still sounded like an Inuit.

"Not until you tell me your purpose here."

"We lost something."

Uki snorted. *Lost something? Aklaq is always "losing things" so he can "find them," then possess them as if he owned them. I'm not that foolish boy.* "Look elsewhere."

"Look, Grandma, maybe we'll just start shooting dogs." The pale one spoke with a New Berlin accent. He took aim at Innuk.

The Inuit pushed his partner's hand down. "Don't be an idiot. If you can't hit all six at once, you'll have the other five chewing on you two seconds later."

"If we don't find—" the pale one started.

"In thirty-six hours it won't matter." He lowered his gun. "Let's go."

The Inuit headed toward Aklaq's palatial home. His pale friend offered a harsh glare then walked away. Aga and Innuk followed about five paces forward but went no further. Once the two-footed vermin were out of sight, Uki lowered her shotgun. All six dogs gathered around her for their coveted reward of head scratches and belly rubs. Kanut, a female whose fur was as white as Uki's hair, darted around the side of the big boulder behind them and howled.

"What's all the excitement, girl?" Uki trudged that way, leaning on Innuk's strong shoulder.

As she drew nearer, a pair of black, lace-up boots in the snow drift got her attention. Kanut stopped her howling and looked up at Uki then back at a man lying prone in the loose, newly fallen snow. The black boots were part of the attire of a working man, but where would he be working this far north? And where did he come from? There were no tracks in the snow aside from the dogs and the sled, but then it had snowed recently. If her eyes were better, she might have been able to make out the slight indentations of recently filled footprints.

Kanut dug in the snow, tossing it backwards through her back legs. Some of the other dogs joined in. Uki added her own efforts to clear the snow away closer to the man's body. His hand clasped a beautiful, dark wood box with angled sides and a glass disk on one end. Carvings decorated the box and blended nicely with a few interlinked, brass-toothed wheels.

So, are you what Aklaq has "lost" this time? Uki nudged the man with her foot. "You all right, there?"

The man groaned and opened his eyes, looking straight into Kanut's snout. He startled and shrank away.

"She won't hurt you," Uki said.

The man tried to turn over onto his back but hit the boulder. He kept a sturdy grip on the box and pressed his other hand to his head. "It all went wrong. It all went terribly wrong."

"What did?"

"Can you help me?" The man reached up to her.

Uki stepped back. Almost a decade ago, her people had offered help to a man from Tethus. Only a few days later, New Berlin airships had dropped explosive devices on them and wiped out much of the tribe. Images of the dead and dying and the sound of their cries still echoed vividly in her head. "Who are you and what help do you need?"

"My name is Dirk." His hand fell back to his side and he sighed. "I just need to get away from Aklaq. Then I'll contact my friends, and we'll take it from there. Can you help me?"

The corner of her eyes burned as she remembered so many people dying in the attack, and yet, she had an injured man here asking for help. Could she turn him away?

There is no tribe for them to hurt this time. The dogs will be fine, and I'm supposed to be dead now anyway. "All right." She whistled Una forward pushed the palm of her hand toward the ground.

The dog lay flat on his belly next to Dirk. The man held on to the dog's neck, and as the dog stood, Dirk came up to his knees. Uki caught him under the arm pit and helped him stand, but he swayed and stumbled against the boulder behind him.

"Easy there, boy." She tightened her grip. "What's happened to you?"

"It's complicated." He clenched his eyes closed for a moment then opened them and shook his head. "We can't stay here. It's not safe. You only scared them off for a moment."

"All right. Let's go. My tent is nearby."

Innuk walked along Dirk's side and Una stayed at Uki's side while Naga raced ahead to scout the area then darted back the way they'd come. The three girls stayed near at hand, with Aga in the lead. Dirk stumbled often, even with Innuk's support, so the trip took twice as long.

Dirk staggered into the tent and collapsed flat on his face. Uki fell to her knees on the permafrost and winced at the jolt through her old bones.

A bitterly cold wind whistled across the ice, but her heavy coat and malamute fur sweater kept her warm enough. The scent in the wind promised snow.

What has happened to you, boy? Uki felt along Dirk's arms and legs to check his bones then ran her fingers through his short hair to look for head wounds. His clothes were dirty, but no blood discolored anything. His skin was clammy and he shook. *Are you sick?* If so, she doubted a little sleep would improve his condition. Fortunately, being ahead of the tribe meant she had more light. That gave her plenty to see by if she wanted to keep going, but the dogs had been running all day, and all of them needed to eat. Worse, if she pushed further ahead, she ran the risk of crossing over into the thawed area where the sled would bog down in muck. The nearest supply station was a several hours' run to the south, but if she made the trip, she could leave Dirk with Old Willie, who ran the station, and get headed back to her trail. Uki covered Dirk with an extra hide and promised to return soon.

There had to be seals or caribou around somewhere close. There usually was. If she could catch their dinner soon and get some sleep, they could get an early start and cross the southern path used by the tribe well before they arrive.

VV

When Uki awoke, the Qamautiik constellation was still below the horizon. Although it was darker than when she'd gone to bed, there was plenty of light to see in the permanent twilight. She looked at her belongings and the sick outsider who had pleaded for her help. A little reorganizing of her usual sled packing, and he'd be a hidden "dog in the basket," just along for the ride and out of Aklaq's sight, even if that pitiful excuse for an Inuit caught up to them.

She gave Dirk a pat on the shoulder. A few hides on the slats would make the ride a little less uncomfortable. She gathered all the hides and the tent coverings and spread them out, folding them where necessary so they wouldn't become entangled in the runners.

Next, she had to get the passenger situated so she could pile everything else around and on top of him.

The tricky part is getting you moved over there.

Crouching next to Dirk, Uki grabbed him under the arms and pulled, but her feet slipped and she landed ungracefully on her rump.

212

"Oof!" She groaned. "That worked well."

One of the dogs nudged her arm. She glanced over at Innuk's face, a white heart-shape around his eyes and snout with black fur covering the rest of him.

Uki ruffled the fur of her lead dog. "Care to help? This seems like a job meant for your strength rather than mine."

Innuk gripped the collar of Dirk's jacket in his jaws and pulled. Uki tried to help, but the big dog was going fast enough that she only got in his way. Once they were alongside the sled, she rolled Dirk onto the slats with the help of dog snouts nudging or tugging from different angles. They all got head scratches for being so helpful.

Once Dirk was situated on the middle of the sled, Uki piled everything around him, strapping the heap down with her homemade ropes to make sure nothing fell off, especially the "dog in the basket." She built up the sides of the sled with the heavier baskets, then piled the lighter ones on top of him, hiding him entirely.

Aga growled and barked, which set the others to echoing her. When Uki snatched up her shotgun, the brass gears on Dirk's box

213

caught her eye. The metal glinted the dull light like a pieces of clean ice. She pushed the box further into a basket full of malamute hair. It should be safe enough there.

Horse hooves clopped closer in the permafrost and ice. The dogs formed their defensive line with Aga in her accustomed front position and Innuk backing her up. The rest formed up according to their rank in the pack with Tamaiijja, the youngest, the furthest back and furthest away.

Aklaq, flanked by the two from the yesterday, came over the rise. The Inuit man standing to Aklaq's left, the one who had encouraged his friend to leave yesterday, now sported a split lip and the beginnings of a bruise around his left eye.

"Hello, Grandmother." Aklaq stopped his horse well back from the dogs.

He sounded friendly enough, but she knew better. She'd sooner trust a rabid wolf.

She gripped the shotgun with one hand and walked past the dogs to give Aklaq no excuse to get close to the sled. "Grandmother, is it? 'Grandmother' when you want something. 'Crazy old hag with the dogs' the rest of the time."

He dismounted, followed by his two goons. "Call off your dogs, Grandmother. I'm just here to talk."

"Then talk. They're not stopping you." She cradled the shotgun in her arms, ready to aim it where it'd do the most good.

He held up both hands to show them empty. "I've lost something, or perhaps more accurately, something was stolen from me."

The carved whale bone handle of his pistol holstered on his hip stood out against his black leather clothing.

"You're wearing your clothes. I see your weapon on your hip. You don't 'own' anything else, boy." Uki shook her head. "That was always the problem with you. Too enamored of things."

His face turned red and he jabbed his finger in Uki's direction. "Don't lecture me. A man stole a camera from me and escaped. He ran this way, into your land. I want him and it back. Now."

Innuk padded toward Aklaq and growled. The fur on the back of his neck stood.

Careful there, Innuk. She kept her gaze riveted on the men in front of her to keep from looking toward the man behind her on the sled. "First of all, this isn't my land. We don't own land any more than we own trees or lichen. I raised you better than that. Second, there are rocks, crevices, and caves everywhere between here and Aqqut. Why do you think he chose this particular spot to hide?"

He pointed to the ground then to the sled. "Those scuff marks. He collapsed here and you dragged him to the sled."

"At my age, do you think I can lift anything of consequence? Do you think sleds move easily?" She aimed her thumb over her shoulder at the sled. "I've been packing, or have you not noticed that the day's run will start as soon as Qamautiik clears the horizon?"

Aklaq's frown deepened. "There aren't that many places he could hide between here and my house, and he was running this way. I'll check those places, and if I don't find him, I'll be back, and I'll start by shooting some dogs. Goodbye, Grandmother." He spat the title as if it were a curse then swung back up into the saddle and left.

Uki watched him go and sighed. Was there any grief greater than a disrespectful child? Where had she gone so wrong with him?

A north wind blew cold against her cheek. Qamautiik was still resting, but she had a full ten hours to go if she wanted to reach the supply station where Dirk could get the help he'd asked her for.

OV

When Qamautiik was overhead, Uki called the dogs to a stop, but she wasn't surprised when she needed an ice hook, the brakes, and several strong repetitions of "Whoa!" to get them to actually quit running. Still, they were happy enough when she unpacked the rest of the seal she'd killed last night and rationed out servings to each dog and herself. When she checked on Dirk, he was in no condition to eat anything.

Her passenger hadn't so much as twitched since he'd fallen. More than once, Uki had checked for his breathing and heartbeat, both of which were slow and weak. Once she got to the supply station, she would use the telegraph line installed there to call in a physician. Whatever Aklaq had done to him was beyond her meager knowledge.

Once everyone had eaten, she attached the gang line to the sled and whistled the dogs over. "Come on. In your places."

Naga, the practical joker in the group, went to the lead dog's place and wagged his big, shaggy tail until Innuk arrived and growled. Naga gave the bigger dog a playful nudge and darted back to Kanut's place as the right wheel dog. The pure white female looked up at Uki and whined.

"Naga! Place!" Uki scolded.

He started for the left swing dog spot right behind Innuk but Tamaiijja beat him to her place and held her ground. Naga the Loon finally went to his place and chased his tail a few times.

Uki smiled and muttered, "Crazy dog." She started with Innuk, attaching his tug line and neck line then slipping booties on his feet. Once he was set, she stepped back. "Line out!"

Her lead dog drew the line out straight and wagged his fluffy black and white tail. She went to the next two, Naga and Tamaiijja in the swing dog positions. Her old knees protested being in a crouch long enough to attach the dogs to the line and slip their booties on, especially with Naga perpetually picking up the wrong foot for her to put a bootie onto. Finally, she got those two set and went on to her wheelers, Kanut and Una, the biggest after Innuk. Fortunately, whatever discipline Naga lacked had been given to Una. He practically took care of himself, and Kanut never gave her trouble, either. That just left Aga. With her dislocating hip, she was no longer a good one for sled teams. She'd served her time on teams when she was younger.

Uki looked around for the black-and-white dog and whistled. "Aga! Come on, dear!"

The old dog poked her head out of the baskets piled on the sled and panted.

"Taking lessons from Tamaiijja, are you?" Uki stepped onto the foot boards and gripped the handle bar.

Aga bolted from the sled and ran to Uki's side. Her fur stood on end in a long stripe down her back and she growled and stared in the direction of Aklaq's mansion.

Aklaq. It has to be. "On by, Aga! Hike! Hike!"

She pushed off the ground with her stronger leg as Innuk led the way. The sled started off slowly but gained speed as the stronger dogs overcame the inertia of the sled on the snow. Aga stayed put, growling and barking.

"Aga! On by!" Uki commanded. "Innuk, hike!" She made several kissing sounds to get the dogs to pull, but really, they were already doing as much as she could expect for starting from a dead stop.

219

When Uki glanced back at Aga, the dog still paid no attention to the command to ignore distraction and get a move on. Too much further, and Uki would have to stop the sled and go back for the dog personally.

"Aga! On! By!"

The old alpha dog turned halfway and looked back then sprinted to catch up with the sled. Instead of jumping on the sled, she ran alongside.

Uki looked down. "Glad you decided to join us, dear."

"Whoa!" Aklaq called from further behind.

Uki gritted her teeth, but none of the dogs even flinched. They knew her voice. She was one of their pack, and they answered only to her.

She glanced back and caught sight of him on horseback a hundred meters behind.

The trail to the supply station, placed there to serve the gold-hunting prospectors in the mountains and the Inuit village that passed through periodically, was a half-day's ride, less if they could go the way the birds go, but it was all downhill. The extra distance followed a series of wide-arcing switchbacks to keep the sled from overrunning the dogs. There were still places where she'd have to stand on the brake. One of those was coming up.

The loud crack of a pistol firing made her duck down.

"Hold your fire, you idiot!" Aklaq scolded.

The rest of his admonition was lost on the wind.

When Uki stood up, Kanut was just passing the first red marker stuck on a stick in the permafrost indicating the turns. She should have given the command when Innuk hit that marker, seconds before.

Uki gasped. "Haw! Haw!"

Innuk obeyed immediately and the other dogs turned with him into the new direction. The sled skidded around, and one runner lifted out of the snow.

No! No, no, no, no, no! A tumble would be fatal, especially with Aklaq so close on their heels. Uki jumped onto the runner that was off the ground, balancing with all her weight on that side.

"Aga! Basket!" she hollered.

The dog would never be able to stick a landing at that angle, but that wasn't what she needed. Aga sped up and jumped, bouncing off the rising side and landing in the snow again.

Her thirty-five kilograms knocked the runner back down. The sled fish-tailed before it straightened out.

Wider turns. She had to pay attention and go for wider turns. She was lucky the gang line hadn't fouled. Uki resettled her weight on both sides in time for Innuk to pass the next marker and start on a sharp but short downhill run.

Uki pressed hard on the brake. "Easy!"

How close was Aklaq? As much as she wanted to spare a look back, she didn't want to risk another badly timed turn. They'd been lucky the first time. However close he was, he was too close.

The dogs slowed as the sled dropped a few feet in just a few yards. She swallowed hard against the rising feeling that she was going to gag on her last meal.

Behind her a horse whinnied in a panic. Thuds and rumbling downhill followed. Uki kept her eyes ahead on the course as the next red flag drew closer.

"Gee!" She called as Innuk came even with it.

The sled turned in a big arc to the right as the dog led the team around the corner of the switchback.

Ahead, between the current part of the trail and the switchback path she'd just turned from, the pale one's horse scrambled to get righted. The rider had attempted to cut past the switchback by going straight downhill, but fell in a depression that was a snow-drift deeper than the poor creature's shoulder.

The blue-eyed rider was half-buried, boots-over-ears in that depression. Aklaq and his Inuit friend were too familiar with snow to do anything so foolish. They followed the runner tracks in the trail. Horse's hooves pounded and crunched the packed snow as the horses breathed hard and the saddles squeaked with motion. She knew the way. They knew that, and she could use that to her advantage.

The next turn was followed by a long straight run, and at the end of it there were actually two places where she could turn. She usually took the second because the downhill part was less severe there, but if she stood on the brake, the dogs could make the earlier turn and the sled would pop right over a collection of runoff rills. The dogs should handle it fine provided their feet landed either between rills or in the bottom of one. Landing on the edge might cause the dog to stumble, a disaster she didn't want to consider. Horses, with their bigger, inflexible feet, wouldn't fare as well.

She gave the command for the next turn and started the long straightaway back in the other direction. With the long run ahead before she gave the next command, she spared a glance back at the two horsemen. They were behind her and wary enough to keep the horses' pace slow on the unfamiliar terrain.

As she neared the next turn, she gave the command to turn before Innuk reached the marker. She applied hard pressure to the brake as he obeyed her and turned the team on the nearer track. The sled jolted as it crossed over the runoff rills but dogs and sled made it fine. When they rounded the corner, the sled passed the horses two dozen meters further uphill coming the other way. They'd closed half the distance.

Moments later, another horse in distress cried out, and a rider behind her smacked into the snow with a muffled shout. Uki winced at the sounds. As much as she wanted to lose her pursuers, she hated the thought of anyone being injured. Was it Aklaq? If so, this chase might be over. She doubted his flunkie would continue the chase without the master giving commands.

At the end of another long run, Uki issued her command for a wide left turn, and Innuk brought them around with the closer dogs in the wheel position handling the heavy part of pulling the sled around the curve. She looked uphill to the previous turn for the last rider chasing her and frowned.

Aklaq. Persistent, isn't he? She looked down at the sled and the man hidden in the middle of it. *He's lost two men and horses and has every reason to expect that I'll find some way to unhorse him, too. What exactly do you have that drives his persistence?*

The next curve required her to brake the sled again to keep the downhill slope from speeding them up and overrunning the dogs in the wheeler positions. Five more turns and a long, straight run would bring her to the supply station, and the underlying ground would be getting rockier with stretches of smooth stone under the snow. As the path straightened out, he'd be more willing to risk greater speed, but the rocks would be a great equalizer.

Heavy clouds loomed in the east, and the scent in the air promised an impressive snowstorm, probably only a few hours away. The wind blew snow into her back or into her face depending on which direction the switchbacks had her facing, but the dogs kept going, listening for her commands to swing around onto the next leg.

As she came around the last turn, Uki caught sight of Aklaq struggling on the previous leg of the switchback. He glared at her as the horse slipped on the rocks and ice buried under the layer of snow.

Her jaw clenched. *You're going to force that poor beast on, aren't you?*

Instead, he stopped and dismounted, walking the horse forward as it pulled against his lead.

Well, maybe there is still a decent person under there somewhere.

Uki watched the route ahead. One last marker showed her the way, and then the straight run all the way to the station. With the station protected by the mountain from the warm Easterlies, the snow was suitable for the sled when her people came through.

The building ahead of them, made of gray stone and metal, looked hardly bigger than a kid's toy in the lower foothills of the mountains from this distance. A wire, which seemed less substantial than the yarn she spun, stretched from the station to the south, held up by wooden poles at regularly spaced intervals.

The dogs ran on unhindered by the need to slow into turns. She watched each dog carefully in case their increased speed on the icy ground made one of them nervous.

The cabin grew big enough to live in, and Uki stood on the brake while she hollered, "Whoa!"

Only after they'd passed the station did the dogs actually stop.

She smiled and shook her head. *Typical. No matter how soon I give the command, you always pass it up.*

After setting the snow hooks, she hopped off and looked up hill. Aklaq still walked his balking horse through the last turn of the switchback trail. He still had a few hundred meters of the final straightaway to go after that. She had time to get Dirk hidden under better cover and get help for him, but only if she moved quickly. For that, she needed stronger help.

For the moment, she left the dogs on the gang line and hurried to the cabin. When she pounded on the door, no one answered.

Odd. Where's Willie? With the mountains to protect him from the worst of the weather and a supply of charcoal to battle the brutal chill of the night, he usually stayed there all year, trading with miners in the area when not buying and selling from her people. Uki's chest felt tight for a moment. *I hope nothing's happened to him.*

Uki stretched and retrieved the key from the top of the doorframe. She fumbled with the key in the door lock and stopped then sighed and closed her eyes for a moment.

You defeat yourself, foolish one. Easy!

Her hands still shook, but she slipped the key into the lock and gave it a turn. For a moment, she reached up to put the key back in its place then stopped and looked uphill at her useless grandson. She might be able to keep him out of a building this sturdy. The stone walls were thick. Roof and doors were made of metal, and the few windows were high on the walls. The key went into a rabbit fur pouch at her waist. The door swung open without a sound, and Aga followed her inside. The old dog limped a bit.

Uki reached down and patted Aga's flank. "A little too much running today, hmm?"

The inside of the station was neat and orderly as always. There were no fancy decorations. Everything had a purpose, and that suited her fine. The note on the table welcomed her to the cabin, invited her to make herself comfortable, and promised that Willie would be back. A date was given in numbers, but she never had gotten used to the outsider way of marking time.

She frowned. *Nothing wrong with Willie, I hope. He's a good man, for an outsider.*

With him gone, she couldn't just leave Dirk here unattended and get on her way. She'd have to delay her departure at least long enough to call in help for him. Uki darted over to a workbench where the telegraph had been installed. The code that used to be tacked to the wall was gone, but in its place was a brass plaque with the dots and dashes etched into it. The birch bark version had been easier to read.

Squinting and leaning back, she could just make out the code. She tapped out a message to the operator at the other end, the fellow who ran a general store in Danu, the nearest town of any consequence, from what she'd been able to gather. She kept it short and to the point.

"Send help. Injured man. Chased by criminals."

After she'd sent it twice, she looked out the window. Aklaq had finished the last turn and was on the long straightaway to the station. He was back on his horse, but the animal still stepped carefully over the ice. She had to get Dirk inside where he'd be safer, but she had to be quick. Uki darted back out to the sled. If she left the dogs hitched, Aklaq could make good on his threat to shoot them all. Loose they could gang up on him or scatter.

Unhitching the dogs took less time than getting them hooked up, and soon she had her half-dozen bouncing, barking malamutes rolling in the snow and chasing each other around.

Uki unloaded her baskets, leaving them next to the sled. She would have brought them in, but there wasn't time for that. She moved faster than her tired old bones appreciated, but Aklaq was closing in. She glanced at him and frowned. Three hundred meters to go and the horse was less hesitant now.

Once she had Dirk uncovered, she sat on the edge of the slats and jiggled the man's shoulder. He moaned and his head lolled to one side, but he stayed unconscious.

"It really would be helpful if you'd wake up enough to stagger into the cabin, but if you can't, I can hardly blame you for that." She gripped his shoulder then looked back toward the door. *I'll need help to get you in there.*

She whistled for Innuk and rolled Dirk into the snow next to the sled. The dog

230

bounded over and pressed his head on her arm. Uki grabbed her shotgun with one hand and mimed grabbing Dirk's collar and pulling with the other. Innuk followed her instructions well, walking backwards and pulling Dirk along. Uki picked up the basket of malamute fur that held the fancy box and walked with them to encourage Innuk. She opened the door for him when he got close. Once inside, the dog dropped Dirk and looked up at her.

"He's still blocking the door, silly. A little further if you don't mind." She mimed grabbing Dirk's collar and pulling again.

Innuk's ears rotated forward and he tilted his head.

"You heard me. A little further."

The big dog pulled Dirk about another two feet and stopped.

At least the door will close now. Uki ruffled the hair on Innuk's head. "Good boy."

Innuk nudged her arm and started back outside.

Dogs! He'll shoot them! Uki grabbed his harness. "Stay here." She leaned out the door and whistled. "Come on! Get in here! Tam! Aga! Naga! Kanut! Una!"

Kanut ran in first. Tamaiijja followed, and Naga chased his tail a few times before he darted in, but Aga and Una stood about twenty meters from the house and barked. As soon as they started, the others joined the chorus, and Innuk tried to squeeze his way out.

Uki blocked the way with her legs and looked down at Innuk. "Stay here. Go sit!" She pointed and watched him retreat, for the moment at least. Uki whistled. "Aga! Una! On by! Get in here! On by!"

Further uphill, Aklaq had halved the distance. Before long, he'd be in gun range to make good on the threat to kill her dogs.

Aga glanced back, but only for a moment before she resumed barking.

"Stubborn, mutt." Uki called for her again. Her stomach unsettled. *You're going to make me come out there and get you. Aren't you?*

Una changed his mind and ran to her. She let him through then grabbed her shotgun and stepped outside, closing the door behind her.

"Aga!" Uki hurried to the dog. She stood in front of the dog and glared. "On by! Come haw!"

The old dog turned left toward the station. Unlike the dogs that still pulled the sled, Aga didn't have a harness for Uki to grab.

"Hike!"

About halfway there, Aga turned again toward Aklaq.

"On by! Come haw!" Uki ordered.

Aga obeyed, but only after she'd gotten in a few more barks.

When they reached the station, Uki let her in and blocked Innuk's new attempt to get out the door.

"No, we're all staying inside." She closed the door, turned the lock, and slid the chained peg into a slot.

The telegraph machine on the workbench tapped like mad, far faster than Uki could translate, even if she were sitting there staring at the marks.

"Slow down! Slow down already!" She darted over to the telegraph and watched a little strip of what looked like very fine, pure white birch bark slide out of the surface of the table. The bark had tiny holes, some bigger than others, in a line. "Very clever."

Comparing the holes to the plaque on the wall, she deciphered the message. "Help coming. Take cover. Stay put."

The message repeated.

She frowned and glanced back at Dirk. "I'll do what I can, but you boys had better be quick about it." *How far away is Aklaq now?*

233

Uki looked up at the windows near the ceiling. She'd have to climb onto a chair to see out of those. The chairs in the station were either too heavy or too rickety to stand on, which meant she'd have to open the door to get an idea of Aklaq's location. If she opened the door, she not only gave the dogs a chance to get out and get shot, but she opened herself up to that same risk if Aklaq had come close enough.

She rolled Dirk over to the set of shelves near the wall of the cabin and moved hides and baskets of goods to block him from easy view of the door. She retrieved a box of shotgun shells from the shelf in the back of the station. Finally, she took a chair from behind a counter and turned it to face the door. With her shotgun across her lap, she waited for that no-good grandson of hers. Her hands shook and her chest ached, but she stayed in her place and prayed for the Almighty to thwart whatever Aklaq had in mind. Time passed as slowly as the stars moved, but she sat and waited. Going to the door to look for him, would just made her more vulnerable.

All six of the dogs stood near the door, giving her warning that danger was closing in. Aga, closest to the door, periodically scratched the heavy metal. The barking echoed off the walls, but she found the noise comforting. They were her protection as much as she was theirs. Aklaq would know for certain that entering this station was unwise.

Someone pounded on the door.

"Open up!" Aklaq ordered.

"Are you sure you want that?" Uki asked. She shifted the shotgun on her lap to make it easier to bring up to her shoulder and aim.

"I need that box. It was stolen from me."

She strained to hear him. "How can a thing be stolen from you? You have your clothes. You have your weapon for hunting. You own nothing else."

The dogs continued to bark and growl. Una and Aga ran from one corner to the other.

He struck the door again. "If no one owns anything, then what difference does it make if you give me back the camera?"

"You are willing to kill at least two people and six dogs to get it."

"Give it to me and no one will be hurt."

"For now, maybe, but whatever is in that box could spell trouble for someone else."

"You don't even know what it is!"

"I know it's important enough for you to want to kill and risk being out in an approaching storm. It was important enough for Dirk to risk his life to get it away from you."

He struck the door harder. "Open this door!"

"That would not be wise. I could never control all six dogs at once, and they clearly don't like you."

His answer to that was lost under the cacophony of angry dogs.

A loud pop was followed by a bang and an equally loud ping from the door. The dogs all crouched lower. Their ears flattened against their heads and their tails tucked. Uki ducked, raising her shoulders as if she could protect her head that way. Her muscles tensed. Tamaiijja crawled over to Uki and whined. After a few seconds, Aga and Innuk resumed barking. The rest followed them, but Tamaiijja barked from her place by Uki's side.

A loud buzzing sound came from the south.

Some sort of airship? Uki looked over at Dirk hidden behind baskets and hides. *Are your friends here?*

The buzzing changed pitch, getting first higher then lower.

236

Another loud pop and bang from Aklaq's gun made all the dogs cringe, but no ping came from the door. In the momentary silence, Aklaq's footsteps retreated in the snow.

Who are you shooting at now? The people in that airship? Uki looked up at the window. *Foolish boy! If you're shooting at the foreigners, they'll kill you!*

Aklaq might be an embarrassment, but she didn't want him dead.

Uki jumped up from her seat and went to the door. With Aklaq's attention on the newcomers, she could get outside where she might be able to talk some sense into one side or the other before someone died.

Another gunshot came from nearby but nothing hit the station. Aklaq had to be paying more attention to the foreigners. Uki unlocked the door and pushed dogs aside so she could squeeze through without letting them out. Aklaq was crouched in the snow twenty meters away from her, trying to hide behind one of her knee-high baskets as if that would stop a bullet. He faced a strange flying machine, very different from the usual airships. This one had two sets of fixed wings sticking out from a wide, closed tube with a tail sticking straight up at the back and a blurry disk in the front. How did that thing get off the ground without a bag of hot air? The strange machine had a broken window in the side. A door slid open and a man leaned out.

Aklaq popped up and shot a small pistol at the flying contraption. The man ducked as the bullet put a small, new hole in the side.

"Stop!" Uki yelled. "What are you doing? Is that box worth dying for?"

He turned to her. "Shut up, old woman."

The man leaned out again. A high-pitched whiz and a pop came from him. Aklaq slapped his neck then looked at a something blue and red in his palm.

The newcomer and a second man stepped into the opening. Both were bundled up against the cold. One of them held some device that looked like a pistol-sized crossbow with brass wheels and no drawstring. They dismounted and the taller man started running towards Aklaq. He came to a halt when her shotgun drifted his way.

"Aklaq may not be a good boy, but he's still my grandson. You will not hurt him."

The taller answered, raising his hands, "Oh, no, ma'am, we won't. We only put him to sleep. We would like to take him with us and ask him some questions, if you don't mind."

"What happens to him after that?"

"Er," the man glanced back at the other outlander before continuing, looking her square in the eyes when he did speak, "Well, probably prison, ma'am. As you said, he's not a good boy."

"Can't say he doesn't deserve that." She moved the shotgun barrel downward.

The man ran forward and patted Aklaq down. The other grabbed a small, leather bag with a handle and came only a few steps closer.

Uki kept her shotgun turned away from them.

The shorter one tugged off his hood. "You telegraphed for help. I'm a doctor. My friend there is law enforcement."

His accent, definitely outsider, was much like the man from Tethus her people had helped so long ago. Even though ten years had passed, she could still hear him begging the tribe for help.

Is that the truth? Or are you another one with a plan and no respect for people?

They had taken care of Aklaq, and the look in his eyes showed more concern than malice.

"Is Dirk with you? Is he the injured man you mentioned? I need to treat him and get back in the air before that storm hits."

"You need to treat him on the plane so we can get airborne now. That storm won't wait for us," his companion insisted. He pulled Aklaq over his shoulder and stood.

"This way." Uki waved the doctor forward and watched the law enforcer jog back to the plane.

Inside, all the dogs were barking again.

Uki opened the station's door and reached through to pat Aga's side. "Easy, Aga. They came to help." She turned her head to the doctor and shouted "Say, do you know what happened to the man who works here? Willie?"

The doctor didn't even try to talk over the dogs the way she had done. But after a couple more barks, Aga quieted, and the rest of the group followed her lead.

"He helped us. Will be back here in a day or so, God willing. Um, how about Dirk?"

Uki waved the man forward. "All right. Come on, but slowly. They'll be wary until they decide you're safe."

The dogs gathered around, sniffing him and nosing the bag he carried. She pushed them all back until she could close the door.

Uki nudged Aga back from the man. "That's enough. Go catch a snow rabbit or something." She led the doctor by the arm through the crowd of dogs.

The doctor walked to the middle of the room and looked around. "Where?"

Uki began moving hides and baskets. "I hid him under here."

The doctor examined Dirk and asked her to summarize what happened. He then prattled on about the importance of whatever mission Dirk had been sent on, exactly what the box was, how the camera revealed vital information on a New Berlin plot to poison somebody important.

She had more immediate problem. If she headed straight north from here, she would invariably run into the tribe, or at least come within visual distance. If she turned east to get ahead of the tribe, she would get to the sunny edge of the twilight and the slush and muck that her sled dogs, for all their skill, wouldn't be able to overcome. She could turn west and head up behind the tribe, but that held the opposite risk. Too far into the darkness, and she and the dogs could freeze to death.

"Ma'am?" The doctor waved his hand in a wide arc.

241

Uki shook herself. "Yes?"

"The box. Do you have it?" He stood and turned toward Uki.

"Yes, of course." She found her basket of malamute fur and dug through to the bottom where she'd hidden it.

The doctor inspected the device then smiled. "Excellent. Thank you."

She adjusted her hold on the basket. "I need to get headed back to my path. This trip is going to guarantee me a couple cold runs while I catch back up to the twilight as it is." *And it put me at risk for running into my family again.*

"Safe travels."

The door opened as Uki got there and the other man, the law enforcer, entered. "Aklaq is secured. You'll have to treat Dirk on the plane. Pilot's getting antsy." He looked down at Dirk.

The doctor offered the other man the box and they spoke briefly in low tones before he added, "We'd better head in before the weather gets worse." He knelt next to Dirk and pulled him up to a sitting position before lifting the sick man on his shoulder.

The lawman stepped closer. "Plenty of room in the plane for you and your dogs, ma'am, but we need to get out ahead of this storm. Let's get your dogs on board."

"I'm not going with you."

"We can't leave you alone in a blizzard. And what about those two men you mentioned to the doc?" When the tall man reached for her, Aga and Innuk growled at him until he backed off.

Uki squinted and turned her head while still looking at the man. "Alone? I'm hardly alone. I have six very excellent dogs. We'll be fine, I assure you, but if you city boys don't get moving, you'll be stuck in a snow bank somewhere."

The physician laughed. "I'm sure the men left when they saw the plane or will soon. No payday for them if we have Dirk. And this tough old bird hasn't lived in the tundra as long as she has without running into a storm or two. Let's go. I don't want to get trapped here." He thanked her and left with Dirk draped over his shoulder.

His taller friend followed him out.

Uki stood in the door and watched the pair jog to their flying machine and load their friend onboard. The physician leaned out the opening and waved to her before he closed the door. The craft turned to face downhill and left with all the grace of a grounded loon.

She stepped outside and looked at her sled. It was still intact, but Aklaq had dumped out half her baskets and made a mess of some of the others. She sighed and shook her head. While packing the sled again, the twilight turned increasingly dark.

The dogs milled around chasing each other and rolling in the snow while she finished preparations for her upcoming plunge into a blizzard, followed by a time in the cold polar night, doing what she had to do to keep her family safe and also stay alive.

She smiled. Qamautiik was still high enough in the sky that she could make some good ground.

END

For King and Planet
by Adam David Collings

Edwin Wakefield clutched the gunwale and took a deep breath. *Eyes off the water.* He shifted his gaze skyward. The sun beat down from overhead, just passed its zenith today. Only eight days till the dark fortnight.

He reached his hand into his coat and felt for the envelope in his secret pocket. Still there.

"You right there gov'nor?" The captain stopped next to Edwin.

"I'll get used to it." Edwin wiped his brow. "To be born on a water planet and suffer sea-sickness. It's preposterous."

"Water planet?" the captain raised an eyebrow.

"Venus is mostly covered in water. We have a much higher water to land ratio than even Old Earth, though it wasn't always like this."

The captain cocked his head.

"I read a lot," Edwin said. "I think it's important to understand the whole world we inhabit, not just the small part that we live on."

245

The captain shrugged. "Well, I don't know much about the planet, as you call it, but I know water." He scratched his beard. "In any case, some men have it, some don't. The sea legs I be meanin'"

"Be that as it may, I can't afford to feel this way the entire trip. I have a lot to accomplish."

"Important mission I understand?"

"Critical." Edwin took another breath. "I need to meet with my crew."

"The mess hall is good a place as any. I'll have somebody send 'em in to ya."

"Thank you, Captain."

"Oh, Mister Wakefield?"

Edwin turned. "The ah, the woman. You see, my men, well they're at sea most of the time and they haven't seen many women for a quite a while. Well, you can imagine they be a bit distracted."

Edwin frowned. "Your men will conduct themselves with the professionalism as befitting sailors in His Majesty's Tellus Navy."

"That they will." The captain nodded.

Edwin shook his head. How had such an odd fellow risen to the rank of Captain? It seemed strange to have a ship's master act so deferential to him, but the minute matters concerning the ship came up, the captain would assert his authority. Guaranteed.

Edwin staggered to the hatch, took one last glance at the blue sky, and climbed below-decks. The mess was near the aft of the ship. Edwin entered and closed the door behind him. The chalk board had been set up for him just as he'd requested. Edwin smiled.

Four rectangular solid oak tables filled the room. Portholes in the far wall let in beams of light.

A knock sounded at the door. Edwin turned. "Enter."

The door slid open and a tall man in an immaculate suit entered. Lawrence Beechworth lived up to his reputation. Not quite a dandy, but close. His bushy moustache curled up at the edges. That would help him blend in when they reached their destination.

"Early am I old chap?"

"The others will be here shortly." Edwin motioned toward a seat.

Lawrence sat on a bench, facing outward, his back to the table. "Putting on a bit of a show, are we?" He motioned to the chalk board.

"All will be revealed when everybody arrives."

"Well, you certainly have me intrigued. Why you'd want a theatre actor for an important mission is beyond me, but for five hundred pounds it doesn't much matter. So, who are my fellow cast members?"

The door creaked open. Lawrence turned. "A negroid?"

"Aboriginal." The man corrected in a rough accent. "I'm originally from Kruchina. My name is Warragul."

"Kruchina? That's ah?"

"Just past Bell. It was colonized by those descended from the indigenous Australians back on Earth. One of the first people-groups to establish themselves on Venus in fact."

Lawrence stood and nodded. "I see." He stroked his chin. "Well," He strode toward Warragul and extended his hand. "Far be it for me to judge a man by the colour of his skin. We're all here for King and country, right?"

Warragul regarded the hand for a second and then shook it.

Edwin smiled. "Please take a seat Warragul. We're just waiting on one other."

"Well, after that surprise," Lawrence said, "I can't wait to see who else you've got."

248

The door opened again. A young woman entered, clothing tight, her hair scandalously short. "How are we all?" she asked in a cockney accent.

Lawrence stood and gaped.

"Gentlemen," Edwin said. "This is Ivy Kidd."

She flashed an entrancing smile and dropped herself onto a bench with no regard for decorum.

Lawrence turned to Edwin. "An urchin?"

Edwin cleared his throat. "Miss Kidd is a highly skilled specialist, and we'll be needing her expertise."

Lawrence crossed his arms. "What's this all about Wakefield? It's time you gave us some answers."

"I agree." Edwin retrieved his bag from behind the chalk board. He removed a large sheet of card and placed it on the ledge that held the chalks. "This is Bishop Johann Eckstein. One of the leading clergy in New Berlin. Not only is he a theologian, but a gifted amateur scientist and official archivist as well. Our intelligence has informed us that a valuable item has been placed in his care for study. Detailed records on how to operate and

249

maintain an orbital platform, from before the United Nations Wars. If New Berlin can figure out how to service the platforms, they'll be able to control the whole world."

"Well that's bad news, to be sure," Lawrence said. "But what can we do about it?"

Edwin smiled. "We, lady and gentlemen, are going to steal it."

Lawrence cross his arms. "Steal it?"

"Problem Mister Beechwood?" Edwin asked.

"I'm not a thief." He gestured toward Ivy. "She might be. Is this really why you brought us all here?"

"This is going to be a complicated heist, Mister Beechwood. It will require the skills of everybody in this room, including you. If we're to gain the trust of the necessary parties you're going to have to convince them that you're New Berlin nobility."

"I don't think you realise who you've hired. I once starred in an acclaimed production of Dr. Faustus in German. The critics proclaimed that I captured the character's descent into damnation like no other before me. Simply put Sir, I am an artist."

"And that is exactly why I need you Lawrence. Nobody else will do." Edwin smiled.

Lawrence nodded slowly. "And if I am recognised? New Berlin is a hub of culture. They're sure to know of my work."

"Then you can claim to be the brother of the famous actor. Perhaps even his twin."

Lawrence leaned back until he hit the lip of the table. "Very well. I will hear more. Continue."

"Bishop Eckstein is holding a reception in his home on the 18th. Warragul here is, among other things, a gifted forger. He will create an invitation for our esteemed nobleman." He nodded toward Lawrence. "And his lady guest." He turned to Ivy.

Lawrence shook his head. "You expect the urchin girl to pass as a lady?"

"I'm 24," Ivy said. "A legal adult in New Berlin."

"How's your Paleo-German?" Lawrence asked.

"I ah, don't speak any." She paled.

"You have until we make landfall to learn." Edwin said.

Lawrence scoffed. "You expect her to learn the language during the trip?"

"No. I expect you to teach her."

"Impossible."

"I'm smart." Ivy said. "I wouldn'a survived this long if I weren't."

"Well be that as it may, I hardly—"

"I have faith in the two of you," Edwin said, his tone hardening. "She doesn't have to be perfect. There are still those in New Berlin whose first language was Modern. Not all are happy about having had to adopt the Germanic life."

"Yes, but they're of an older generation than Ivy here."

"She was raised in the country by her elderly grandfather."

Lawrence shrugged. "Do go on."

"I have a question." Warragul raised his hand. "You say you want me to forge an invitation. Based on what? I need to know what the legitimate invitations look like."

"Our contact in New Berlin will direct us to the home of an invited guest. Ivy will steal it."

Warragul nodded.

"Incidentally, during our sea voyage, I'll need you to create travel papers for us, in case we are intercepted on our journey from the shore to New Berlin." Edwin turned back to Lawrence. "Once the two of you have gained admittance to the reception, you'll make yourselves known. Ivy will slip away under the pretence of needing to freshen up. She will change into serving clothes and pass into the rear of the building, allowing Warragul and I to enter through the back door."

"How are we supposed to reach New Berlin shores?" Warragul asked. "Before we can even consider any of this we need to evade the patrols."

"I was getting to that. Firstly, we've timed our journey so that we will arrive during the night cycle. Even if winds are unfavourable and we are delayed several days we will still have the cover of darkness. In addition, Major Wood is sending an airship to create a diversion for us. They will keep New Berlin forces busy so we can slip in. When we're close enough, the four of us will take a row-boat to shore. We brought this ship for a reason. As a cutter, she's faster than a paddle steamer, but she's also silent."

Warragul nodded. "So we've all gained entrance to the house."

"After that point it gets a little tricky. We don't know its the exact layout, so we can't predict where the Bishop's lab is located. We do know that it is a secure location, so the plans are unlikely to be kept anywhere else. Lawrence, while Ivy is letting us in, you'll be using all the charm at your disposal to gain information from the Bishop. Let him know you share his interest in the sciences. If you can, find out where the lab is."

"That's a tall order lad, and a little vague. Are you sure you've got this whole plan figured out?" He contracted the space between his eyes.

"It's not perfect," Edwin admitted. There is only so much we can plan for while an ocean separates us from our goal. Improvisation will be important. That is something that you're all good at. Lawrence, you improvise on the stage during live shows all the time. Ivy, you grew up on the streets. Your entire childhood required you to improvise and adapt to circumstances. And Warragul, you left your homeland to make a life for yourself in Tellus - an entirely different culture."

"This whole thing sounds intriguing, but dangerous." Lawrence scowled. "I'm not accustomed to risking my life." He crossed his arms. "How are you to gain entrance to the lab when you find it?"

"Warragul is a professional locksmith. In addition to that, Ivy here is a notorious cat burglar. If necessary, she can gain entrance through the exterior of the building."

"And what about you lad?" Lawrence asked. "What makes you qualified to be in charge of all this? You're not military. Are you an intelligence agent?"

"Not exactly. Major Wood recruited me because of my past. I used to run a heist crew in my younger days. I was a career criminal."

Lawrence leaned forward. "Well I'll be. You don't look the part."

Edwin shrugged. "My life is very different now. I served my time. My debt to society is paid." He cleared his throat. "Now, shall we get back to it?" Edwin turned to the chalk board.

ℚℚ

Edwin watched the crew file out of the mess hall. They'd gone through as many of the fine details as he'd worked out. These people were good at their jobs. It would all work out. So why were his palms sweating?

You shall not steal. The words of Exodus 20:15 mocked him. It had been so much easier back in the day. There'd been no doubt. No regret.

255

Edwin hadn't stolen anything since he'd converted. Since he'd found the path of Christ. All the old feelings were coming back. His blood was pumping. The adrenaline surged through him. This was what he was born to do. He shook his head. It was different this time. He was doing this for a higher purpose. Everything would be fine. He just had to keep his eyes on the real goal. The true plan. Both his missions.

VV

"Vee Entzerkent"

Lawrence frowned at Ivy. "No, you're saying kent at the end. It's an oo sound, like in good. You need to tighten it up a bit. Like this. *Wie entzueckend.*"

"*Wie entzueckend.*"

"Better." Lawrence folded his arms. "But you're going to have to work on that accent. They'll spot you as one of us immediately if you speak like that."

"*Wie entzueckend. Wie entzueckend.*"

Lawrence stood and began to pace. "Why don't we take a break."

"No, I want to get this. *Wie entzueckend.*"

"We've been doing this for three hours, girl. Where do you find the stamina?"

Ivy shrugged. "If I don't get this right I could get locked up or killed. That means I gotta get it right. Welcome to a day in my life."

Lawrence bit his lip and extended his hand to Ivy. "Stand, girl. For my sake if not for yours. We need a break"

Ivy squeezed his hand in a surprisingly masculine fashion and stood.

"I'll call for tea."

"Nah, I'll do that." Ivy opened the door. "Tea!" she yelled, then closed the door. "Done."

Lawrence let out a breathy laugh. "You fascinate me, girl."

"In what way?"

"So rough, and yet so...substantial."

"What ya' mean by that?"

"I'm not sure how to explain it, it's just there is...well...more to you than I expected."

Ivy shrugged. The door opened and a yeoman entered carrying a tray with two cups and a pot of tea."

"*Sollten Sie sich kümmern meine Dame für eine Tasse?*" Lawrence asked with a wry smile.

Ivy furrowed her brow for a moment. "Say that last bit again?"

257

"*Sollten Sie sich kümmern meine Dame für eine Tasse?*" Lawrence said, repeating the entire phrase.

"*Ja bitte. Das wäre entzueckend*" Ivy raised her chin gave a satisfied smile.

"Try to keep your responses short." Lawrence poured a cup and handed it to her. "The less you say, the less chance you have of saying something awkward. You just told me the tea is adorable."

"Well...it is." She raised her cup as if in toast.

Lawrence shook his head and paced the small cabin. What was he thinking? This was a street urchin. Was he actually starting to feel something for her? What was it? Sympathy? Friendship? Attraction? Well, there was no denying she was attractive to look at, but no, maybe if she were ten or so years older. But try as he might, it was becoming difficult to despise the girl.

"You have obviously learned to do whatever is required of you to survive. Stealing, manipulating." He regarded her figure. "Perhaps...other things?"

Ivy frowned. "There are some lines I don't cross." She took a sip. "It's a tough world out there for one like me. Gotta be tough yourself to survive."

"Yes, but, you're an adult now. You could have found some poor peasant to marry. You'd have a much easier go of it then. You could be settled into a normal life. Why do you continue to live like a street child?"

Ivy put down her cup. "What, and become the property of a man. That don't sound like much of an improvement."

"Well..."

"I'm me own boss. I do what I want and go where I please."

"Not at the moment. Right now, you're going where Edwin wants, and you're doing as I instruct."

"I'm here by choice. I'm earning a lot of money doing this job, when it's done I'll be on my way."

"Yes, but—"

"Can we get back to work please?" Ivy stormed across the room and dropped back into her seat. "*Wie entzueckend.*"

"Very well." Lawrence slumped his shoulders and carried his cup back to his seat.

OV

"Zero point five kilometres to target Captain," The young navigator said, on the bridge of the airship *Salisbury*.

Oscar Whitlock tugged his beard and glanced over his right shoulder. "Steady as she goes Ensign." He stood. "Ready the bomb."

"Aye Captain," the bombardier said.

"Visual contact with enemy," the first officer said.

"Blimp or Jet?"

"It's … it's a biplane Captain."

"Hang it all, that's unexpected. Man the guns."

The tell-tale rattle sounded as the water-cooled guns spat bullets toward the enemy.

"We have to abort Captain," the first officer gripped the back of Oscar's chair. "They'll shoot us down before we complete the task."

"We don't have to destroy the shipyards, Frank, just keep the enemy occupied long enough for Wood's team to reach the shore. We'll just drop one bomb, then flee."

A high-pitched whine swept from left to right. The biplane.

"Stand by to drop," Oscar said to the bombardier.

"In position now," the navigator said.

"Release."

The bombardier pulled the lever. "Bomb away."

Oscar peered into the bombsight. One of the large sheds erupted as bright yellow flames spread across it.

"Come about," Oscar said. "Time to withdraw."

The biplane buzzed past again, its guns rattling.

"We're taking fire," Frank said.

Bullet holes appeared in the bulkhead. About fifteen, all in a row. An ensign grabbed his arm and screamed. The boy pulled his hand away. Blood.

"Power up the new fans," Oscar yelled.

◊◊

Edwin held the sides of the row-boat and took a deep breath. The miniscule vessel rocked as Lawrence climbed in and settled in a seat behind him. Ivy came next, holding a large knapsack. The boat hardly moved. The cat burglar was light on her feet. Finally, Warragul dropped into the front seat, his motion rocking the boat moderately.

261

"You all right, old chap?" Lawrence asked.

"I'll be fine." Edwin gripped the oars, his knuckles almost bursting through the skin. "And for the record, I'm younger than you."

"Just an expression lad."

"And one that makes me feel like a child. My name is Edwin."

"Touchy."

Edwin craned his neck back. The captain looked down from the gunwale of the cutter, like a benevolent god from above.

"I don't know if we'll be able to stay here," the captain said. "There be a lot of lights down the coast, in New Hamburg. We be a sitting duck just anchored here."

"Wait, if you leave, how do we get home?" Lawrence started to stand. The rowboat almost capsized.

"Sit down, you fool." Edwin glared at Lawrence.

"Won't nobody be here to take you home if we get sunk," the captain said.

"I trust you'll do what's right," Edwin said. "Besides, I think Captain Whitlock is keeping the Berliners occupied."

"Let's be hoping so." The captain stepped away from the gunwale.

Edwin pulled back on the oars and the boat began forward motion. The sooner they reached shore and got out of this accursed vessel the better.

❦

The engines roared from behind the cabin. The biplane passed by, it's engine a decidedly higher pitch than the *Salisbury*'s. A staccato rattle sounded from the machine guns as they fired at the enemy.

"A squadron of biplanes approaching from starboard," Frank said. "I count six. They're gaining on us, but gradually."

"Can we get any more speed out of the engines?" Oscar asked.

"Our new engines are at their maximum, Sir. We're at 190 kph. No Tellus airship has gone this fast before."

"Open fire the moment they're in range." Oscar rose from his seat and walked to the starboard side. Large windows gave a broad view of the outside. The second and third biplane bore down on them like angry wasps.

They drew closer. And closer.

The gunner opened fire. The acrid scent of gunpowder filled the air.

Seconds later, the biplanes returned fire.

Oscar's heart raced. These planes were only a little faster than the *Salisbury*, but they were much more manoeuvrable. The only hope was to outgun them. The *Salisbury* had three port guns, three starboard guns, and one aft.

"One big target, compared to seven small nimble ones," Frank said.

The deck shook.

"They just took out one of our cells." Frank shouted over the rattling of the guns.

"Concentrate your fire on a single target at a time," Oscar ordered the gunners. "Our attack is too haphazard."

A biplane roared past. A port gunner opened fire. A direct hit to the fuel tank. The biplane erupted into flames.

Oscar clapped his hands together. They'd lost one of seven cells, but they'd taken out one of seven planes. This would be a close fight.

The deck shook.

The ship dropped suddenly, leaving Oscar's stomach behind.

"Another cell gone. We've lost altitude."

"Take those planes out," Oscar yelled. "They can keep fighting with only one plane.

We can't stay in the air if we lose many more cells in the envelope."

VV

Edwin's back strained as he pulled the oars. It was no small challenge to propel the boat quickly through the water while making minimal noise. A lone lookout swept the bay with a directed lantern. It was not enough to cover such a large area. *Well done Whitlock.* Through careful course corrections, Edwin had been able to avoid detection.

He glanced up at the cloudy sky. The *Salisbury* was over the water now. Four or five biplanes buzzed about it, the whine of their engine carrying across the still night. A flash of orange flame lit up the envelope atop the *Salisbury*'s cabin. The giant airship was beginning to droop. Would they make it? The odds weren't looking good. A biplane exploded in a brilliant ball of flame.

Nothing Edwin could do. They were buying him the opportunity he needed to complete his missions - both of them. The *Salisbury* was in God's hands now.

Not a word had been uttered since leaving the cutter. Even Lawrence had kept quiet. They all knew what was at stake.

Just past a rocky outcropping was an area of dense vegetation. That would be a good place to hide the boat until they needed it again.

They were ten kilometres south of New Hamburg. Seventy kilometres from New Berlin. Even if they pushed themselves, they'd be lucky to walk that in a day, but, with Warragul's forged travel papers, they should be able to catch the train.

With each pull of the oars the boat surged forward. Edwin's back strained but he pushed on. Before too long they reached the shore.

"I'm glad we don't have to worry about tides," Edwin said.

"Tides?" Lawrence asked.

"Back on old Earth, the water level would rise and fall twice daily. It was something to do with the gravitational pull of their moon." Edwin was met with silence from the others. "Am I the only person who reads?" More silence. "The nature of our world, when compared to the birthplace of our people, has always fascinated me.

"You're an odd one," Lawrence said.

Edwin climbed out of the boat and motioned for his companions to disembark. First Warragul, then Ivy. Finally Lawrence. Once they were all standing ashore Edwin climbed out. The icy water stung his ankles.

He dragged the boat up onto the grass. Warragul stepped forward and helped him push it into the bushes. The leaves rustled as the wooden vessel vanished into the foliage. That should remain hidden.

"*Wer geht dahin?*" A voice called out from the other side of the bushes. *Who goes there?*

Edwin's eyes widened. He looked to Lawrence who rolled his eyes and stepped out into the open.

"Pardon me, just out for an evening constitutional," Lawrence said in Paleo-German.

"Nobody is permitted at the shoreline after dark. Are you not aware that we're at war?"

"Do you *really* think the Tethus/Tellus alliance are going to jump out of the shadows?"

"An attack is underway at this very moment. Return to your home."

"Very well."

Lawrence's footsteps began, and started fading away.

"Wait!" The guard shouted.

"What were you doing behind those bushes?"

"I told you," Lawrence said. "I was just out walking."

"Wait there."

The guard's footsteps brought him closer. Every muscle in Edwin's body tensed. They would be discovered. He glanced at Warragul and Ivy. Warragul was difficult to read, as always. Ivy's eyes held an unexpected fire. There was no fear, just a determination. What was she planning?"

Ivy reached into her jacket and held something close. She turned and backed further into the bush.

Seconds later, a tall man wearing a spiked helmet peered in. He drew a flintlock pistol.

"Come out of there, all of you."

Edwin considered his options. If they ran, the guard would shout for backup. The alarm would be sounded. If they cooperated, they'd buy themselves a few more seconds to come up with a plan.

Edwin motioned for Warragul to follow him out of the bushes. Ivy was already out of sight.

Edwin raised his hands.

"What were you doing in there?"

Leaves rustled a few meters down toward the water. The guard glanced that direction. Edwin followed his gaze. Nothing.

The guard turned back to Edwin.

"We were chasing an animal." Edwin winced at the words. The first thing that came to his mind.

"An animal?"

Without a sound, Ivy crept up behind the guard. Wasting no time, she leapt forward, reached out, and swiped a knife across the guard's throat. A gasp sounded. Edwin looked away. The guard crumpled to the ground. Clothes rustled.

Edwin covered his mouth and glanced down. The guard continued to thrash.

"What have you done?"

"Saved our lives," Ivy said. "We were discovered. He didn't buy Lawrence's act. This was the only option."

"But … you killed him."

"This *is* an operation for the military 'aint it? We are at war with these people. I thought you were some big-name criminal."

Edwin let out a long breath. "I was a thief. A long time ago. But in all my heists, I never found it necessary to take a life."

"Oh, grow up Mister."

"Ethical considerations aside," Lawrence said, emerging from the other side of the bushes," we now have a problem. We need to dispose of this body effectively and rapidly."

"And even then, the alarm will be raised when he doesn't check in with his superiors." Warragul said. "The New Berliners will know somebody came ashore."

"That spells danger for us, but it also puts the ship at greater risk of discovery. One of those ironclads in New Hamburg could easily take her out."

Edwin closed his eyes for a moment. This wasn't how it was supposed to go. "All right. There'll be time for regrets later. Lawrence is right. We have to deal with this body quickly and then get away from the shore."

OV

Edwin drew his jacket around himself against the cool air. Hydrogen gas lanterns lit the cobbled street as they made their way through the outskirts of New Berlin.

The train ride to New Berlin had been uneventful. It had given Edwin a good opportunity to steel his thoughts, and Ivy a chance to listen in on some native German conversation. All up, the journey from shore to here had taken almost two hours.

Most citizens would be well and truly asleep at the moment. It had always amused Edwin that society operated on a traditional 24-hour daily cycle here on Venus. It was completely arbitrary with a 672-hour day. Then again, the body needed rest some time, so the natural cycle of old Earth was as good as anything else.

"We need to find diggings for the night," Edwin said in Paleo-German.

"Shouldn't we get on with our mission?" Warragul asked.

"We're tired after our journey," Edwin said. "The city guards will be extra-vigilant with the attack on New Hamburg, even here. We'll look suspicious moving about while everybody else is home asleep. No, a few hours sleep will do us good."

271

"So, you want us to sleep where?" Lawrence said in Modern, his voice incredulous. "On the street?"

"I'll admit it's not glamorous, but it will do, and please speak German."

"Oh you boys," Ivy switched languages. "You're such amateurs. I'll find us a decent place. This after all, is my life."

"I can't believe my life is in the hands of a street urchin." Lawrence said.

"A well-educated urchin."

"I think you meant to say *ausgebildete* not *unterrichtete*," Lawrence whispered.

"Let's try up here," Ivy pointed, ignoring him.

"There should be a shelter somewhere," Lawrence said.

Ivy shook her head. "First place the coppas will look. Especially when they find that missing guard. We'll blend in better up 'ere."

Edwin glared at Ivy. Her face dropped.

"Sorry." She switched back to German.

They walked on for another block. Then Ivy stopped at a shop with a large sign. Closed Down. She strode into an alley at the back of the building. "This'll do just fine." She hunkered down behind a metal rubbish bin.

Lawrence grimaced.

"You wouldn't last a day in New Whitechapel." She turned to Edwin and Warragul. "How about you two then?"

"I'll manage." Edwin dropped to the ground and leaned his back against the wall.

The alley was only about a meter and a half wide. Tall bridge walls were separated by a floor of large stone blocks. There was an occasional wooden door, or boarded up window. Apart from the rubbish bins, it was empty.

"Me too," Warragul said. "I've slept in the bush many a night. Sleeping outside don't bother me."

"So why's this orbital platform so important then?" Ivy asked. "We're risking a lot to steal these plans."

"It's not just about stealing them," Edwin said. "Having the information for ourselves is just a bonus. The real goal is to deprive New Berlin of the information."

"I still don't understand how panels in the sky can provide light and heat. Some say that fairies live up there. That the light fairies all died out, which is why they don't make the light during the fortnight of darkness, just heat to keep us warm."

273

"Don't pay attention to such stories, lass," Lawrence said.

"I never said I believed them," Ivy protested.

"The panels are just a piece of technology," Edwin said. "If the Berliners were able to control the panels, they could decide who gets light for their crops; they could decide who freezes in the cold. They'd have even more power over the planet than they do now."

"They'd have to get up there first," Ivy said, "and I don't see that happening."

"Actually, intelligence suggests that they've almost finished rebuilding a V2 rocket. They're well on their way to putting a man in space. That means they'll have direct access to the platforms. This is more urgent than most people realise."

Edwin pulled his jacket tighter against the cold.

"I hadn't realised it was this serious." Lawrence grunted, having finally relented to laying on the hard ground.

"There's even more to it," Edwin said. "Venus isn't the only planet in the solar system. There's Old Earth, Mars, some writings even suggest there could still be people living under the surface of Mercury. I don't think ours was

274

the only world to suffer a great setback after the United Nations wars. Whichever planet gets back on its feet first will control the Solar System. Do we want New Berlin to have that kind of power?"

"Personally, I couldn't care less about other worlds," Lawrence said. "Tellus is all that matters."

Ivy shrugged. "It don't seem so bad 'ere. Are the Berliners really as bad as you say? Didn't they bring technology to Tellus?"

"Some, yes. And they also brought the Christian teachings of the Lutheran Church, for which I personally am grateful, but they also stifle our trade. A dictatorship is never a good thing."

"I can tell you their advances were not welcome on Kruchina," Warragul said. "My mob have a history of Europeans coming in with their fancy technology and occupying our home. We weren't gonna stand for it again. We came to Venus to get away from all that."

"And yet you live in Tellus," Edwin said.

Warragul shrugged. "Livin' in the bush wasn't for me. My people deserve to be left alone to live the way they choose, but doesn't mean I have to stay with 'em."

Lawrence grunted. "I believe we came here to get some rest. Perhaps we should do so."

"He's right." Edwin said. "Goodnight all."

VV

Ivy sprung awake. Somebody was close. She reached for the dagger hidden in her clothing and leapt to her feet.

A man with a trimmed beard and bowler hat startled in the dim lantern light. He raised his arms in surrender.

"Relax. I'm here to help."

"We don't need your help," Ivy clenched her fists and stepped toward him.

"My name is Herbert," he said. "I'm an agent with his Majesty's government."

"He's our contact." Edwin sat up. "We were supposed to meet you in Bismarck Park."

"I came looking for you early. You need to be more careful. The police are on the lookout for you. I've been searching alleys for over an hour. It's not safe to stay out here."

"Then perhaps we should get on with our mission," Edwin said.

Ivy unclenched her fists, took a deep breath and stepped back.

"My thoughts exactly," Herbert said. "I have the address for the house where you will steal the invitation."

Herbert handed a piece of paper to Edwin. "Memorise it then destroy it. *Freiherr* Albrecht's study is on the first floor, by the tree. Let your forger have a look at it, then return it. If the *Freiherr* finds it missing there will be too much suspicion."

"Will that work for you?" Edwin handed the note to Warragul.

"If I have a few minutes with it, I can memorise what I need to know." He glanced at the note for two seconds and handed it back.

"Just a few minutes?" Lawrence raised an eyebrow.

"I have an eidetic memory."

Herbert nodded. "The other address on the paper is a safe-house. Once you've seen the invitation, meet me there. I'll have supplies so you can create your own."

"Thank-you for your help." Edwin shook Herbert's hand.

"Until later." He tipped his hat to Ivy and left.

Ivy opened up her knapsack and removed tight black pants and shirt. No way she could climb up into a first story window in a dress. She undid several clasps and let her dress fall to the ground. Even in just her drawers and a linen chemise she was completely covered. She'd never been one for corsets and petticoats. Not with her lifestyle.

Lawrence's face turned red. His mouth dropped as he tried not to look at her.

"Have you no decency urchin?"

"None at all." She winked at him and pulled on the pants.

Lawrence folded his arms and turned away.

"Are you more offended by my unmentionables, or the fact that I'm putting on trousers?" She laughed.

"The house is just a few blocks away," Edwin said. "We can be there in a few minutes. Judging by the sound of commotion it must be morning. We can move about without drawing so much attention."

Ivy pulled the shirt over her chemise and smoothed her clothes.

"You really should put the dress back on over that until we reach our destination,"

Edwin said. "You'll look suspicious walking the street dressed like a cat burglar."

Ivy grabbed the dress and popped it over her head.

"And you should walk a little behind us. Not right for a woman to be walking with three men."

"Anything else?" Ivy crossed her arms.

Three blank faces looked back at her.

"Okay, then let's go."

The men left the alley. Ivy counted off thirty seconds and then followed.

Hansoms rolled down the street, with the occasional steam car. Men chatted over cigars by the glowing street lamps. Ladies in puffy dresses strolled on pathways. Ivy had never seen the point of the fancy clothes most women wore. It was surprising how much they stood out in the dark with those bright colours. She'd be almost invisible without this dress over her black clothing.

Edwin, Lawrence and Warragul stopped at an intersection of two streets, outside a row of five or six city houses right next to each other. They all had identical triangular roofs, three stories each, with a single attic window at the peak.

279

"All right." Edwin pointed to the house closest to the corner. "This is the address."

Ivy stepped up to join them. "This is where I save the day then," she said, approaching the side wall. She took the dress off again and tossed it to Lawrence. He grimaced, like it was soiled with dog droppings.

Ivy laughed as she removed her shoes and tested her toes in the gaps between stone bricks. Easy. She gripped her fingers into gaps above and began her ascent. It took only a few minutes to reach the window. She slid her knife into the soft wood of the windowsill. It made a good makeshift handhold. She used her free hand to pry at the window. It was locked.

Ivy reached into her back pocket and removed a small file. Using it, she was able to pry the window latch up. The window slid upward with a slight scrape. Ivy ducked down, letting her knife hold most of her weight, her toes clenched into the gaps in the wall. Anybody who may have heard the window would likely have glanced and seen nothing, then turned away. She raised herself back up and peered in. The study was empty. Perfect.

Ivy climbed in the window. There was a small kerosene lantern on the *Freiherr's* desk. She turned the knob and lit it with a nearby match. Dim illumination flowed across the desk. Papers lined most of the surface in piles. Ivy wasted no time going through them.

While she'd spent countless hours learning spoken German from Lawrence, there had been little training to read it. Instead, she'd been taught several keywords to search for: *eingeladen*, *Bischof*, and *Eckstein*.

She flipped through letters and invoices. Nothing. She moved to another pile. There it was. The stiff card was decorated with swirls. There in fancy cursive writing were all three keywords. She grabbed the invitation and headed back to the window.

Edwin, Warragul and Lawrence had separated. Good thinking. Warragul spotted her and ambled toward the house.

Ivy removed a small contraption from her pocket. A reel of fishing line and a paperclip. She attached the invitation to the clip and dropped it out the window, keeping a firm hold on the line so she could pull it back momentarily.

Warragul grabbed the card and began to study it. As soon as he gave her the signal, she'd pull it back up.

"Where's that invitation my dear?" A gruff male voice called out in German. The voice came from a nearby room. Ivy's heart seized. She hung the reel on her knife, pulled the window down and dove behind a couch.

The door opened. Ivy held her breath. She clenched her hands into tight fists. They started to sweat. Footsteps on the carpet took the man - Albrecht himself most likely - to the desk. The sound of flipping papers sounded. What would he do when he couldn't find it?

"*Was in Himmel?*" The man sighed loudly. Heavy footsteps stormed from the room. There wasn't much time. Hopefully the *Freiherr* would look elsewhere before returning. Warragul had better have finished looking at that invitation.

Ivy dove for the window, pulled it open and grabbed the reel. The crew looked relieved to see her. She wound the reel up quickly and retrieved the invitation. She ran back and placed it at the bottom of one of the piles. No doubt the *Freiherr* would find it and wonder why he'd not noticed it before.

Ivy slipped out the window, pulled it closed, and grabbed her knife.

It was tempting to let herself fall straight down to the ground, but a release from this distance would injure her. Instead, she patiently climbed, until she was only a meter up, and then dropped.

"Well done," Edwin whispered. "Now let's get out of here."

V

The safe house was a small wooden cottage on the outskirts of the city. Unlike Albrecht's house, it was separated from its neighbours by several meters of grass on all four sides. The inside was cosy. Nicer than a lot of places Ivy had stayed. Herbert was waiting for them by a crackling fire with mugs of hot coffee.

"No tea?" Lawrence asked.

"In New Berlin, coffee is king." Herbert handed him a mug.

Ivy dropped into a comfy couch and put her feet up on the coffee table.

"Did you get a good look at the invitation?" Herbert asked.

"Yes." Warragul tapped his head with his forefinger. "It's all up here."

"All your materials are on the desk. Will you be able to duplicate it effectively?"

Warragul strode over and took a seat. He looked through the materials.

"This card is too stiff."

"I'll see if I have anything lighter," Herbert said.

"Well." Lawrence clapped his hands. "While he's doing his work we need to get you something suitable to wear to the party."

Ivy raised an eyebrow. "I brought a dress with me."

Lawrence chuckled. "Yes, you brought a dress. You didn't bring a gown. Come along, we'll see what the stores have." He turned for the door then stopped and looked over his shoulder. "And I trust that this time you'll make use of the proper changing facilities?"

Ivy stood and gave a mock curtsy. "I wouldn't want to make you blush, gov'nah."

VV

Ivy crossed the road, Lawrence dragging her by the arm.

"Come along. Anybody would think you didn't want to go. Aren't women supposed to enjoy shopping for new dresses?"

"I wouldn't know," Ivy said. "I've never done it."

Lawrence stopped on the pathway and turned to face her.

"Never?"

Ivy shrugged. "What would I need with some fancy dress?"

Before leaving the safe house, Ivy had changed from her house-scaling outfit back to her simple dress. It was comfortable. It felt like home.

"We'll make a lady out of you if it kills us. Come on."

They stopped outside a small boutique named "*Kultivierte Kleidung*."

"Well in you go." Lawrence motioned toward the door.

"Aren't you coming in with me?"

"I'm not sure a gentleman entering a women's clothing store is entirely seemly."

"Why not?"

"Well..." He scratched his chin. "They might sell... unmentionables."

Ivy rolled her eyes.

"Which you might do well to acquire," he added.

"But how will I know what to get? What if I can't communicate well enough?"

"Oh for the love of Venus. Just pick something that looks elegant. The shop assistant will help you. That's her job."

Ivy worked up a smile and entered the store. The interior was well-lit by gas lights hanging from the ceiling. Two other ladies browsed the lines.

Ivy staggered over to a rack and stared at the dresses.

How to choose? She glanced over her shoulder. Outside, Lawrence mimed to her. He was reaching out and touching something that existed only in his imagination. He wanted her to touch the dresses.

Ivy obeyed. After a moment of awkwardness, she released the dress and grabbed another. She stared at it a moment.

"Can I help you with something?" Ivy looked up. A girl, not much older than herself flashed a wide smile. "Please call me Gretchen."

"Ah, I'm looking for something to wear to a party tonight."

"What kind of party?"

"A reception. At a bishop's house."

Gretchen raised one eyebrow. "Well you must be up in the world if you've been invited to the bishop's reception." She leafed through the rack and removed two gowns.

"These look your size. Go try them on."

Ivy's eyes went wide. Her heart beat against the inside of her chest. "I'm...that is to say...I'm not sure how."

Gretchen's eyes went a little wider. "Oh. Well, no matter. I'm here to assist you. You're not expected to put on a gown like this all by yourself."

She led Ivy to a change room. Ivy immediately pulled her dress over her head. Gretchen looked away. Hadn't she come in here to help?

"Oh my, you're not wearing a corset. You'll be needing one. I'll get one for you."

She disappeared. Ivy took a moment to breathe. What must the girl think of her? No doubt she'd picked up on her poor command of German.

Gretchen returned and fitted the corset around her torso. This wasn't going to be pleasant. Gretchen then tried to kill Ivy, pulling the thing so tight she couldn't breathe.

"New to the city, are you?"

Ivy nodded.

"Well that's all right. We often have newcomers from further down the Ulfron. Takes a while to get used to all the rank and formality of New Berlin." She pulled again. *Ouch.* "Have you had a pleasant day so far?"

287

How was Ivy supposed to speak, let alone breathe? She gasped in and answered. "Yes."

"It's been slow in here today. Business is always slower during the night cycle. People prefer to do their shopping in the light." She yanked another tie and the corset tightened further. She wouldn't be able to move in this. "My aunt runs this shop. She dislikes the dark fortnight. All the extra cost of running the lamps. The dark depresses her."

"I can understand that," Ivy said.

"Did you hear about all the commotion last night?"

"Uh, no."

"Airship attack from the Tellus, down in New Hamburg. That's not so unusual, but apparently, they found a ship hiding off the shore. They think it brought spies to our city, but the Ironclads destroyed it."

Ivy swallowed. "That can't be good."

"*Nein.*"

Ivy began to sweat. If the enemy took out the ship, they'd have no way to get home. They'd be trapped."

"All citizens have been told to be on the lookout for spies, and to report anything suspicious."

"Aren't we always to be on the lookout for spies?"

"Perhaps." Gretchen lowered her voice. "You know, I've heard of some people helping the spies."

"Why would they do that?" Ivy asked.

"Because many in this city don't like this war any more than our enemies do."

"Hmm, is that so?"

Gretchen tipped her head wordlessly.

War. It was never simple. Under different circumstances, Ivy could be close friends with this girl.

With the corset now fitted, Gretchen helped her into the gown. Once it was on, she regarded herself in the mirror. The transformation was incredible. She looked like, well, one of those fancy women who went to balls. It wasn't her, it really wasn't, but she couldn't deny that she looked pretty. Prettier than she'd ever looked.

"It suits you," Gretchen said. "Shall I help you out of it?"

"Oh no," Ivy said. "If it's all the same I'd like to wear it home. Save me having to change back into it later."

Gretchen frowned. "Well, if you're sure."

Ivy was positive. With no other women back at the safe house she'd have no one to help her into it.

Gretchen smiled. "You'll stun everybody at the reception."

Ivy returned the smile and turned to leave. Oh! Payment. She chuckled to herself. Paying for something was a bit of a novelty. She counted out several gold certificates and handed them over.

"Is this right?"

Gretchen nodded.

"Nice doing business with you." Ivy strode toward the door.

VV

Edwin turned as the door opened. Ivy entered, in a glorious gown, followed by Lawrence.

"Wow."

"Thanks." Ivy's face brightened just a tad.

"Yes." Lawrence closed the door. "Ivy will make a stunning lady this evening. Assuming of course that we can get in. How goes the forgery?"

"See for yourself." Edwin motioned toward the desk where Warragul sat at work.

Ivy gasped. "That's incredible."

"It's serviceable," Warragul said. "I'm still a little concerned about the thickness of the card, and this colour isn't quite accurate." He pointed to a blue swirl.

"The untrained eye will never notice the difference, lad," Lawrence said.

"Yes, but how trained will be the eyes of the doormen?"

Lawrence nodded and dropped into an armchair next to a coffee table with glasses of water. "That is a good question." He turned to Edwin. "Ivy heard some disturbing news while we were out."

"Oh?"

"Apparently, the ship has been destroyed."

Edwin bit his lip. All those people. The captain. His crew. Lost.

"That means we're stranded, with no way to get home," Warragul said.

Edwin turned to Herbert. "Any Ideas?"

"Me?" Herbert pointed a finger into his chest.

291

"You're an agent of His Majesty's government. You must have a way of moving people about."

"I'm permanently stationed here in New Berlin. We had a method for getting you here and back. It was the ship."

"So you can't organise an alternative?"

Herbert ran his hand through his hair. "Possibly. I'll have to give it some thought. What you ask is not easy."

"So what do we do?" Lawrence asked. "Not much point in stealing the plans if we can't get them back to Tellus."

Edwin scratched his chin. "Even if we can't possess the information, destroying it is still a valuable goal. Maybe we'll find a way home, and maybe we won't. That is not ours to worry about. We still have a duty to perform. We'll go in tonight and pull the heist. After that, it's up to Herbert."

"Thank you for that. Much pressure."

"We go ahead as planned."

The others stared back at him, looking for assurance. If only he had some to give.

"For King and Country," Lawrence said, and raised a glass of water.

"No." Edwin picked up a glass of his own. "For King and planet."

"For King and planet," they all said in unison.

◊◊

Edwin strolled through the park that backed on to Bishop Eckstein's property. Warragul followed close behind.

Lawrence and Ivy would be arriving soon by coach.

"Over there." Edwin pointed. There was a vantage near a gnarled oak tree where they could see the arrivals at the front of the house.

"Now we wait?" Warragul asked.

Edwin nodded. He opened the newspaper he'd purchased on the way here. There was just enough light, spilling from the well-lit entrance of the house, to make out the words. He remembered reading about how Old Earth's moon provided some illumination at night. Such a thing would be very useful here on Venus.

An article on the third page expatiated upon Bishop Eckstein's reception tonight. It spoke of his work within the church, and as an archivist, his gifts as an amateur inventor in accordance with the technological plan, and the rare pearl earrings he had inherited from his late mother. Having never married himself, those earrings would likely fall into the hands of the church upon his death. Eckstein was quoted as saying their financial value was great, but their importance to him was sentimental as they reminded him of his mother.

Edwin rubbed his eyes. Maybe it wasn't such a good idea to read in the dark. He folded the paper, bowed his head and began to pray for the success of the mission.

"Edwin?" Warragul said.

"Yes?"

"You praying?"

Edwin nodded.

"For our success?"

"That's right."

Warragul was silent for a minute.

"You're a Lutheran, right?"

Edwin turned to face his companion. "Yes I am.

"And it was New Berlin who introduced Lutheran Christianity to Tellus."

"What are you getting at Warragul?"

"It's just, you're here praying to their god for the success of our military operations against them.

294

"Don't you think that in this city there are others, maybe Eckstein himself, who are praying to that same god for New Berlin's victory against our rebellion?"

Edwin nodded. "I believe that to be accurate."

"Don't you see that as a problem? I mean, what's a god to do?"

"My friend, I hear what you're saying. In fact, I'm more aware of this issue than you can know."

VV

Lawrence leaned back into the cushy seat. He'd been on many a hansom ride back in Tellus, but to ride in a luxurious fully enclosed carriage, this was wonderful. It definitely helped him find his character. The monocle that Herbert had given him didn't hurt either.

"Are you looking forward to the reception my dear?" He said to Ivy.

"Give it a rest Lawrence." She glared at him like he had no head. "It's just the two of us in 'ere."

"I'm getting into Character. You should try it. Imagine yourself a young lady, filled with pride that she gets to accompany a rich aristocrat like myself."

"You 'aint that high up the scale mister. You gotta be low enough that people won't think twice about not having heard of you."

Lawrence shrugged. "It's not like the Kaiser himself will be here. Now, do try to make an effort will you."

"Very well, *my lord*." She sneered the last part. Lawrence shook his head. How could he be expected to work like this?

They rounded a corner. The Bishop's mansion was brightly lit. There had to be near a hundred lanterns hanging from the stonework.

The carriage came to a stop. A footman approached and opened the door. Lawrence motioned for Ivy to exit first. She took the footman's hand. Immediately, her rough exterior melted away. Her bearing became stiff and regal, yet shy and vulnerable. By the mines of Mercury - the urchin could act after all.

Lawrence disembarked and took Ivy's hand. Together they walked up the pathway to the house. A butler stood by the door, awaiting invitations.

Lawrence clutched the cardboard in his left hand. *No don't sweat all over it.* This was where they would see if Warragul's efforts were worth anything.

Lawrence had to show more confidence. He was an invited guest who was eager to attend. *Here goes...*

They stopped before the butler, who eyed Ivy. Before the man could ask, Lawrence handed his invitation over. His breath caught. His pulse boomed in his ears.

The butler glanced at the invitation, and returned his gaze to Ivy, then made eye contact with Lawrence.

"Welcome *Freiherr* Müller."

The butler walked in ahead of them and announced boldly. "*Freiherr* Müller and Fräulein Fischer."

Lawrence nodded to the butler and led Ivy inside.

It worked!

QV

Lawrence soaked in the atmosphere. The ballroom was smaller than he expected, but then this was the home of a bishop, not a Lord.

Imperial moustaches abounded. Ladies sported elaborate dresses, mostly in blue, pink or cyan. A quick assessment suggested that, in

Lawrence's subjective opinion, Ivy was the most attractive of the female companions in the room. Probably also the youngest. That would be helpful. Gentlemen would want to engage with him, if for no other reason than to catch a glimpse of his lady. It was hard to believe that under it all, she was still just an urchin. Such a transformation.

A small ensemble of strings were set up in one corner of the room. They played a quiet waltz, though nobody danced at present. There wasn't really room for it.

"I don't believe I know you Sir." A gruff voice came just from the left.

Lawrence turned. A man with military bearing and a uniform jacket. He sported a handlebar moustache. The only thing missing was the spiked helmet.

Lawrence extended his hand. "Freiherr Müller."

"Generalmajor Albert Garver." The general shook Lawrence's hand tightly.

"Are you a close acquaintance of the bishop, *Freiherr*?"

"No. In fact I am yet to meet him. My invitation was arranged for me by an adviser to the Kaiser. I have recently moved to New

Berlin from the country. It was felt that I should begin to mingle with the urban nobility."

"Quite wise."

"Might I introduce my companion, the lovely Fräulein Fischer?" Lawrence motioned to ivy.

The general's eyes brightened. He took her gloved hand.

"Indeed a pleasure, Fräulein."

Ivy smiled at him, and then looked at the floor without a word. She had this shy girl character down pat.

"Perhaps I could regale you with a story of my exploits in the country," Lawrence said.

"By all means."

Lawrence smiled. Yes, this was the role of a lifetime.

VV

Ivy did her best impression of enraptured attention as Lawrence droned on and on about his make-believe sons and their adventures. She giggled at his jokes.

Ugh. Kill me now.

She swept her eyes around the room. An antique vase stood on a stand near the servant's door. A priceless tapestry hung behind her. There was so much valuable loot in here. So much more than was necessary for a basic existence. Of course, most of it would be very difficult to offload.

Ivy shook herself. She wasn't here to case out the place. She had a job to do.

"And what was your part in all of this *Fräulein*?" A ridiculous woman wearing half a bowl of fruit on her head asked.

"Uh, I didn't yet know the *Freiherr* at that stage," she said, testing her German. Nobody appeared alarmed by her lack of command of the language. Good.

"Yes, I didn't make the acquaintance of this young lady until well after the passing of my late wife Adelina. May God give her rest. The interesting thing about Adelina was..."

Ivy tuned out. She'd played the part long enough. It was time for her to make her way to the back of the house.

"If you would excuse me *Freiherr*," she said quietly, while avoiding eye contact.

"Certainly my dear."

Ivy took her leave, ambling across the room toward the back door.

"Oh, Fräulein Fischer." A voice called. It took Ivy a second to remember that was her.

She turned. It was the fruit woman. Anyone but her.

"I would like to introduce you to Freiin Burgstaller."

"But—"

"This way." The fruit woman took her by the arm and almost dragged her to another corner of the room. There she was presented to a blond woman several years her senior.

"Fräulein Fischer, please meet *Freiin* Burgstaller."

"A pleasure," the blond said.

Ivy clenched her fists and released them. There wasn't time for this. Edwin and Warragul would be wondering where she'd gotten to.

"Fräulein Fischer is the companion of Freiherr Müller."

"Really," Burgstaller said. "Please tell me about that."

What excuse could she make to get out of here? *I need to pee.* She almost said the words. It would be a good excuse but a proper lady would never speak of such things. Not around here.

"Ah, well," Now this was going to test her command of German. Ivy strained her

301

memory for the story Lawrence had concocted of how they met. "You see I was..."

A waiter wandered past carrying a tray of drinks. "Oh my throat is dreadfully dry. If I am going to tell this story I might need a drink."

"Waiter," Fruit woman called.

The waiter approached.

"A drink for Fräulein Fischer, please."

The waiter nodded and held out the tray. Ivy gently grasped the glass and took a sip. This stuff was strong. She couldn't afford to drink much of it if she wanted to keep her wits about her."

"You see I was—"

She twisted her wrist as she spoke, and tipped the contents of the glass all down the bodice of her gown. Did that look suitably accidental?

Burgstaller gaped. Fruit woman gasped.

"Oh, dear me, I am such a fool," Ivy said. She handed her empty glass to Fruit woman. "Would you please excuse me; I need to make myself presentable."

Both women nodded. Ivy turned and headed for the door. It was all she could do to keep from running.

Ivy let out a long sigh of relief after passing through the double doors. To her left was the servant's area. To the right, the powder room, and then stairs that rose to the rest of the house.

The atmosphere in that ballroom had been stifling. So many people. No, not people. Not real people. They were all so fake. Just as fake as her Fräulein Fischer.

She strode right and found the powder room. It was bigger than expected. A white basin stood next to the wall. Above it - taps. This house had running water. The old bishop's parents *must* have been rich.

There was a window on the far wall. Ivy unlatched it and pulled. The window was stiff, but a second heave managed to lift it. She peered out. Warragul approached, glancing over his shoulder every few steps. He passed a small parcel through the window to her. A servant's uniform. Shame the window was too small for a person to climb through.

Ivy closed the window and began to unfasten her dress and let it drop to the floor. The corset was much harder to get off all by herself. She sighed and closed her eyes when it finally came off. What a joy to be rid of that thing.

She slipped into the uniform dress and fastened it.

She unpinned her hair, letting it fall into a more natural style — the type a servant might wear.

Now, where to hide the gown? She opened the window again, and pushed the gown out through. There was a rustle of leaves as it landed in the bushes. It probably wouldn't be found until dawn, which was several days away.

Ivy closed her eyes and took a moment to adopt her new persona. Then she left the powder room and strode down the hall toward the servant's area.

VV

The quiet hallway was suddenly active. Two waiters strode past carrying platters of finger food.

"What are you doing wandering the hallways?"

Ivy spun. An older woman hovered over her. Ivy shrank backward.

"Ah…"

"You should be in the kitchen."

Ivy searched for words. Then had to translate them.

"You *are* the new scullery maid, aren't you?"

"Oh, yes."

"Then take yourself back to the kitchen and start washing dishes."

Ivy curtsied and walked down the hallway in the direction the waiters came from.

The kitchen swam with activity. Cooks were cooking, and more waiters were getting ready to wait.

The most important thing now was to locate the back door to let Edwin and Warragul in. She also needed to find where to wash the dishes, just in case that fat woman saw her again. She wove among the waiters, trying to give the impression she belonged, and knew where she was going.

Okay, there was the back door. In full view of everyone. That would be a challenge. How would she explain two servants coming in from the back yard? What would they have been doing out there?

To her left a little doorway led into another room. She followed it.

Never had she seen so many pots. What kind of a person would willingly live a life like this?

A girl around her age stood at the basin, scrubbing a pot. She turned at Ivy's footsteps.

"What are you doing here?"

"I've come to wash dishes."

"What? I'm the new scullery maid."

"Well apparently, there's two of us." Ivy crossed her arms. She was starting to get the hand of conversing in German.

"Well don't just stand there. Grab a pot and get scrubbing. There's plenty here for the both of us to do."

Ivy surveyed the pile. It looked pretty unsteady. It wouldn't take much more than a shove to bring the whole lot crashing down.

Washing dishes in here would definitely take away any suspicion people had and would remove the unfamiliarity of her face. You didn't question a hard worker, but she really needed to let the others in. She'd taken too long already.

Tentatively, she picked up a large pot. What she really needed was a diversion. The pot was filled with gungy water. It had obviously been soaking.

"Well don't just stare at it," the maid said. "And don't empty that in my washing water. Go empty it out back."

Perfect. That was just the excuse she needed. "Ah, right."

Ivy turned, and stuck her elbow out at an unnatural angle. With mock-clumsiness she strode forward, her elbow impacting with the pile of pots and pans.

Hopefully that had been enough. She needed to disrupt the pile enough to cause a fall, but not before she left the room. She strode with the noxious pot in arm out the doorway into the main kitchen. Just as she reached the back door an almighty crash sounded from behind.

People looked about, stunned. Several of them heading in the direction of the washing room. Ivy threw the back door open and went through.

She tossed the noxious contents from the pot, almost soaking Warragul. He jumped out of the way.

No time to apologise. "Get in there now. Head to your left."

Edwin and Warragul strode in. Ivy followed.

307

Only one or two people were looking their direction when she walked in and closed the door. She wasted no time in putting the pot down and following Edwin and Warragul out into the hallway. She passed the double doors and the powder room. The steps were just ahead. Edwin was already climbing them.

Heavy footfalls were coming from behind. They had to get up and out of sight before the fat woman rounded the corner. She'd not expect them to be going up there.

Leaving decorum behind, Ivy ran. She ran up the stairs two at a time.

She reached the landing and spun around.

"Where is that girl?" The fat woman's voice sounded from below.

They'd made it.

VV

Lawrence took another glass of champagne from a passing tray. He sipped it, making it look like he was taking a longer drink. He needed his wits, but wanted to portray a character who'd not be shy with his beverages.

Ivy had made her departure some time ago. That meant the plan was in full force. His only task now was to continue interacting with guests, keeping attention away from anything his colleagues were up to.

The bishop stood tall and straight just several meters away. Lawrence had not yet made contact with him. Perhaps it was time. He made his way in the general direction.

A fat woman in servant's garb strode in, red-faced. She walked directly to the bishop.

"Bishop, something is amiss with the servants."

It was not difficult to listen in. The woman's voice was raised with anxiety.

"We have a girl I do not recognise."

"Didn't you employ additional staff for tonight?"

"Yes, but we seem to have two scullery maids, and one of them has gone missing."

Not good. Ivy's presence had raised some alarm. Time to do some damage control. Lawrence stepped in.

"Pardon me, Bishop. My name is Müller. Freiherr Müller." He extended his hand. The bishop took it distractedly. "I wondered if I might indulge you in a discussion on the subject of justification."

"I'll be right with you, *Freiherr.*" The bishop turned to the servant. "Please Miss

Geiszler, can you not handle this situation yourself? You are in charge of the female staff after all."

"Yes, Bishop." The woman bowed her head slightly and strode out of the ballroom.

"So sorry *Freiherr*. You were saying?"

OV

Edwin took a moment to steel his nerves. It wasn't that he was worried, but his entire body tingled with the excitement. He'd missed this life. His arteries pounded. Likely there would not be anybody up here. All the guests and servants would be downstairs.

He took a moment to survey the house. Near the back was a heavy wooden door. It was the only locked door on this level. That was the bishop's lab.

"Warragul," he called.

Without any further instructions, Warragul removed his lock-picking tools and started work on the door. He'd have it open in a moment. Edwin turned to Ivy.

"I have another task for you. I need you to find the Bishop's mother's prize pearl earrings. They'll be in his bedroom somewhere."

310

"What are pearls?" Ivy asked.

"Little white spheres. Kind of shiny. They came out of a kind of fish back on old Earth that was never transplanted to Venus."

Ivy's eyes became carriage wheels. "You tellin' me that earthlings used to hang bits of dead fish from their ears?"

Edwin shrugged.

"No wonder their civilisation fell."

"Just get the pearls, and keep yourself hidden."

The door swung open. "Why are we bothering with pearls?" Warragul asked?

"That's our payment." Edwin gave his preprepared answer. "The maintenance plans for the platform are for Tellus. The earrings are for us." Edwin turned back to Ivy. "Once you have them, get out of the house unseen. Wait for me on the corner of Moorboden and Kaffee roads."

She nodded.

Edwin stepped through the door.

IV

Like most rooms in this house, the bishop's bedroom was bigger than Ivy expected. The bed sat against the left wall. On

311

the closest side, the bedside table sported a daguerreotype of a man and a woman. The bishop's parents? Ivy picked it up. The metal plate held a lifelike black and white image. She placed it back on the table.

On the other side of the bed, another table sported a big thick black Bible. A hip bath sat in one corner, with a wash pot.

To Ivy's right was a dressing table. That had to be it. She began to rummage through it. No doubt the bishop's mother had once sat at this table making herself presentable. One of the drawers contained assorted jewellery. She noticed gold, silver and the odd gemstone. No white spheres.

Ivy bit her lip. Where did the bishop keep his dead-fish earrings?

On the far side of the room stood a wardrobe. Ivy strode over and began to look through its contents. Jackets, shirts and trousers hung neatly inside. No white spheres.

Ivy's ears perked. Footsteps on the staircase.

"Girl?" The fat woman's voice.

VV

Edwin closed the lab door behind him. The room was cramped. A kerosene lamp provided dim illumination. No doubt Warragul had just lit it.

Bookcases lined almost every wall. A wide variety of theology texts and science books. Against the far wall was a large safe. That's where the orbital platform plans would be housed.

"What do you think?" Edwin asked.

Warragul shrugged. "It's a safe. I crack them. Won't be a problem."

"All right. Get started. The sooner we're out of here the better."

"Girl!" A woman's voice called out. Edwin's heart clenched. Surely she wouldn't attempt to enter the bishop's locked laboratory, but what about Ivy?"

OV

The fat woman was looking for her. No doubt she'd realized that Ivy was, in fact, not the scullery maid. It surprised her that the woman would venture up here into the Bishop's private area of the house, but to catch an intruder, why not?

313

Ivy had to hide. There was no room under the bed for a person to wedge. She made a frantic spin about. She had only one option.

She dove into the wardrobe and pulled the door closed. She hunkered down amongst the jackets, pulling them close around her.

"Girl?"

The fat woman stood just outside the bedroom door. Would she dare to enter the bishop's room?

Footsteps. She had entered.

Ivy held her breath. She tightened her body so not a muscle would twinge.

More footsteps. Don't open the wardrobe. Please don't. If she found no evidence of anything amiss, the woman might decide she wasn't up here and resume her search downstairs. Otherwise, she might call guards to do a thorough search.

The footsteps receded.

Ivy let out a short breath.

She'd remain here in the wardrobe for a time. Just in case.

VV

Edwin strained to hear, ear up against the door. Nothing.

314

"I think she's gone." He turned to Warragul. "How are you going?"

"Getting there slowly." Warragul concentrated on the safe, listening to the inner workings with an ear-piece as he slowly turned the wheel. "This safe is a little different to those in Tellus. The basic principles are the same but the specifics vary. In all my years working as a locksmith and safe engineer, I've never worked on one quite like this."

"So how's it feel breaking into a safe without the owner's permission?"

"Surreal." Warragul put the ear piece down and took out a small booklet from his pocket.

Edwin suppressed a chuckle. "It's funny how life works out isn't it. I spent so many years stealing, only to give it all away when I converted to the teachings of Christ. You're a legitimate locksmith, and are now working on the dubious side of the law."

"Don't forget I'm also a forger. But as you said, we are doing this for King and planet."

Edwin nodded. "While I agree, I doubt the New Berliners will see it that way."

Warragul let out a sigh and dropped the booklet.

315

"Trouble?"

"Whatever gave you that idea?"

"Anything I can do to help?"

"Grab the drill out of the knapsack for me, will you? I may have to bore into the safe's weak spot."

"You're the boss." Edwin collected the device.

"I'll give this one more try." Warragul put the ear piece up against the safe again.

Edwin silenced himself. Warragul strained, eyes closed. Edwin prayed that would work. It could take a long time to drill all the way through the thick metal.

"I think I've got it."

Warragul pulled on the handle and the door swung open.

Edwin's heart soared. This was the life he'd lived for. Words couldn't express how he'd missed it.

Together, the two men peered into the safe. The only contents were a small metal box. Edwin reached in and took it. He turned the box over. He saw no visible opening. It wasn't a box. Several holes congregated together at one end. Edwin gave the object a little shake, close to his ear. No moving parts inside.

"What is it?" Warragul asked.

"Our worst fears realised," Edwin said. "The plans are not on paper. This is an electronic storage medium. The New Berliners are rumoured to still have some left-over computers from before the United Nations Wars. It's how they have so much knowledge of past technologies.

"But how are we supposed to read the information?"

"We can't. We'll have to destroy it."

"If we destroy it, the orbital platforms will never be fixed."

"At least they still give us heat. We'll just have to live with a fortnight of darkness, as we have for decades."

"And if the heating stops working some day?"

"We can't let the Berliners control the technology." Edwin took a hammer from the bishop's desk. "I just hope they don't have any additional copies."

IV

Ivy daren't move. There was some kind of commotion up here. Footfalls sounded out in the hallways. Nobody had yet re-entered this

317

room, but they were definitely searching for someone.

It was getting cramped and uncomfortable in here. Ivy had spent plenty of time in uncomfortable positions during her life. She'd hidden from worse people than the guards in this house, but something hard dug into her back.

Careful not to make any sound, she eased herself forward slightly and reached her right hand backward. Her fingers made contact with a small wooden cube. She grasped it and moved it out of the way.

She then leaned back again. What a relief to not have that box sticking into her. She opened the box and felt inside. Something small and round. She felt around. Could it be?

She cracked the wardrobe door, just enough to let in a sliver of light.

Yes, pearls. She'd found the dead fish earrings.

VV

Edwin held the cool box in his hand, the hammer in the other. Part of him had still hoped that they'd be able to bring these plans home for Tellus. Now it was clear - that had never been possible.

Still, there was the other mission. The real reason Edwin came here to New Berlin. As long as Ivy had done her job, he still had hope.

"So now what?" Warragul asked.

Before Edwin could answer, the door opened. Edwin spun. Two bulky guards entered. A fat woman stood behind them in the hallway.

"Don't move," one of them said in German.

Edwin raised his hands. Warragul followed suit.

"What might you two be doing here then?"

W

They dragged Edwin and Warragul downstairs, through the corridor, and down another flight of stairs into a basement.

A tall clean-shaven guard pushed each of them down into a chair. Edwin grunted.

There was no sign of Ivy. Had they found her? Maybe she'd been successful.

"First thing's first," the taller of the two guards said. "Where's the other one?"

319

"Other one?" Edwin asked.

"The girl. Geiszler tells us there was a servant girl. Mistook her for the scullery maid at first. She seems to have disappeared. I was surprised she wasn't with you."

"It seems you're mistaken. Clearly she was not with us. Maybe you're just attracting thieves tonight."

The guard grinned. "Don't you worry. We'll find her." He leaned forward. "So you thought to steal the bishop's private belongings, did you?"

"We had our reasons."

"Your German isn't very good. Who are you? Spies from Tethus?"

"Tellus actually," Edwin admitted.

The guard's eyes widened slightly. "Oh, so you plan to be cooperative? Nice to see a criminal who's willing to be forthcoming."

"We can hardly deny it."

"You'll probably hang for this. Both of you."

"Well before that happens, I'd very much like to speak with the bishop."

The guard grunted. "Now why would the bishop waste his time with thieving scum like you?"

"Tell him to go check on his mother's earrings." Edwin smiled.

The guard's face contorted. "You took his mother's earrings?"

He nodded. "The serving girl."

"Of course we'd be willing to return them, in exchange for a conversation."

He turned to his companion. "Go search the main bedroom." He turned back to Edwin and snarled. "I'll search these two."

IV

Ivy climbed out of the wardrobe. She clutched the earrings tight.

There'd been a commotion across the hall. Edwin and Warragul had been captured. Things couldn't get much worse.

Sure, she had the earrings and she imagined they'd fetch a pretty price, being from Old Earth and all, but without the information they came here for it had been a very long and dangerous trip for a trinket. If she were captured, she'd be killed as an enemy spy. Why had she agreed to be a part of this?

She tucked the earrings into her pocket and fastened it. Her hands now free, she peered out of the doorway. Empty. Should she attempt

321

to rescue the others? It wasn't exactly her strong suit.

Edwin had told her to meet them at a rendezvous point. A strange instruction. She'd expected to remain here and help with the main heist. Why had he been so keen for her to leave with the earrings?

And what of Lawrence? Now that Edwin and Warragul had been taken they'd surely figure him out, too. They'd investigate his back-story more fully and arrest him too. She'd be the only one that survived. Would Herbert be willing to help her escape back to Tellus?

Ivy hung her head. She didn't wish execution for any of her colleagues. Even Lawrence. But the fact was, there was nothing she could do. Those guards sounded big.

Footsteps and yelling. She spun toward the exterior wall. One window.

She flipped the latch and pulled with all her strength. The window came up. She climbed out and clung to the outside wall of the house.

Using her right foot, she pushed the window down. It clicked, cutting off the voice of a guard. "Check in the bedroom—"

Ivy clambered upward and grabbed hold of the lip of the roof. She pulled herself up and turned around.

On the roof, she had a splendid view of New Berlin.

The layout of the streets was less orderly than she'd expected. Rather than a perfect grid, there were various angles, with triangular blocks. It all managed to fit together somehow. Lights stretched far into the distance. To her left she could make out the airfield, where they launched New Berlin's infamous jets. To the right, a train puffed its way toward the coast.

Time to plan her next move.

⊘⊘

After a thorough and very uncomfortable search, the tall guard allowed Edwin and Warragul to put their clothes back on.

The other guard, shorter, bald, and sporting a toothbrush moustache, appeared at the bottom of the stairs. The tall guard wandered over and they conversed for a moment.

The tall guard strode back over. "All right. You have our attention. The earrings are missing, and are not anywhere on either of your persons. If it were up to me I'd have you shot right now, but the bishop has agreed to meet with you."

Edwin smiled. "I thought he might."

The guard leaned in close to Edwin's face. "One wrong move and you'll get it, understand?" His voice reeked of bratwurst.

"Completely."

The guard stepped back, giving Edwin some personal space. "The bishop wishes to see you in his private study."

"The laboratory?"

"That's what he said."

Edwin nodded. "Lead the way."

Edwin and Warragul stood. The guard put an arm out in front of Warragul.

"Not you, just him."

Warragul raised an eyebrow but sat back down.

Edwin shrugged and followed the tall guard.

VV

The bishop waited in the lab for Edwin. He'd even brought in a second chair. He was a tall man with a white beard and kind eyes. A twinge of guilt assaulted Edwin at the thought of what they'd done to him. In the past, he'd stolen from rich aristocrats who almost deserved what they got. This man was different.

"Please take a seat. I am Bishop Johann Eckstein. May I have the courtesy of your name?"

"Edwin Wakefield, sir." He sat.

Eckstein turned to the guard. "You can leave us now. Wait outside the door."

"But Sir,"

The bishop raised his hand. The guard nodded and stormed into the hallway, closing the door behind him.

Eckstein turned back to Edwin. "You've stolen something of great personal value to me, Mister Wakefield, and you tried to take something else that is of value to the whole world."

Edwin shifted in his chair. "The earrings were just to ensure a meeting. I meant nothing personal by it. As for the plans...well, that was for my country."

"Why do you resist so the efforts of New Berlin to make life on Venus better? We only want to improve things for everybody on this planet."

"I'm sure you believe that Bishop."

Eckstein chuckled. "I can imagine your surprise when you found a solid-state data storage device. My government has banks of computers underground, you know. We know of technologies you could only dream of."

"Then why have you not implemented them?"

"Not all technologies were good. We aim to prevent repeating the mistakes of the past. That's why we have chosen the current level of technological and cultural development. This world is based on a time when moral values were held in great esteem." Eckstein removed his glasses. "But I'm more interested to know what it was you wanted to discuss with me, Mister Wakefield. You've gone to a lot of trouble, so speak."

"Bishop Eckstein, I am a Christian. A Lutheran just like you."

Eckstein nodded, then rubbed either side of his chin with two fingers.

"Doesn't it seem odd to you that we're fighting each other? We're not supposed to be enemies. I wanted to talk to you about peace."

"Peace?" Eckstein scoffed. "You break into my house, commit an act of espionage, steal my mother's pearls, all so you can discuss peace? Forgive my scepticism."

"Bishop, I knew getting away with the plans was a long-shot. I knew I would likely be captured. I also knew that was the best way to get a face to face meeting with you."

"You've certainly gone to a lot of trouble, so say your piece, Mister Wakefield."

"Your ultimate goal is to get to the orbital platform and repair it, right?"

Eckstein nodded.

"Don't you see how counter-productive it is for us to be working against each other towards that same goal? So much divided effort. Think how much we might achieve if we worked together rather than apart. We're both Christian nations, yet we oppose each other. It shouldn't be that way."

"Your Tethus / Tellus alliance started this war, Mister Wakefield."

"In response to New Berlin aggression. You're trying to rule the world." Edwin stopped himself. "I didn't come here to debate politics. Look at what's happening here, Bishop. Your leader takes the name Kaiser. Look back at history. The last time a man called himself

Kaiser he led old Earth into a global war. How long until we face the same thing? Right now, you're facing rebellion from two nations. How long before the rest of Venus rebels? You'll pull in allies on your side, and Venus will be engulfed in a world war. Then what happens to our efforts to reach the orbital platform? We'll be so distracted killing each other that we'll forget all about it."

Eckstein nodded slowly.

"You present a problem, Mister Wakefield. I can see some of what you suggest coming true. Which begs the next question, what is your solution?"

"Our governments are far from being willing to talk to each other, so let's bypass them altogether. Let the church lead the way. We can begin the process of peace by establishing a dialogue. Let's agree in principle to strive toward peace. Rather than praying to God for the victory of our own nations, let's agree in prayer as one voice, asking God for peace, and a way forward for the entire planet."

Eckstein stood and began to pace his lab. Edwin watched the bishop's progress as he walked back and forth. Finally, he returned to his seat.

"In principle I agree with most of what you say. This war certainly has fractured our relationship with the Tellus and Tethus arms of the church. I agree that peace should be the goal of God's people. We are called to be peacemakers, after all. But how far do you expect this to go? Do you envision me speaking out publicly against the Kaiser? You suggest a line that is dangerously close to treason."

"I'm not asking you to betray your people. I'm asking you to open up the lines of communication."

"And who will speak out for your side? You ask me to put my neck on the chopping block, but I don't see anybody doing the same in Tellus."

Edwin reached into his secret pocket and withdrew the envelope.

"This is a letter from Bishop Shaw, authorising me to negotiate on his behalf with you."

Eckstein took the envelope, opened it and began to read.

"He could have simply sent this letter to me."

"He wanted me to deliver it in person, to demonstrate that his desire for peace is genuine."

329

"I will give it consideration." Eckstein folded up the letter. "In the meantime, where might I find my mother's earrings?"

"My colleague is waiting on the corner of Moorboden and Kaffee roads."

"That's not far from here."

"Please don't harm her."

"Of that you can be assured Mister Wakefield." He opened the door. "Guard, please take this gentleman back down to the basement.

VV

Ivy hugged herself. Goosebumps rose on her forearms. The servant's uniform was hardly designed to keep out the nightly cold. Haze swirled around the gas streetlights.

She must have been standing here ten minutes at least. How long should she wait? What was the likelihood that Edwin and the others would escape? The chances were low. Surely getting captured wasn't part of the plan. Still, she'd give him another twenty minutes or so. After that, there'd be no point.

She'd have to make her return to the safe house by an indirect route - just in case somebody was following her.

330

Something moved behind her. She spun about. Nothing. Ivy reached for her knife. It rested against her left thigh. She strained her ears. This wasn't a very defensible position. Too many bushes where people could sneak up. She stepped right up to the edge of the road.

A hansom rode past, one driver and one passenger.

With no warning, the passenger leapt off the moving vehicle. Ivy pulled out her knife. The man was moving toward her. She raised her blade.

A hand grabbed her wrist from behind. She struggled to no avail. Her knife clattered to the ground.

A second pair of hands grabbed her from behind. No way she was breaking free. Her heart thumped. Not like this. Not after everything she'd been through. It couldn't end here on these foreign streets.

Edwin had betrayed her. He'd set her up from the start. So, this was his escape plan. *Her.*

The man from the hansom stood close and leered at her.

"Where are the earrings?"

The guard forcibly pushed Edwin back into his seat. And bound him with heavy rope.

"What were you talking about up there?" Warragul asked.

"I proposed something to the bishop."

Warragul shook his head. "What's your game, Wakefield? You've been doing your own thing since we got here. It was never about the plans, was it?"

Edwin gave a bitter smile. "I'm just trying to save the world, Warragul."

"Well that's nice. Do you have a plan to get us out of here?"

"That's in God's hands."

Warragul rolled his eyes. "Brilliant."

"I never asked you, do you believe? I don't even know if Christianity made it to Kruchina."

Warragul sighed. "Lutheran missionaries from New Berlin were not well-received. That's not to say my people don't have their own Christian heritage though. Some of the early aboriginal settlers brought a Christian faith. My father was a preacher in the New Uniting Church of Venus."

"And you?"

"I never really saw much need for religion in my life."

"But what about faith?"

Warragul shrugged. "There's always room for faith."

The door opened and a guard pulled Lawrence in. They'd found him out as well. It was a credit to the actor that he'd lasted as long as he did.

"Evening gents," Lawrence said. "This is a bit of a pickle, isn't it?"

They waited in silence for a time. Maybe half an hour. Edwin struggled against the bindings. His wrists ached under the pressure. Finally, the door opened. Eckstein entered.

"Guards, please excuse us."

The guards scowled but left the basement.

Eckstein approached and stopped in front of Edwin. "I've given thought to what you said, Mister Wakefield. In all seriousness, I'm not convinced that we can prevent the coming global war you describe. Eventually though, it will end. Wars always do. In the meantime, I'm willing to establish talks between the arms of the church. I am also willing to pray with you for peace."

"Thank you Bishop Eckstein. I am eternally grateful."

"As a show of good faith, I give you this." He placed a booklet into Edwin's shirt pocket. It is a hard copy of the plans you came here seeking."

Edwin's eyes grew wide. "Bishop. I never thought—"

"No need for thanks. It might give your government a stronger bargaining position with mine. Perhaps it will help our nations reach an agreement. Or perhaps it won't.

You can imagine what I've just done may be considered treason. That puts me in a dangerous position, so you know I am genuine in my desire for peace. There is however, one thing I'm not willing to do. I cannot just let you go."

Edwin's heart clenched. It was never going to be that easy, was it?

"That would be an outright and public sign of betrayal, one which I cannot make. I will remand you to the custody of New Berlin authorities. If you escape, you will need to do so on your own."

"So you give us the plans, but then send us to a certain death?" Warragul asked.

334

"Let's say I'm leaving your fate in the hands of God."

OV

Edwin squirmed on his seat under the watchful gaze of several guards. Each of them pointed revolvers. One for each member of the team - himself, Warragul and Lawrence.

The cart bumped down the street, pulled by two horses, likely taking them to the local jail.

So, this was it. Short of some kind of miracle they weren't getting out of this. All three of them would be hanged for espionage. The whole thing had been insane. What kind of person came up with a plan like this? A futile effort. All of it.

They approached Moorboden Road. The cart slowed to a stop. Ivy stood there, in the custody of two more guards. She seethed.

They manhandled her into the cart. She dropped in the last remaining spot on the bench.

"Evening Ivy," Lawrence said.

She ignored him - instead glaring at Edwin. "You set me up."

One of the guards wound a chain around Ivy's legs and fastened it with a lock.

"I wouldn't describe it that way, exactly," Edwin said. "But I wasn't completely forthcoming about my plan."

"You put them onto me so you could escape. Nice to see how that worked out for you."

"I wasn't trying to escape, Ivy. I needed the earrings as a bargaining tool. I exchanged them for a word with the bishop."

Ivy scoffed. "A word with the bishop?"

Edwin nodded.

"You went to all this trouble, to talk to someone?"

Edwin stared at the floor of the cart.

"You must be an idiot."

"I won't argue with that, Ivy."

A commotion arose among the guards. Edwin looked up. Over the road, a small wooden shed caught fire. The bright red and orange flame stood out in brilliant contrast to dimly-lit city.

"Get some water," somebody shouted. "You don't want it to spread!"

"We have spies in our custody," another voice yelled.

336

Movement caught the corner of Edwin's eye. He looked to the left. Somebody vanished into the bushes after taking a glance over his shoulder. That face. Was that Herbert?

A low hum emanated from somewhere up above. What was that? An airship?

Tracer bullets spewed out of the darkness. The area around the cart illuminated. The horses whinnied and startled but didn't bolt.

"What in heaven's name is going on?" One of the guards asked.

Two men dropped, impacting the ground with hard thuds, parachutes billowing over them. They unclasped the chutes and drew Lancaster pistols.

Bang. One of the guards dropped to the floor of the cart. The remaining two, eyes wide and mouths open, shook off their surprise, pursing their lips, and raised their pistols toward the paratroopers. Pistols gave almighty cracks, which echoed all around. Both guards dropped.

"Mister Wakefield, we're getting you out of here."

The driver leapt from the cart and bolted toward the cover of trees at the side of the street.

"Let him go," one of the troopers said. He threw off his parachute and climbed onto the cart. "Hold out your chains."

Edwin extended his arms. The heavy chains strained his biceps.

The trooper pulled a long metal contraption, like shears, but stronger, from his belt. He placed the tip over the chains and clamped it shut, breaking a link. The remaining chain crashed to the floor.

Edwin jumped from the cart as the trooper freed the others.

A rope ladder dropped from the sky. Edwin didn't wait to be instructed. He started climbing the rope. His biceps burned as he pulled himself up, handhold after handhold. The higher he got, the more of New Berlin he could see. Pinpricks of light spread out across the land. The hum from above grew louder and louder.

Warragul climbed directly beneath him, followed by Lawrence and Ivy. The troopers came up last.

Edwin reached the top of the ladder and a burly crew member pulled him into the airship.

"Thanks," Edwin muttered as he sprinted for the nearest door. He threw it open and stepped onto the bridge.

"Welcome aboard, Mister Wakefield."

Edwin nodded. "Captain Wilcock. I'm surprised to see you still in the area."

Wilcock shrugged. "Turns out the *Salisbury* can shoot down as many biplanes as those Berliners could throw at her."

"All aboard," a voice from behind called.

"Full speed ahead," Wilcock yelled. The airship surged under the power of mighty engines.

"What about New Berlin's jets? Won't they come after us?"

"We've been flying low to avoid detection as long as possible. We'll keep altering our course. That, plus the speed of the *Salisbury* means that by the time they can dispatch a squadron, they'll have a hard time finding us. Relax Mister Wakefield. It's almost over."

Edwin leaned back against the steel bulkhead and closed his eyes. His hand touched the booklet secured in his pocket.

VV

Edwin looked out through the wall to ceiling window. Far below the ocean sparkled. He closed his eyes and swallowed down an attack of nausea. It seemed air travel didn't agree with him any more than sea travel.

A presence appeared beside him. He glanced over. Ivy. No wonder she made such a good cat thief, with those silent footsteps.

"Still hate me?"

Ivy bit her lip and inclined her head. Finally, she shrugged. "Guess I had the wrong idea about you. You weren't actually trying to betray me to the guards. It was just part of your plan. Pity though you didn't explain it beforehand."

"Sometimes the leader of a crew has to hold some things back."

"So what you gonna do when we get back to Tellus? We could keep the gang together. Lots of opportunities for a good thieving crew back 'ome."

Edwin shook his head. "My thieving days are behind me now, Ivy. This job was just for King and planet. Tempting as it was for a bit there, I'm not going back to it. No, I think I might even take up something of a diplomatic position within the church. If they'll have me of course."

"Shame to waste all that talent."

"I just hope it wasn't a waste. What about you?"

Ivy shrugged. "Back to the old life, I guess."

Edwin smiled. "Well, if you ever want to settle down into something more stable, just let me know. It would be my delight to help you any way I can."

"That's sweet Edwin, but it's still a man's world out there, and I like me freedom too much."

"Then God go with you, my friend."

"Yeah, you too."

Edwin turned back to the window and watched the first glimmers of the sunrise. The day cycle had arrived. A new day on Venus.

END

Secrets Kept
by Kat Heckenbach

I crouched behind the staircase, peering through the scrolled iron railing. It mirrored the row of buildings on this side, two-story brick structures with staircases arcing in pairs like brick and iron wings. Homes and businesses mixed together, apartments above and storefronts below, although some lived in both levels if their work required no storefront. Shadowed alleyways gapped between every few units.

He'd told me not to be seen entering the building across the busy cobbled street. The strange man I'd met the evening before, delivering a package that was oddly heavy for its size. He'd answered the door—the same door I stared at now—and snatched the package from my hands.

Ash was smeared in greasy stripes across his sweaty forehead and clouded his gray work shirt and trousers. His dark hair, thick and wavy, stood out in every direction as though he'd not combed it in days. Or maybe he had, but he'd run his long, skinny fingers through it and undone the work.

342

"Not this door, you fool!" he'd hissed. "Did you not read the instructions?"

I opened my mouth, but the words of my protest scrambled up and jammed in my throat.

Then his expression changed as he looked me over. His pale blue eyes narrowed and a single eyebrow rose.

I know my eyes had to have been wide with shock at his words, his tone—but more so the way his eyes suddenly lit before he pressed aside my waiting hands and whispered, "I've much better than measly coin for you, boy. Come back tomorrow. Don't be seen. Secrets kept secret, eh?"

The broad wooden door snicked shut in my face. The same door he'd forbidden me to return to, and which loomed before me now like a giant warning sign. *Do not enter here.*

Where then? I *hadn't* seen his instructions, so I knew of no other entrance.

And *why*? Why could I not be seen?

More importantly, *why had I come back?*

The man had ordered me to, but I had no obligation. He hadn't paid me, obviously had no intention of paying me.

Secrets kept secret, eh?

343

He had a secret. Just knowing that was enough to drive my curiosity to impossible lengths. A secret in this town, where the Victorian façade had been taken to extremes. I hadn't figured out yet whether the façade actually ran deep, or if everything below the surface was secret. Surely there had to be some for whom this was a farce.

No progress allowed. Even though they were allowed in New Berlin, steam-powered vehicles were banned from our cobbled roads by our own town government's choice. You walked, or rode a bicycle. Simple technology was permitted only for necessity, not luxury. Muscle power remained our top resource, and our town folk prided themselves on independence from anything that might move us toward the devastation caused by…

Fear lanced through my mind, and I gripped the iron railing and sank lower so I could lean my head against the side of the cold brick steps.

We didn't talk about those times. We were not to even *think* about them. We were to be happy in our created world, to rest assured we would not make the same mistakes as our ancestors.

I breathed deeply and lifted my head once again.

People shuffled past on foot in both directions, the noise of their chatter and clicking footsteps allaying my fear of being heard as I tried to control my breathing. It would be easy enough to cross the street; no one would notice me in my plain shirt and trousers, my worn leather boots. Even my too-large vest was nothing to turn someone's eye. I did better than blend in—I faded out. A poor boy, old enough to work but still not so much as fuzz on my chin, out on delivery. I even bundled an old canister in newsprint and wrapped it in twine to make a fake package.

But the door. The impossible door.

There must be a back entrance, but I would be noticed skulking around the shadowed side of a building, searching, and then…what? Was I to knock? Simply wait? The man obviously wanted no attention drawn to his home, if he insisted on avoiding the front entry.

Well, I had no choice.

I inhaled, swallowed as I held my breath, then released the air, leaving myself nearly dizzy. Still, I stood.

Acting as though I were on an ordinary delivery, I slipped between men in coats and silk hats, and women with layered skirts beneath tightly corseted waists. I shuddered at the thought of being squeezed so for fashion's sake, and moved past the throng to the other side of the road.

I refused to even look at the door I'd visited the day before.

Instead, I walked up and down as if checking the addresses and comparing them to the one on my package. It gave me the opportunity to pass the alleyway next to the man's building. Completely shadowed, it afforded no view of the wall, and therefore I couldn't tell if there was a doorway hidden back there.

What to do? I stood, contemplating, turning the package and squinting as though the writing on the label was unclear. Pedestrians moved around me, most ignoring my presence, thank goodness. Maybe I had overthought this whole thing. Perhaps no one would care about me searching for a back entrance when there was obviously a front door. Perhaps the man routinely had deliveries made to a back door and no one would think oddly at all…

Just as I had made up my mind to dive into the alleyway, a gentleman dashed past me, waving a lace handkerchief—"Miss! Oh, Miss, I believe you dropped this!"—and grazed my shoulder, knocking my fake package to the ground as he chased down a young woman in a frilly layered skirt and bonnet. The package rolled with a metallic hum into the alley.

"Sorry, young man!" the gentleman shouted over his shoulder before disappearing into the crowd.

At least I had my excuse now.

I darted into the alley, following the package by sound as I scanned the wall with my eyes. Nothing but brick. No sign of a back door at all. The packaged thumped into the tall iron gate at the end of the alley, and I stooped to pick it up.

I stood back up, package still lying at my feet.

A gate. Of course—the back door must be behind the building. But a padlock secured the gate, and I had nothing with me to even attempt to pick it. The vertical bars of the gate were too close together for me to squeeze through…

I would have to climb.

347

I peered over my shoulder, out toward the opening at the end of the alley. Pedestrians continued past, completely unaware of me. How stupid of me to think otherwise. A delivery boy, unimportant and uncared for. No one would think twice about me scuttling down an alley because no one even noticed me unless the package in my hand was for them...or unless they, having slammed into me *because they hadn't noticed me*, knocked the package out of my hand and into an alley.

I sighed and turned back to the gate, then shimmied up and over, leaving the fake package on the ground. And there, around the corner on the back wall of the building, was a door. It was set a good eight inches above the ground, as the gap behind the back of this row of buildings and the back of the row opposite the gap served mainly as a ground level gutter, collecting rainwater and shunting it into storage wells during rainy seasons. It stood mainly dry now, with a few muddy puddles here and there.

Steeling myself, I stepped up to the door and knocked.

Waited.

Just as I lifted my hand to knock a second time, a slot in the door slid opened, and a set of pale blue eyes peered out at me.

348

The slot slid shut with a thump, followed by the click of a lock turning. The door swung inward, and the man stepped into the open doorway.

A smile lifted one side of his mouth. "Much better. Come in, then." He stepped back into the building.

I stared up at the empty doorway for a moment, chewing the corner of my mouth, before stepping up and hauling myself inside behind him.

We were in a sparsely furnished room—a lone sofa and plain wooden end table topped with a gas lamp sat against one wall, across from a fireplace with a small wooden stool beside the hearth. The floor was dusty other than his footprints, including the small round rug that lay slightly off-center as if it had been thrown down with no thought to placement and then forgotten. Obviously this was not the door at which he routinely received deliveries.

The man shut and locked the door behind us; then without a word he crossed the room to the door opposite, where he stopped and turned to face me. The angled shadows of a hallway filled the space behind him.

I slid my hands into my pockets, in case they decided to start trembling. What had I done? I knew nothing of this man, and now I was locked in a house with him. He obviously had no one living with him, or the room I stood in would have not been left to neglect.

"Sir…" I scooted backward toward the door behind me. "I think there's been a mistake…"

I turned, yanking my hand from my pocket, only to find the lock on the door required a key from the inside. Spinning back around, I found the man holding a brass key between long fingers. The lopsided smile slit his face eerily in the shadow of the doorway. My heart slammed into my breastbone.

He stepped over to the fireplace and set the key on the mantle, then slid back to his spot in the opposite doorway. "It won't stay shut properly if not locked. If you've no heart for secrets, take the key and be gone. Perhaps I misjudged you."

He spun on his heel and disappeared into the dark hallway, footsteps silencing in moments.

What now? The man had done nothing to hurt me, never even stood within arm's reach. He'd left the key and bid me leave if I chose. Was he genuine—or was this a trap? Did he mean to snare me with my own curiosity?

My gaze fell on the key. So easy to leave. But I'd come here for secrets. At the very least, I needed payment for yesterday's delivery. I had barely enough coin for a loaf of bread and had no deliveries lined up for today because of my eagerness to visit here. It was time to make my trouble worth the time and effort.

Shoulders back, I marched through the doorway through which the man had disappeared, and followed the dark hallway past closed doors on my right and solid wall on my left, which opened up to the base of a carpeted staircase. This must be why his footsteps had silenced so quickly; he'd taken the stairs up. Which meant, that's where I would go.

My hand trailed the banister as I climbed. The downstairs living space felt abandoned and lonely. Sunlight barely filtered through the heavily curtained windows on the front of the building, and the stairway grew darker as I ascended, but the staircase turned abruptly and the space opened into bright light.

I halted at the top of the staircase, gripping the open doorway for support. The door, swung in against the wall to my left, had no less than seven deadbolts. This was not a room the man wanted seen.

Yet, here I stood, gazing at the wonder that lay before me, and he not only allowed it, but had invited me.

I swallowed, steadied myself, and pushed forward.

Thick wooden tables lined every wall of the expansive room. Above each table, a window was covered with a brazen metal sheeting. I wondered at its purpose. Could it reflect sunlight during daytime so from the street one might think lights were on, while keeping the upstairs unseen through the windows? Were there curtains on the other side? Was it merely to reflect the sunlight to keep the room cool?

Above the covered windows, strange tubes of light hung from the raftered ceiling, setting the room in full illumination.

In contrast to the dusty room downstairs, this one gleamed from use. The floor was polished, although grease stains marred the wood here and there. The tables glistened with brass instruments, all looking as though quite regularly wiped down with the many dust cloths that lay strewn about. A chemical odor and a metallic tang edged the still air.

My jaw had gone stiff, and realized my mouth hung agape, but rather than close my open mouth, I placed my hand over it and stepped farther into the room.

The instruments, the tools…they drew me like moth to flame. Such beauty and practicality, such strength and precision. Large hammers and tiny mallets, screwdrivers from a half meter long down to a mere few centimeters, the smallest with head meant for the most delicate of work. Spindly-legged contraptions that clicked and ticked. Lenses of varying thickness and diameter. Scales and balances, glass dishes filled with tiny screws and bolts. Stacks of metal sheeting, massive tinsnips, spools of wire…

It was a feast for my eyes, and I allowed my gaze to creep its way from corner to corner as I inched my way toward the center of the room.

The man had said nothing. I glanced in his direction to find him leaning against a column by the door through which I'd entered the room. Behind the column, an alcove dipped deep into the corner. And inside the odd space, a machine stood.

Easily three meters high and not quite two across, it was cylindrical in shape, but for the square base on which it sat. Pipes stuck out from everywhere, with wires woven between and around them. Gauges were fixed in a neat row down the front, like buttons down a jacket, and their hands either spun or ticked back and forth. Steam issued from a broad pipe at the very top in not quite regular intervals, but it had a rhythm, almost like the beat of a song.

It was the loveliest thing I'd ever seen.

I lowered my hand, but did not turn to look at the man, who I knew was staring at me.

"What is it?" I asked, voice creaking with astonishment.

Movement drew my gaze to him. He had pushed away from the column, and now stood with his arms crossed. The lopsided grin looked far less eerie in the bright light. And the fire in his blue eyes told of excitement, of mischief but not misdeed.

"That, my son, is," he said as he stepped up beside me, "or rather, *will be*, a time machine."

I couldn't stop the laugh that bubbled up through my throat, nor the words that followed. "Are you mad?"

He made no move, and only allowed his smile to fall slightly. "What's madness is this society we live in that is so afraid of technology.

354

It's foolishness to be frightened of computers and communication. Such things have as much power to bring the world together as they do to tear the world apart. It is not the object itself, but the purpose and method of using. The user. *We* are the problem, dear boy."

I crept back a step. My heart began to pound against my breastbone like a bird frantically trying to escape its cage. The man was daring to speak plainly about this! The Great Devastation that was to remain nameless so that we would not repeat our foul mistakes.

But it was not his openness that scared me…

The words he spoke, the ideas he held—they were the same thoughts that had traveled through my mind so many times.

Had he somehow known? Was there something about me, in my demeanor or expression, that told him I felt the same?

Was it something others could see as well?

"Sir, I…"

He snapped his hand into the air, and held it palm facing me. "Don't bother. I see the way you look at this, the curiosity in your eyes. I had hoped that would be the case."

355

I shook my head and stepped back again. This was dangerous. No matter how I felt, no matter my agreement with the man's opinions, my life, such as it was, would be in danger just by being in this room and having this conversation.

"I'm sorry, sir, but I think I need to go."

He stepped quickly to the side, crossing his arms again and blocking the doorway.

"And where, exactly, do you need to go? Your home? You have a mother and father waiting for you in a nice cozy house somewhere?"

"Yes, and they were expecting me—"

"Don't lie to me...*boy*." His eyes narrowed with that last word, and I found myself struggling to swallow a lump that suddenly grew in my throat.

My eyes burned as though tears wished to form, but I would not allow them. Boys my age did not cry. I straightened my shoulders and crossed my arms to mimic his stance. "All right, I don't have parents, or a home. Does that please you?"

The hardness melted from his expression, and his words matched in softness. "Of course not. Everyone should have a family."

I had to struggle more now to keep the tears at bay. The way he looked at me now, with such pity, such compassion. It had been so long since I'd seen a face gaze at me with genuine kindness. This was a cruel place for those without status of family or manhood. And I stood before him with neither. Either he meant what he was saying, or he was a very talented actor.

"I'm sorry if I frightened you," he said, uncrossing his arms and hooking his thumbs into his pants pockets. "You understand the importance of secrecy here."

I only nodded, not trusting my voice at the moment.

"I knew you would. The moment I scolded you at the door yesterday. And you did not disappoint." He smiled crookedly at me again, amusement crinkling the corners of his eyes. "Such lengths you took to avoid the front entry." He leaned forward, and the smile dropped. "I'm sorry I deceived you about the instructions on the package. I had to see your reaction."

I blinked. Had I heard him correctly? It had been a test? A ruse to discover my reaction?

The man straightened again and cleared his throat. "What I'm offering you is a job," he

357

said with a renewed air of formality. "And a home. I have plenty of room for you here. You will have your own bedroom and a private bath. Three solid meals a day. No worries about safety as long as you keep quiet about my project." He paused, and his expression deepened. His next words were laced with heavy meaning that I feared to pinpoint. "The only part of your previous life I require you keep is delivering my packages yourself. I will be receiving a few more items of…questionable nature. I do not wish to have a curious delivery boy open these packages."

His words filtered slowly through the haze that had formed in my mind. A job. A home. Not just my own bed, but my own room and private bath. All in exchange for delivering a few more packages and helping him with this insane project.

A time machine. Ludicrous.

Finally, my voice solidified. "Why are you doing this?"

His mouth twitched at the corner. "Because you—"

"No," I said, turning away from him and spreading my arms to indicate the room around me. "This. Why are you doing this? Why build such a thing?"

"Can you really not guess?"

I spun back around to face him. Our eyes met, and somehow my nerves didn't falter. It was so obvious now. "You wish to return to the past, before the time of the Great Devastation."

One eyebrow rose into a curious curve above his piercing blue eye.

"You wish to stop it." I could not help the awe that infected my voice. It would be such wonder to have the charade over with—to have it never have happened in the first place. To regain the progress that had been made before the world overreacted. To have a life outside this Victorian prison. Outside this society that had chosen such antiquated ways, such backwards thinking, in which children were dismissed and women were forced to squeeze into corsets and mountains of fabric, in which men lorded over both and hoarded opportunity…

I inhaled to quell the anger that caused my pulse to thump painfully in my temples.

A smile formed fully on his lips now, including both corners of his mouth this time. "I knew I'd chosen wisely."

Now that I understood his purposes, I could not help wondering…

"Fine, then, you may continue what you were saying before. Why me?"

His gaze moved from me and then tracked the breadth of the room behind me, as if he were looking over every tool and mechanism exactly as I had done when I'd first arrived. He drank in the scene in great gulps, stopping when he reached the so-called time machine in the corner alcove.

"Because," he said, pausing to lick his lips, "I see in you much of myself. Someone different, someone alone. Someone…"

He shifted his gaze directly at me.

"Someone who can keep a secret."

The weight of his stare was nearly physical. My shoulders slumped forward and I found myself wanting to pull my cap over my eyes. It took all my will-power to not adjust my overlarge vest.

Not that it mattered. I could see in his eyes that he'd guessed. He knew my secret long before he told me his. I forced my shoulders back and returned his gaze, eye to eye.

His head cocked to the side. "Do we have a deal?"

I hesitated, and he stepped closer.

"You have my word," he said.

I believed him, even if he was on a mission of madness.

"Then yes. We have a deal, Mister…."

He held out his hand. "Jacobson."

I gripped his palm with mine. "Secrets kept secret?" I asked with one eyebrow arched.

"Absolutely."

I nodded and shook his hand. "I'm Margaret." A smile pushed at my cheeks. "Let's build a time machine, Mr. Jacobson."

END

Bear Publications is a Christian publisher of science fiction, fantasy, and other forms of speculative fiction in short story anthologies and novels. We also publish non-fiction that's related to speculative fiction.

Find out more at:
www.bearpublications.com

For more information on the writers who contributed to this anthology, see:
http://bearpublications.com/our-authors/